EVACUE

To Michael & Norma

EVACUEE'S RETURN

BY

TOM FARRELL

with thanks for your encouragement!

Tom & Liz

Illustrated by

PETER ROGERS

New Generation Publications

Published by New Generation Publishing in 2018
Text © Tom Farrell 2018
Illustrations © Peter Rogers 2018
First Edition

British Library Cataloguing in Publication Data.
A catalogue record for this book is available from
the British Library.

ISBN 978-1-78719-710-7

www.newgeneration-publishing.com

 New Generation Publishing

For Liz

In grateful memory of those patient teachers
who didn't give up on me.

CONTENTS

CHAPTER ONE

HOME AGAIN

The Grandfather clock downstairs had just struck ten, Muriel and Joe, the Crab Mill Farm children, and Shirley, his sister, would probably be asleep, but Tim was still awake. The angry drone of bomber engines high over the peaceful Shropshire countryside told him there was danger in the air. The Luftwaffe had arrived again, right on time. Farmer Everson said that Germans are never late for anything.

He slipped out of bed and crept quietly across to the window, opened it and leaned out to look up. It was easy to pick out the enemy planes. There seemed to be hundreds, like a battalion of ants, on the march across the steel-blue canvas of the night sky. There was a chart in the Farmer's Home Guard cupboard showing the silhouettes of enemy bombers, and Joe and he had memorised most of them. This night's visitors were Dorniers and Heinkels, as usual, and going by the weather-vane over the farm dairy, he didn't need to guess where they were heading. On their present flight path, which looked like due North, on a bright, moon-lit night like this, a navigator's dream, they would soon pick out the River Mersey. They would just follow its course to reach Liverpool, his city, and its eight miles of docks.

He frowned. This was the seventh night on the run that he had watched the Nasties, as he called them, passing high overhead with their deadly cargo. Liverpool was sixty miles away, but, if he stayed awake, even at this distance, he would know when they had reached their target. Search-lights would be sweeping the sky to the north, across the horizon there would be a tell-tale orange glow from burning docks reflected on billowing clouds of smoke, and if the wind was from the north, he would hear the sound of exploding bombs. Not that he wanted to see or hear any of it. His Dad would be there, in the thick of it, high up on the factory roof, on the look-out for fires, while right under his feet lay tons of sisal and manila fibre, an enormous bonfire waiting to be set alight by a stray incendiary bomb. His Mum would be there too, not exactly in the line of fire, but cooped-up in the Welbeck Avenue air-raid shelter, holding hands with someone more nervous than herself and joining in songs like 'Pack up your troubles in your old kit-bag, and smile, smile, smile!' - a useless attempt to steady her nerves and keep out the sound of the bombing.

For the people of Liverpool during these first days of May 1941, there wasn't much to smile about. The city centre was half in ruins, the docks had been burnt down time and again; the fire-fighters and the builders working around the clock to repair the docks were exhausted, and there were no Spitfire squadrons this far north to keep the Luftwaffe away. The city was cut off.

He watched the last of the ants disappearing off the canvas, closed the window quietly, whispered a prayer for his Mum and Dad, and was soon asleep.

At breakfast there was no mention of bombers. Tim wasn't going to admit that he had disobeyed orders and stayed awake and, if farmer and Mrs Everson had been bomber-spotting themselves, they had decided to say nothing. The doctor had said that Shirley was making herself ill by worrying about her Mum and Dad in 'the danger zone'. They didn't want to make matters worse.

That night, although Tim hated the bombers and the bombing, curiosity once again kept him awake, as he waited for the tell-tale throb of bomber engines; but the clock downstairs had already struck ten, and the night sky was empty and silent. Several minutes passed, and still there was no sign of raiders. Was this their night-off, or had Adolf Hitler finally decided to call-off his flying 'dogs of war'? Whatever the reason, Dad could spend the night at home, and Mum wouldn't have to put up with the discomfort of the air-raid shelter. He allowed himself a grim smile, and was asleep almost before his eyes closed.

The next night, ten o'clock came and went, and again there was no sign of the enemy. Tim was falling asleep at his post, and the Shropshire countryside and people of Merseyside were left in peace.

The rest of May slipped by, there was no sign of the Luftwaffe, and Tim had given up his late-night vigil.

Breakfast was almost finished one morning in early June when Farmer Everson came into the kitchen.

"Germany has attacked Russia! It was on the seven o'clock news."

Hitler's 'dogs of war' had a new enemy to get their teeth into.

"Perhaps, they'll leave us alone now."

Shirley clapped.

"Does that mean that we can go home?" She stopped, and bit her lip. She didn't mean to be rude.

Mrs Everson understood. She smiled.

"We'll have to wait for your Mum and Dad to get in touch."

Tim was in two minds. According to Mrs Everson he was 'quite a Shropshire lad', now, and was even talking about becoming a farmer one day. He was in no hurry to leave; but, every morning, Shirley was up early, dressed and waiting to way-lay the postman; and, if he hadn't come before they left for school, her first question when she came home, was always, "Is there any post?"

Then, at last, the letter she was waiting for arrived.

'The bombers have done their worst,' Mum wrote, 'and we think they won't be coming back. So we'll be coming soon, to bring you and Tim home.' Shirley ran upstairs to start packing.

On the first Saturday afternoon of the summer holidays, Mum and Dad drove down in Uncle Bill Brett's Morris Eight. There was tea and a lot of talk. Mum said a tearful 'thank you for all the kindness' shown to the evacuees. Mrs Everson said how brave Shirley had been, and hoped that now that the bombing had stopped and she would be back at home, she would recover from her illness. She said some nice things about Tim, too, not mentioning the times she had sent him back to the bathroom to wash the back of his neck. She smiled.

"He dunna like soap much!"

To set the record straight, Mr Everson said how well Tim had done as the Crab Mill egg-collector.

"He can sniff out a well-hidden nest as well as any weasel!"

Tim promised to come to visit in the holidays.

Then they were off, back the way they had come the first time, almost two years before, through Cheshire, skirting Birkenhead and the ship building yards, through the Mersey Tunnel and out into the centre of their war-scarred city.

Just after six o'clock, the Morris turned into Welbeck Avenue and pulled up outside Number 6. Within seconds, as if by some kind of telepathy, doors opened and familiar residents spilled out onto the pavement. Tim spotted Mrs Impitt, next door neighbour at number Eight, and Mrs Thompson, his friend Billy's mum, from over the road at Number Seven, and they were all smiles! The evacuees from Number 6 were back! He grinned. A 'Welcome Home' committee all to themselves! In the excitement he noticed old Mrs Ferguson from number Twelve beaming in his direction, which was surprising, he thought, considering the number of times his football had landed in

her front garden, upsetting Henry, her parrot. He had heard his Mum say that being absent 'sometimes makes people love you more!' Perhaps it was that! He beamed back.

Bill Brett drove off, the evacuees finally made their escape from the reception committee and went indoors. Straightaway everything felt strange. Number 6 seemed so small compared with Crab Mill Farm. Tim went upstairs to his bedroom, unpacked his carrier bag, stacked his Beanos on a shelf and rolled his football under the bed. Hanging his Spitfire and Hurricane models from the ceiling took longer; but now he was back in circulation, more or less. He felt better and went downstairs.

A few moments later the front-door bell rang, announcing that Grandpa and Grandma Oliver had arrived. He knew it would be them. Mum always laid out the 'red carpet' for Dad's Mum and Dad. They lived in a big house in Stoneycroft, one of the more posh parts of the city and were used to a fuss being made; especially Grandma, who eyed Tim cautiously, he thought. Had he forgotten to comb his hair? Where was the mirror? He couldn't remember. He played safe and retreated to the kitchen. A few moments later Mum's parents were ushered in. They were more down-to-earth. Grandpa Dodd was keen on football, so Tim and he spoke the same language. The next to arrive were Uncle Arthur and Auntie May, Dad's sister, unselfishly armed with most of her current week's sweet ration, to be presented to her 'favourite evacuees'. Mum's jolly friend, honorary 'Auntie' Freda, was the last to arrive, and that completed the quorum of eleven, the absolute maximum number which could be fitted into a Welbeck Avenue front-room in any comfort.

Mum had used up almost all of the week's margarine ration on sandwiches and all the sugar ration on a sandwich cake topped with a thin layer of white icing and WELCOME HOME in royal blue.

Dad, normally a man of few words, said more than a few, with a slight wobble now and then, expressing what was on everyone's mind - joy, that Shirley and Tim were back home, and hope, that 'they will never again be evacuees'.

Shirley smiled happily. There was no way that she would be an evacuee again. If the bombers did come back, she would stay at home with Mum and Dad, bombs or no bombs. Tim wasn't sure how to react to the out-pouring of emotion. He grinned and sipped his fizzy drink.

The chatter went on for an hour or more, questions coming from all directions; but staying awake, perched on the arm of the settee in the warm, crowded front room was difficult. It had been a long day. He said "Night, night!" and headed upstairs.

CHAPTER TWO

TIM DOES A RECONNAISSANCE

Tim opened his eyes, stretched, and swung his legs out of bed. He sat on the edge, thinking about nothing in particular, then walked over to the window to pull back the black-out curtains, frowning. Why had he bothered pulling them across in the first place? The Luftwaffe had gone off to bash the Russians, so what was the point? Well, according to his Mum, they might decide to come back, so the black-out was still in force, the Air Raid Wardens were still on the prowl at night, and they would all be in trouble if he forgot it!

He looked down over the yard into the back lane. The air-raid shelter was still there, neglected and looking sorry for itself. According to Dad, it would also be staying until the war was over, and Tim already had plans for it.

Pressing his cheek up against the window, he could just make out the railway embankment at the end of the Avenue which carried the main-line traffic to and from the city and docks, high up in line with the roofs. Mr Impitt, who claimed to be 'a bit of an expert' on aerial warfare, said that such things as main railway lines were 'bound to be strategic targets for the Luftwaffe', and everybody knew how strategic this particular stretch of line was, linking the city and docks with the rest of the country. Even more importantly, in the opinion of a keen train-spotter, on this very stretch of line, The Coronation Scot, known as THE SCOT, the world's fastest express, could be seen pounding past twice a day without fail. He rubbed his eyes and looked again. Yes! The embankment and lines were all there still. If the Luftwaffe had targeted them, the bomb-aimers had got their calculations wrong. Back at base, heads would roll!

He turned away from the window, glanced up at the Spitfire,

nudged it into circular motion and trudged towards the bathroom. Hovering over the wash-basin, he ran a dribble of hot water onto a flannel, wiped his face, flicked the flannel in the direction of the back of his neck, and reached for a towel. Dressing took even less time, and he was on his way downstairs, when there was a knock at the front door. The doctor had come to examine Shirley, now that she was back at home. Dr Minitt, elderly, staid and a byword for wisdom about all things medical, nodded to Tim and followed Mum upstairs. Dad had already gone to work.

After a quarter of an hour, the doctor came down to speak with Mum. Tim picked up snatches of the conversation, and guessed that the news wasn't good. The doctor left, and Tim glanced across the table.

"Is Shirley very ill, Mum?"

"Yes, Tim. It's what the doctor calls a nervous disease, with a rather strange name - St Vitus's Dance. It isn't the kind you can catch from someone else, like measles or chicken pox; but it's very serious all the same. The Doctor thinks that worrying so much about Dad and me here in the Blitz was partly why she became ill. He said that, in war, there are all kinds of casualty and our Shirley is one of them. He says that Herr Hitler has a lot to answer for."

"Will she have to go to hospital?"

"No. But she'll need a lot of rest and quietness. This will be her hospital, and we'll all have to be her nurses...yes, you too, Tim!" He frowned. "Don't worry." she smiled. "Nursing's not only about bandages, bed-pans and that kind of thing! Often it's simple things, like taking the patient a cup of tea, holding hands and chatting. You could tell her how the school football team's getting on, or about your favourite subject at school. It should be fun!"

Tim wasn't so sure. For one thing, Shirley wouldn't be interested in the latest football scores, and, to tell the truth, he couldn't think which was his favourite subject at school. They were all a bit dull. As for holding hands, that certainly wasn't his idea of fun. On the whole, he thought he wouldn't be much good at nursing. And now he had other things on his mind. For instance, he wanted to know what damage had all those Dorniers and Heinkels done to the neighbourhood while they were asleep far away in the countryside?

Welbeck Avenue was more than a mile from the nearest docks, but it had had its own special moment of danger. It was the night the war came to Welbeck Avenue. Shirley and Tim had been away in their safe place for three months, but there was no sign of any bombers, so, like most of the evacuees, they had come home.

Then without any warning, the Luftwaffe arrived overhead, and they were trapped. For two frightening nights they sat huddled together in the shelter with the rest of the Welbeck residents, listening to the sound of explosions. On the second night they had just settled down and the sirens were still sounding, when there was a shrill, whistling sound followed by a ground-shaking thud, as the dim lights flickered.

"That was a 'dud'", Mr Impitt muttered. They could breathe again. But the 'dud' had made a big impression on number 12, Mrs Ferguson's house, next door but one to the Olivers' house. The whole of its front had disappeared, as if it had been hit by a giant hammer and, where the neat little front garden had been, there was a deep hole, with the dud bomb lying at the bottom next to Mrs Ferguson's talkative parrot, Henry, still in his cage and complaining at the top of his considerable voice. The bomb had been defused and carted off to be re-fitted with a new fuse and, at the suggestion of the residents, dropped on the enemy, 'to give Adolf a dose of his own medicine!' Mrs Ferguson had attained something like celebrity status as 'a notable survivor of the Blitz', and number 12 had a brand new frontage including a privet hedge.

But what about the rest of the Avenue? Had it survived the May blitz? He was keen to find out, and slipped out into the street to inspect. The sticky tape was everywhere, still. Nothing which was considered breakable had been left uncovered. Mrs Thompson at number 7, who was extremely nervous, had been particularly enthusiastic, with an extra-sticky, anti-blast variety, and said to Mrs Impitt, strictly in confidence, that, if Mrs Ferguson's bomb hadn't been a 'dud', her sticky tape would have been properly tested! Mrs Impitt replied that, if Mrs Ferguson's bomb hadn't been a dud, it would certainly have tested the sticky tape at number 7, but there would probably have been nothing left of number 12, and only bits of number 10 and 14!

Tim strolled on up the Avenue. The white lines were still there on the lamp posts to remind everyone that, although the bombers had gone elsewhere, the war was still going on; but the enthusiastic painter hadn't stopped there. Daubed on the sandstone wall which brought the Avenue to a dead-end, was a large, unmissable, white cross, to warn any unwary, night-time road-user that that was where the Avenue ended and the London, Midland and Scottish Railways took over. Otherwise the Avenue seemed to be as the evacuees had left it, and the residents had survived.

The little children at number 16 had been taken to safety in Ruthin, a pretty town in North Wales where their mother was renting a cottage. They would be staying there until the war was over, she said. She wasn't taking any chances!

Harry Simpson's Mum at number 17 had mentioned to Tim's mum that Harry was serving on a Destroyer protecting convoys. "He's somewhere on the high seas," she said proudly. She couldn't say exactly where, and wouldn't, even if she knew.

"After all, careless talk costs lives, as we all know! It's very dangerous out there, with all those nasty U-Boats lurking about waiting to sink you! But I don't worry. I just pray for my Harry and his brave sailor-comrades." She mustered a brave smile. "I feel that that's my little part in the war effort."

'Poor, lonely Mrs Simpson! Another casualty!' Tim thought, although, judging by what the doctor had said about Shirley, almost everyone in Welbeck Avenue was a kind of casualty of war! Mrs Ferguson being bombed out of her home, and having to go and live with her talkative sister in Knotty Ash. Mrs Thompson, fretting about her Billy away from home in far-off Wales, and his own mum, hiding from the bombing in the cold, draughty shelter, worrying about her kids sixty miles away. Dad, too, sticking to his post on the factory roof, whatever the weather, dodging bombs and risking catching his death of cold. And what about himself? Far away from home and Mum and Dad, enduring eighteen terrifying months under the all-seeing eye and heavy hand of Mrs Low, the village Headmistress, and falling miles behind at arithmetic! Didn't that make him a casualty? Yes. Their street had its share of casualties. And that was just one street! Multiply Welbeck Avenue by a few thousand, and that was just one city. Multiply that by dozens or more! The Doctor was right! Adolf Hitler had a lot to answer for.

By now he had reached the end wall. This was his favourite place, where he and Billy had spent hours with note-book and pencil before the war, checking on the railway traffic. It had also survived the bombing! It took only a moment to locate the foot-holds that he and Billy had scraped out. He scrambled up on top, found a smooth place to sit, and looked around. In front of him, the railway embankment rose steeply to the tracks which drew his eye through Wavertree Station, a hundred yards to his right, and beyond, towards the Edge

Hill sidings - THE GRIDIRON - with its spaghetti-like lines, hot and shimmering through a mirage in the mid-July sunshine. A passenger train rattled past, it's windows covered in tape, followed by a goods-train on its way towards the docks, loaded with what looked very like tanks and armoured cars, thinly disguised under flimsy covers.

He frowned. Don't they realise that there are spies about?

In the quietness, he thought about the strange September morning, almost two years before. He had been sitting in that very spot, watching THE SCOT rushing past, just a few minutes before their country declared war on Germany. The next morning, he and Shirley were evacuees, on their way to Shropshire and Crab Mill Farm.

Now, alerted by some kind of sixth sense, his heart-beat quickened. He sat up straight, shaded his eyes and focussed on a spot a few hundred yards away, beyond Wavertree Station where, at any moment, THE SCOT should be heading towards him. It must be well after ten o'clock, he guessed, and it was never late; but the seconds ticked by, and a shocking thought crept into his mind. Perhaps it wasn't coming! Was THE SCOT yet another casualty? He had meant to ask his Mum.

He was thinking more dark thoughts about Herr Hitler when it came into view - the Prince of Steam in all its shiny, dark-maroon glory, its famous bullet-nose buckling in the mirage, hurtling through Wavertree Station towards his ring-side seat. He dug his heels hard into the wall. An elbow sticking out of the driver's cab was all he could see of the footplate action. Never mind. There would be plenty of opportunities to catch the driver's eye. Now he could write to Billy and the others who had been evacuated to Wrexham in North Wales with the school, and let them know that their precious SCOT had survived.

He slid down off the wall and started off, at a run, down the Avenue, across Penny Lane and into Dovedale Road.

CHAPTER THREE

RECCE CONTINUED

Considering that education now ranked at the very bottom of his list of important pastimes, to anyone interested, it would have come as a surprise to learn that, to Tim, Dovedale Road Junior School ranked second only in importance to the Welbeck Avenue end wall, for two reasons. Firstly, it was where he and his best friends met up every week-day during school term time. If they couldn't be enjoying a game in the park, they could at least be together at 'Dovedale Road', as the school was known. They had no choice, of course; but, in Tim's case, it made life at school bearable.

The second reason was a stretch of grass in one corner of the playground where keen footballers played every break-time. It wasn't a proper 'pitch'. Nobody bothered about such things as penalty areas, centre circles, side-lines or even goal posts. But to Tim it was the most important place in the school. Far away on the dusty playground of Lyneal village school, he had thought about it every day while he was showing the village kids how to dribble and shoot. He had to know; had it survived the Blitz, or had one of those stray bombs wiped it out?

To someone on foot and in a hurry, the school was only a two-minute run from Welbeck Avenue. Once inside the gates he ran quickly across the yard and pulled up, frowning. The precious grass was still there! The Luftwaffe had left it alone; but someone had painted white lines all over it; not the kind one would find on a football pitch; just straight lines, about five strides apart, making avenues, each divided into boxes. What was it all about? He turned away, and had almost reached the gates when he spotted Mr Spinks, the caretaker, crossing the yard. He would have an answer. Tim ran across.

"'Scuse me, Mr Spinks, but what are those white lines doing on the field, please?"

"They're for the allotments."

"What allotments?"

"For you kids to grow vegetables."

"You mean it's going to be DUG UP?

"That's right…for the war effort. The Head says so."

"But that's not fair. It's where we play football!"

"Not any more, you can't!"

"Where are we supposed to play football, then?

"That's what the playground's for."

"But the ball bounces about too much on the playground."

"That'll make you better at ball-control!" The caretaker grinned.

Tim frowned. This was taking digging for victory too far, and certainly no grinning matter. Obviously the caretaker didn't know much about football. If he did, he would know that it's supposed to be played on grass!

"Well, I'll talk to Mr Donaldson about it when he gets back from Wales."

"I don't think that will make any difference!" Mr Spinks shook his head, and went on his way.

Tim was not in a good mood as he trudged home. He grabbed his football and vented his annoyance practising shooting at the cross on the end wall. Pitch or no pitch, he intended to be ready for the coming football season.

After a disgruntled lunch, he set out for the next destination on his recce. THE TUCK SHOP was very popular with Dovedale Road pupils, but the south end of Penny Lane, where it was situated, was close to the main Liverpool to London railway line, and, bearing in mind Mrs Ferguson's ruined frontage, he knew how inaccurate the Nazi bomb-aimers could be. It would be just their luck if a stray bomb had blown the shop away, plus the entire stock and Mr Wattleworth, the owner, who was very popular with the kids, and would be difficult to replace. Mum said she thought the shop and owner were still there, but he wanted to make sure.

It was a five-minute walk away from Welbeck Avenue. A good runner could do it in less than two. He turned the corner into Penny Lane at speed, and pulled up, fingers crossed, smiling. THE TUCK SHOP was all there still, the orange polka-dots covering the windows, a weak attempt to disguise the fact that there wasn't much to see on the shelves - just a token selection of Sherbert Dabs, Liquorice All-sorts, Everton mints, Pear Drops and Mint Imperials. Not exactly mouth-watering! It was no good blaming Mr W, as he was known. Everyone knew who was to blame!

A notice invited all discerning sweet-lovers to step inside and blow the whole of the week's ration on the spot. Unfortunately, this could only be a fact-finding mission. He was penniless, and it would be Saturday before he could come back as a paying customer. But, having come this far, he decided he might as well make contact with the important Mr W.

He pressed down on the latch, pushed open the door and stepped inside. The portly, white-haired Mr W was at his usual post at the counter, and behind him, a large poster carried the usual grim announcement.

SWEET RATIONING
4 OUNCES PER PERSON PER WEEK ONLY

Tim shook his head.

How could anyone be expected to survive the week on four ounces of sweets? The rationing was as cruel as the bombing! Back at Crab Mill Farm he had been lucky. When the sweet ration ran out, there was a mountain of sugar-beet in the barn. They could help themselves, and gnaw away to their heart's content; and, as a last resort, there was the cattle-cake, which might look like chunks of saw-dust, but tasted all right once you got used to it. It was better than nothing. Another sign said....

DON'T FORGET
YOUR
RATION BOOK!

As if he would!

He noticed that Mr W hadn't lost any weight while they had been away. Do sweet-shop owners have ration books, like everyone else, he wondered; or are they allowed to help themselves? It would probably be rude to ask.

The shop-keeper smiled across the counter.

"Well, it's the young evacuee come home! I'm glad to see you! When all you Dovedale Road kids went away, I lost most of my regular customers!"

Tim nodded sympathetically, as if to admit that it was his fault that Mr W's regulars had deserted him.

Mr W continued.

"I hope the shop-keepers in the countryside have been looking after you."

"Yes, they have!" Tim thought he might mention the village Postmistress who took pity on the little evacuee and sometimes added an extra Everton mint or Aniseed ball to his ration. Then he decided not to. She might get into trouble. He headed for the door.

"Cheerio, Mr W. I'll be back on Saturday... and cheer up! The others'll be back soon!"

Now he retraced his steps along Crawford Avenue to destination number four. The Wavertree Playground was a vast area of grass, stretching away into the distance, with hardly a bush or tree in sight, better known as 'THE MYSTERY', although nobody seemed to know why. It had certainly seen much better days, and the war hadn't helped. The ornate iron gates at the three entrances had been taken down and carted off to factories, to be turned into tanks, guns, bullets and such-like, although that was good news for local footballers. At closing time, the Park Keeper could shout and blow his whistle until he was blue in the face. There were no gates to close! They could stay as long as they liked and there was nothing he could do about it.

But as he walked up, another doubt crossed Tim's mind. The main-line ran along the whole of one side of the playground. Suppose some of the bombs intended for the lines had landed on it! It was certainly big enough. They could hardly miss. He feared the worst as he jogged through the entrance and up the main path.

Straight ahead lay the sports pavilion, a strange, wooden pagoda-like edifice, with enough changing room for hundreds. Gaunt and lonely against the sky, with peeling paintwork, it seemed to underline the impression of bleakness. A squadron of sea-gulls had ventured inland, and with the whole playground to choose from, had camped-out in front of the main entrance, like a crowd of supporters waiting to cheer the players as they clattered down the steps on the way to their allocated pitches, which was what he had come to check on.

The Mystery might not be very scenic, but the pitches, stretching end-to-end and side-by-side, as far as the eye could see, more than made up for that. He stood there smiling. It was a footballer's paradise, a reminder of the city's proud footballing history, where generations of young hopefuls, including himself, had dreamed of playing, some day, at Anfield or Goodison Park. For all its dreariness, the MYSTERY must surely rank with the Cathedral, the Liver Buildings, the Adelphi Hotel and St George's Hall, not to mention eight miles of docks, among the city's most important places, and the bombs had missed it completely! Or had they? The grin on his face died. Some of the pitches had disappeared!

He frowned. There could be no doubt. Where penalty areas had once been the scene of goalmouth scrambles, rows of vegetables were flourishing. He might have known! First the precious school field, and now this!

He wandered across, peered over the fence, and noticed that someone's carrots were flourishing. He had planted some at Crab Mill Farm as his personal bit of digging for victory; but the local rabbits had found them. Perhaps the Wavertree rabbit population had gone to ground when the May blitz started, and hadn't surfaced yet. More probably they had been nabbed by hungry locals, and made into pies.

On the higher ground behind the pavilion, there was a fenced-off area where a squad from the Kings Own Regiment had hoisted a barrage balloon high over the playground. How effective it had been in dissuading the bomber pilots from flying over the city and docks was anyone's guess; but no bombs had landed on the allotments, and, having done its bit, the balloon had gone, and its crew with it. He shook his head. The evacuees always seemed to miss the interesting action!

He now retraced his steps, leaving the MYSTERY to the sea-gulls and headed along Smithdown Road towards the final destination on his reconnaissance.

Situated only a minute's walk from Welbeck Avenue, via back lanes, the GRAND CINEMA had an impressive frontage to match its name. Eye-catching Roman columns flanked the entrance and, when films were showing, an elderly gentleman would appear on the pavement in a military-type, navy-blue frock-coat, with gold-braid piping, tassels tumbling from each shoulder, and peaked cap. His official title was Commissionaire, although, to regular customers, he was known as 'The Colonel'. Behind his back the boys called him 'The Fuhrer'.

It had to be admitted that, compared with other cinemas such as the Allerton PLAZA, which boasted a stunning, mosaic-lined goldfish pond in a spacious foyer, THE GRAND was one of the poor relations of the city's cinema scene, but in Tim's opinion, it always lived up to its name. The grandeur was what was on the silver

screen. Once inside and focussed, preferably on an adventure film with lots of action, not too much talking, and no kissing, he would be transported quickly into another world, riding for justice with the Lone Ranger, repelling visitors from outer space with Flash Gordon, or outwitting the Gestapo with the Resistance. A bomb might blow the roof off during a performance, and he wouldn't notice.

Now as he approached, the tall figure of the Colonel loomed up where they had left him when the blitz started.

"Hello, Colonel," Tim tried to sound cheerful.

The Commissionaire frowned down at him, tweaking the ends of his moustache.

"Oh. So you're back, then!"

Tim grinned.

"Yes, and I thought I'd come to see if you've still got a job."

"Well, as you can see, I have! So push off!" The same old friendly Fuhrer!

Tim smiled, politely. He wouldn't trade punches.

"The others will be coming home from Wales any day now." He knew this wouldn't be good news to the Colonel, who loathed the kids' matinees...all the noise and pushing and shoving. Again he tweaked his moustache, frowning.

"Oh."

"Yes. They're all looking forward to seeing you again." That wasn't true, and the Colonel knew it.

Tim grinned and saluted.

"See you on Saturday, Colonel!"

The Colonel sniffed and turned away as Tim headed for home.

To sum up the morning's mission...so far so good. Either the Luftwaffe had considered the main line not worth targeting, or their bomb-aimers were worse at their job than he had thought. But he knew that that wasn't the whole picture.

CHAPTER FOUR

DEFIANT CITY

It was the evacuees' first Saturday back at home. Shirley was under orders to stay in bed, so this was an ideal opportunity to catch up on Tim's latest exploits in Shropshire. Lunch was moving slowly, as questions and answers criss-crossed the table.

"I hope you remembered to clean your teeth every night, Tim."

He frowned. As chief interrogator, Mum had asked the same question every time she had visited! That and the one about combing his hair. They were two of her little obsessions.

"Yes, Mum."

"...And combed your hair before school?" He frowned again.

"Yes...usually." That was a long way from the whole truth.

"And paid attention in arithmetic lessons?" Another obsession!

"I tried to." Arithmetic lessons were a blur.

"We hope you were polite to the Headmistress."

"Everyone was polite to Mrs Low!"

"And did you remember to say your prayers at bed-time?"

"Sometimes. But sometimes I was too sleepy."

More questions followed, including one about football. He could answer this one confidently. He had taken his ball to school to show the country kids how to dribble and shoot.

"...That's when Mrs Low didn't confiscate the ball."

The third degree finally came to an end, lunch was over and Dad reached for his hat.

"Come on, Tim. I'll show you what was happening to your city while you were coaching football. "

It was a one minute walk to the tram-stop, and they joined the queue. High up, a goods-train clattered over Smithdown Road bridge heading south. Tim counted the trucks.

"That's twenty three! I wonder what it's carrying?"

"Food, probably. That's one of the main reasons we had to keep our docks working. Hitler couldn't make us give in by bombing us, but he knows we rely on lots of food from overseas. So, while his U-Boats were targeting the supply ships to stop them getting through, his bombers were doing their worst to put our docks out of action. Then, even when a ship made it into port, there'd be nowhere to unload its cargo, and we would starve."

"That was cruel!"

Dad nodded. "The Luftwaffe's favourite weapons were fire-bombs - incendiaries, you've heard of them. From my fire-watchers post, I could see them cascading down through the search-lights in their thousands."

"That must have been scary!"

"Yes. Incendiaries can do even more damage than ordinary bombs. Fire spreads quickly, especially in a strong wind. So what isn't knocked down by high-explosives is finished off by fire. My job was to spot where a fire had broken out, and phone the fire-fighters to tell them where to look. Mine was the easiest part! They had to find their way there, dodging through the rubble and around craters. And that wasn't the only danger. Down there, especially on the Dock Road where the warehouse walls are well over a hundred feet high, they couldn't be sure that they wouldn't just topple over and bury them and their hoses.

"They should all get medals!"

"You're right, Tim. And they weren't the only ones! There were the rescue teams, digging people out of the rubble, the ambulance men, the doctors and nurses. They knew they were in great danger, but kept going. It shows you how brave people can be when they've got their backs to the wall! Ah...come on. This one will do!"

A tram with the words PIER HEAD on the destination board, was pulling up at the stop. Tim led the way smartly up the stairs, and bagged two seats as they lurched forward under the railway bridge, heading for the city centre.

The first few hundred yards were on the level, between rows of shops, the windows criss-crossed with sticky tape or boarded-up, where windows had been blown out. Tim spotted a notice on the pavement saying 'Walk in! No windows, but business as usual!' Now they started to climb, stopping now and then, to let passengers off and on, until they reached level ground running along a ridge. It was one of the highest points in the approach to the city, with a first view over the river. Crossing the ridge, they began a long, rapid descent, down a wide road flanked by rows of impressive, Edwardian residences, a reminder of the hey-day of one of the world's great sea-ports.

It was less than two months since the end of the May blitz and, from their bird's eye position, everywhere they looked there were gaps where someone's home had once been. Tim spotted an ornate fire-place still in place, hugging a wall, as if determined not to drop off. Here and there, faded wallpaper fluttered in the light breeze. He pointed.

"It must have been terrible to come home after an air-raid and discover that your house wasn't where you left it! I wonder what happened to the people who lived there?"

"Most of them would go to stay with relatives or friends, like our Mrs Ferguson; but some would have to spend the night in a church or a school hall...even a cinema."

Tim grinned.

"Imagine that, a whole night at THE GRAND!"

Dad smiled.

"They wouldn't be watching a film, Tim!"

Now the tram was running on a downhill slope, and a massive building loomed up on the sky-line.

The Cathedral, built from the reddish sandstone on which the city stood, lay less than a quarter of a mile from the nearest dock. Tim pointed.

"No wonder it wasn't knocked down! The bombs probably bounced off!"

The tram rattled on its way, and he was thinking hard.

"D'you think God made them miss...I mean, because a church is supposed to be His house?"

"You might think so, Tim; but churches got the same treatment as everything else. Some were ruined, like Coventry Cathedral. The bombers were aiming at the munitions factories and the Cathedral got in the way! All that was left were the outer walls. But it didn't stop people worshipping. They cleaned up the floor, brought in some chairs and carried on as usual. Our Cathedral didn't escape altogether. The outer walls were damaged, but most of the stained-glass windows ended up on the floor."

"We should send Hitler the bill!"

There was more squealing of metal on metal as they swung left, past Central Station, and Dad was pointing.

"That was one of the safest places in the city when the bombing started. If you were caught in a raid, you could drop down to the Underground station and spend the night on the platform. The trains didn't run during the raids, so it was safe down there, and quiet, once the singing stopped!"

Down below, the pavements were crowded with shoppers, mostly mums with children in tow and ration books in hand, looking for school uniforms and equipment. The summer holidays were nearly over.

Tim sighed.

They were in Lord Street now, and he was pointing, open-mouthed.

"Just look at that!"

Over to their left, instead of the rows of towering, three, four, and five-storey shops and offices which he remembered, there was just one vast, empty space.

"That was a land-mine!" Dad muttered, "maybe two! They're super-bombs, as big as a pillar-box, intended for the docks and warehouses. They come down on parachutes and can easily miss their target, especially if there's a strong wind blowing. But wherever they land there's usually very little left standing!"

Tim was sitting quietly, trying to take everything in, as the tram screeched its way slowly up to another ridge. Now they could see along Castle Street to the Town Hall, almost invisible behind a wall of sand-bags. It was the same wherever they looked...offices, banks and shops engulfed by sand. Tim grinned.

"It's lucky that New Brighton's so close, Dad. We'll never run out of sand!"

Among the crowds below he could pick out soldiers in Khaki, airmen in blue and a surprising number of officers of the Royal Navy, some with an impressive array of gold rings on their sleeves.

"They're probably Admirals...or at least captains!"

"You could be right, Tim. I've heard that the top brass, as they're called, are here, somewhere under these streets, planning ways to tackle the German U-Boat packs in the Atlantic. That's one of the battles we've got to win if we're going to beat Hitler."

By now they had reached the business centre of the city, towering buildings everywhere, with open spaces where a bomb had made a direct hit. Dad pointed to an ornate doorway standing by itself in an open space.

"That's all that's left of our grand old Corn Exchange. Just think, Tim. It's been here for well over a hundred years and it took the Gerries a couple of minutes to blow it away, except for that doorway! But it didn't do them much good! The next day the businessmen were back, top hats, brief cases and all! It was business as usual, out in the street, as if nothing had happened! The doorway was a kind of rallying point. That's determination for you, Tim, the 'bull-dog' spirit, and it was the same up and down the country. Most of our biggest cities and sea-ports took a pounding, and you wouldn't have seen a white flag flying anywhere! Hitler must be wondering what he's got to do to make us give in!"

Now they had to hold tight again as they lurched forward, dropping down to sea level, under the Overhead Railway and onto the open space of the Pier Head. They shuddered to a halt and Dad led the way.

"Come on, let's catch a ferry."

They had arrived at low-tide, so the gangway dropped steeply to the landing stage, and they had to dig their heels into the floor for balance. A ferry, THE BIDSTON, was just pulling alongside, and they joined the crowd. The crew tied up, the gangplank slammed down, and the passengers flooded out onto the stage, bracing themselves for the stiff climb to the quayside. Then the waiting crowd surged over the gangplank and onto the lower deck. Dad led the way up a flight of stairs to the upper deck and Tim ran ahead to find a seat with a good view of the Captain on the bridge. With all that gold braid in mind, he had decided that it would be fun to be in charge of a ship. He would think about it.

The last passengers had come on board and the crew swung into action, raising the gangplank and sliding the barrier across to make an adventurous late-comer think twice about leaping aboard. The mooring ropes were untied, and the engine throbbed under their feet as they pulled away from the stage in a broad sweep, out onto the river. Now Tim was on his feet, pointing.

"Just look at that!"

The river was almost gridlocked. Ships of every kind, flying a variety of allied flags, made their way to or from one or other of the bigger docks. Two troop-carriers, a mass of khaki, were riding at anchor, waiting for orders to sail and, further west, nearer the mouth of the river, a whole convoy of merchantmen had formed up, preparing to venture out into the perilous Atlantic. Their Destroyer escort would be waiting for them as they left the safety of the river. On the south side of the river, streams of traffic headed to or from the Ship Canal. Here and there, a posse of tugs fussed about, pulling or nudging huge ships into a dock or out onto the river. The Pilot boats were out in force, key-players in all the activity, and, to complete the mix, the ferries, going about their routine business, but steering anything but a routine course.

For once Tim was speechless, and Dad did the talking.

"Now you can see why the Luftwaffe wanted to burn our docks down!".

At this point the Bidston was manoeuvring around the stern of a troop carrier.

"The ferries came in very useful during the Blitz. They were under orders to tie-up alongside the troop-carriers, it was called *stand-by* duty, so that, if there was a direct hit on one of them, the troops could be transferred to the ferry and safety. It was dangerous work! The Royal Daffodil II, one of the oldest ferries, was on stand-by one night. She received a direct hit near her engine room, and went down."

"That was bad luck!"

"Yes, and it might have been far worse; but the blast from the explosion went straight up through her funnel into thin air; otherwise she would have been blown out of the water!" He pointed towards the Seacombe landing stage. "She's still down there in thirty feet of water, very wet, I should think, and filling up with sand, but still in one piece. They say they're going to try to re-float her."

By now the Bidston had negotiated a gracefully-curved approach to the Birkenhead landing stage. Dad paid the fare and, back on board for the return trip, they leaned over the side-rail, observing the twentieth century armada which had taken over the river. A group of soldiers waved from the deck of their carrier. Tim waved back.

"I hope they'll all come back."

"Yes. We must hope and pray that they will."

The helmsman was again performing wonders, steering them back towards the Pier Head. As they emerged, they had a perfect view of the water-front and the giant, imitation Cormorants, perched high up on the top of the Liver Buildings - the Liver Birds, twin, silent witnesses of the blitz. They had ridden out the Luftwaffe storm, and now, with wings out-stretched, waving 'good riddance' to the retreating raiders, they seemed to symbolised the city's defiance.

THE BIDSTON drew alongside the landing stage and they joined the rush up the gangway, this time on their toes, back to terra firma and the tram home.

Back at Welbeck Avenue the news was out. The Dovedale Road evacuees were coming home. Mrs Thompson said they would be arriving at Wavertree Station, Platform Two, at 2.30pm, the following Monday.

CHAPTER FIVE

EVACUEES REUNITED!

Tim had been waiting since two o'clock, and Platform Two was seething. As the train steamed into sight, heads and shoulders hanging out of windows, an ear-splitting cheer went up from the crowd, and it had hardly screeched to a halt, before doors flew open, and bodies and baggage tumbled onto the platform, to be seized by blubbing mums. A few dads, stiff upper-lipped, hankies at the ready, hovered in the back-ground. Last off were the long-suffering teachers, overjoyed to have finally arrived, and the guard, muttering that it was 'the rowdiest train-load' he had come across in his long service with London, Midland and Scottish Railways!

"I can't understand why they're so happy to see 'em back. Should've have left 'em in Wales!"

Tim soon spotted Billy, who was being hugged by his mum. Mrs Thompson was in quite a state, vowing, through sobs, that she would never, ever let him out of her sight again! Tim caught Billy's eye and waited for his friend to detach himself and push his way through the crowd. Then he spotted his other close friends, Sid Shaw and Ken Cox and waved them over. There were slaps on the back all round, and, at Tim's suggestion, it was agreed that they would meet at his house the next morning, at half past nine, to inspect the air-raid shelter behind Number 6. They remembered it as a good place for robbers to hide from cops, and that kind of thing. Tim hoped he could convince them that, now it wasn't needed as a shelter, it would make an ideal den.

When the others knocked, he was waiting. He led the way around to the back lane, pushed open the shelter door and went in. The friends followed and immediately had serious doubts. The pungent smell of cement was even stronger than they remembered; the metal doors, one at each end, wouldn't stay closed, and the solid -glass, slit-windows, even in the bright afternoon sunshine, seemed reluctant to admit any more than a miserly amount of light. The furniture lay where it had been left by the retreating residents after the last of the May raids – a couple of card-tables and rickety chairs; Mrs Impitt's old sofa, well-worn, mildewed and uncomfortable; a faded, striped deck-chair, and Tim's wobbly bunk with his name still on the side - all sentimental reminders of the intrepid Welbeck Avenue Resistance, but long past their best. The shelter had served the older residents well in their hour of need, but, now that that hour had passed, it had to be admitted...it was hardly 'ideal' as an Headquarters for much younger ones.

It was a great disappointment to Tim who felt a strong personal attachment to his shelter. After all, he could tell the true story, exaggerated in parts, of how he had ventured out of that very shelter in his dressing gown, during an air-raid, with enemy bombers overhead, at dead of night, hunting for shrapnel, and how he had found the nose-cone of a bomb, which his Mum immediately and heartlessly confiscated, as a punishment for 'reckless behaviour'.

To sum up, while his shelter might look and smell like a pile of bricks and cement, it had a history of its own. The others had heard it all before and sympathised; but the truth had to be faced. It was smellier, gloomier, draughtier and untidier than any of them remembered, and they voted, three to one, to move on. But where to?

It was then that Ken mentioned that, as the brand-new air-raid shelter in his back garden wasn't 'doing anything much', they might as well take it over, with his Mum's permission, of course. This was greeted as enthusiastically as Tim's idea had been turned down. They decided to go and look it over.

But first things first. At ten o'clock precisely, according to Ken's watch, they left the shelter, trooped around to the end wall, shinned up on top, and found seats on the smooth sandstone.

It seemed ages since they had had the honour of witnessing

THE SCOT going by, and it was due at any time. Now they looked at Sid, who had unusually sensitive hearing and claimed that, if the atmospheric conditions were right, he could pick up the sound of an approaching express as far as two miles away. He raised his hand and motioned for silence, cupped his hand over his ear and closed his eyes. Nobody spoke as a minute went by, and another. Then he nodded slowly.

"It's on its way!"

A minute later, THE SCOT thundered into view, more glorious than any of them remembered, through Wavertree Station and past their ring-side seat, gigantic wheels a deafening blur, paintwork sparkling in the sunshine, and lucky passengers smiling down, understandingly, at the little congregation on their sandstone pew below, arms raised in homage. The worshippers sat quietly, watching the guards-van disappearing in the direction of Mossley Hill Station. The moment had been well-worth waiting for. Being evacuated had its compensations.

They agreed to re-convene at Ken's house at two o'clock, to ask permission to inspect the family air-raid shelter, with a view to taking it over as a den.

The Cox family home in Greenbank Road was situated on the other side of the main-line from Welbeck Avenue. The houses there were bigger and could boast back-gardens with space for such things as a family-size air-raid shelter. So, when, in 1939, the newspaper headlines were about 'PEACE IN OUR TIME' and 'APPEASEMENT,' Ken's Dad had snapped up one of the new Anderson shelters, at a price drastically reduced, on account of the possibility that it might never be used.

It had been delivered in *Easy to Assemble* parts - corrugated-iron sides, roof and door, timber interior, complete with slatted bunks and duck boards. Mr Cox, a keen golfer, was determined to hang on to the neatly-trimmed back-lawn which he used for putting practice; so, to make way for the large hole into which the Anderson would have to be sunk, the rhubarb patch in one corner of the garden had had to be sacrificed. Mrs Cox was not pleased.

According to the Instructions for Assembly, the shelter would measure five feet wide and seven feet long and high, protruding three feet above the ground, with an arc-shaped roof. Over the roof, father and son had toiled to lay a thick layer of soil, and Mrs Cox, not wishing to be left completely out of the action, had offered to plant a mixture of geraniums on top, 'as a sort of camouflage.' The rhubarb had been re-sited, in pots, at the side of the cycle shed.

When the shelter was finally in place and the geraniums had been sown, Mum, Dad and Kenneth, as Mum insisted on calling him, had gathered to admire and declare it 'operational'. Dad could pronounce the Anderson 'a sound investment', and history had proved him right.

According to official records, although the Luftwaffe had raided the city more than sixty times, the shelter in the back garden of number Thirty-five had kept them safe, and, as a bonus, with Ken safely away in Wales with the school, Mum and Dad had had the

shelter all to themselves. So, on nights when the invaders droned overhead and the odd, wayward bomb whistled down into a nearby garden, with the door shut, to keep the candle-light in and inquisitive rats out, they had sat safely holding hands, listening for bits of news on the wireless and hoping that the Ack-Ack gunners were having some success.

Then the Luftwaffe lost interest in the docks, and Ken's Mum's spirits rose, lifted by the thought that the Anderson could be unearthed and her rhubarb patch would be reinstated. But the ever-vigilant Mr Cox insisted otherwise.

"They might come back, my dear. You never know, in war… we're still a nuisance to Herr Hitler! Our little bunker must stay!" So the bunker had stayed, unvisited and unused since the end of the blitz.

Thus what, to a casual passer-by, might have seemed a white elephant cluttering up the garden, to the discerning eyes of a group of returning evacuees without a den, might well be considered a desirable residence with vacant possession.

At two o'clock, Billy, Tim and Sid, with Ken as the spokesman, appeared before Mrs Cox to request that, since the Anderson 'probably wasn't needed any more as an air-raid shelter', they might make it their new den. Mrs Cox, hoping that she had already descended into the mud for the last time, was inclined to hand it over there and then, no questions asked. For one thing, it's noisy new tenants might help to keep any rats away. It would also be nice to know where Kenneth might be from time to time. She waved a hand in the direction of the back garden.

"You can have it all to yourselves!"

The boys made grateful noises, then trooped around to the back garden to look more closely at their new premises. They agreed that even if it was 'a bit on the damp side', it should make a pretty good den.

It was sound-proof, once the door was shut, far enough away from the nearest civilisation, which was Ken's house, cleverly camouflaged behind the runner beans, and just the right size for four tenants. They decided to meet the next morning to take possession and make plans for the last few days of the holidays.

By mid-day they had moved in, and were enjoying the kind of satisfied feeling that people have on being handed the keys to a new home. Above the door, in chalk, a notice said THE DEN and, under that, another one declared GIRLS NOT ADMITTED. Inside, the walls had been brightened up with pictures of fighter planes in various operational modes - taking off, climbing, banking and diving, and Ken's favourite - a Spitfire, upside down, half way through a Victory Roll. When the air-raids started, Ken's Dad had added some extras - a shelf for a kettle, tea-pot, cups, and saucers, and a mirror for shaving. He had knocked three large nails into the wooden frame just inside the door as gas-mask hangers. The masks had gone indoors, but the nails must remain, he insisted, 'just in case'. On duck-boards in between the lower bunks, they had created a 'table' - a short plank resting on two piles of bricks salvaged from a nearby bombed-site. A well-worn tartan rug, donated by Ken's Mum, ripped in two and spread over the lower bunks, made two easy chairs. On one of the top bunks, called THE LIBRARY, they had piled various comics - Rovers, Wizards and Hotspurs, having decided unanimously that the Beano and Dandy were 'kids stuff'. The other top bunk was reserved for games gear - Ludo and Draughts, Tim's football, extremely grubby after almost two years' farmyard treatment, Ken's cricket bat, a cork ball minus its coat of red paint, and a set of stumps of varying lengths. The bails had gone missing.

Now they sat, two on each side, quietly taking in their new accommodation.

"You were very lucky to have a shelter all to yourselves, Ken," said Sid, "you and your Mum and Dad." Ken nodded thoughtfully, although secretly, he would rather have taken his chance with everyone else, in a shelter like Tim's, passing biscuits around and singing confident songs. He also had a hunch that Tim's shelter, with its roof of six-inch concrete might be a safer bet than the Anderson, with its covering of geraniums, but hadn't mentioned that to his Dad.

"My Grandpa's house has got a cellar," said Tim. "He and Grandma sheltered there during the raids, but I think that was a bit risky. I mean, if the house had been hit by a bomb they might have been buried alive...perhaps for days!"

"Old people don't seem to worry as much as everyone else," said Sid. "My Auntie Sybil's like that. She's quite old and lives all by herself in a block of flats. The nearest shelter's at the very end of the street and Auntie can't move very fast, so when the sirens started, she refused to budge. She just put a deck-chair under the staircase and sat there with her knitting and the cat. She said she wasn't scared, and, if she was going to be killed by a bomb, she would rather it was in her own home, with her cat."

Billy frowned. "That was brave! But my Mum says everyone should go to a proper shelter if they can. She says that two trams were caught in an air-raid one night, and everyone had to get off. They took shelter in Durning Road School which was nearby. It was one of the old schools, built of heavy stone, so they thought they should be safe; but there was a direct hit by a land-mine. The whole building collapsed and fell on them. A hundred and fifty people were killed, including quite a few kids."

"That was bad luck," muttered Tim. "Billy's Mum's right. It's always better to go to a real shelter - one like yours, Ken!" The others nodded, as Ken smiled, modestly.

"So what'll we do tomorrow?" asked Billy. "It's back to school on Monday."

"I vote we go to the Cassie," said Tim. "Mr Impitt says that Hitler couldn't beat us in the air, so, next time, he'll probably send his troops in by land. He's bound to go for the docks, and the Cassie's close by. It's smooth and sandy, perfect for landing craft to drop off troops and tanks and things. Billy and me went to look last year. There was just a roll of barbed wire and a few concrete blocks. So the defences are bound to be much better now...you know...Ack-Ack

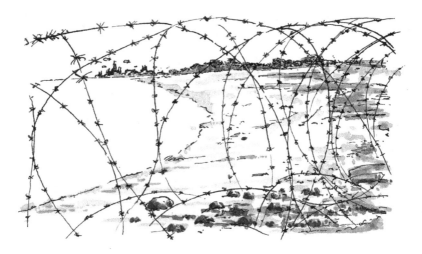

batteries, Pill Boxes, tank-traps, trenches, that kind of thing...and probably quite a few soldiers patrolling."

The others nodded, and it was agreed that they would meet up at the newspaper kiosk at ten o'clock the next morning, with sandwiches, to go and check out Mr Impitt's theory.

CHAPTER SIX

TROUBLE ON THE DOCK ROAD

Tim was waiting when the others arrived. The kiosk was Mr Erskine's little newspaper kingdom. The latest edition of the ECHO was always on sale, but anyone short of time or cash could read the news headlines for nothing. In large capital letters, on a special bill-board, they were usually headlines with a difference, written personally by Mr Erskine, who liked to inject a note of mystery into them. It was his way of 'lightening up the news', he said, which in late August,1941, tended to be on the gloomy side.

The day's headlines proclaimed RATS KEEP FOX AT BAY!

"I wonder what that means?" said Sid.

"Why don't we ask, while we're waiting?" said Billy. They walked over to the kiosk where Mr Erskine sat in an elevated position surrounded by newspapers.

"Mr Erskine,...what does your headline mean, please?"

The proprietor smiled down.

"Well, boys, our 8th Army's fighting the Gerries' Afrika Korps in North Africa, and there's a very important little sea-port on the Mediterranean called Tobruk, with a British and Australian garrison. Part of their job is to stop General Rommel - he's known as the Desert Fox - taking it over. He needs it to get supplies to his army. The Luftwaffe's been bombarding it for months, but there's lots of caves and tunnels there, and when the bombing starts our chaps just go underground! Then, when the bombing stops they come out and get on with their defending. Goebels, Hitler's right-hand man sneers at them. He says they're 'rats caught in a trap'. But the Desert Rats, as they call themselves, don't mind. They're holding the Fox up!"

"Thanks, Mr Erskine," said Billy. "We're going to the Cassie, to check our defences!"

"Well done, boys!" He gave the thumbs up sign.

A tram signed Aigburth was just pulling up at the stop, and, after a short ride they reached the Dingle, and set off for the Cast Iron shore, a stretch of muddy sand on the north side of the river known as 'The Cassie'. If Mr Impitt was right about German tactics, and Tim's hunch was correct, it should be worth investigating.

After a few minutes, they left the road to walk down onto the shore and pulled up short, with frowns all round. The barbed wire was still there, rustier than Tim and Billy remembered, and the concrete blocks were where they had been twelve months before. But where were the new defences that Tim had almost promised...the tank traps, Ack-Ack gun-emplacements, pill-boxes? There wasn't even a trench; and if soldiers had been on patrol they had either gone on leave, or home for a cup of tea. If the Germans were really thinking of invading by land, they obviously weren't expected to come this way! The Cassie was a big disappointment, a damp squib; but fortunately, if the shore wasn't bristling with defensive activity, there was plenty of interest elsewhere.

The Cammel Laird ship-building yards lay across the river from where they were standing. The Ark Royal aircraft carrier, Britain's Flag

Ship, had been built there in 1939, in time to send its fighter bombers to finish off the German flag ship, Bismarck, with their 'tin fish' torpedoes. The towering, dockyard cranes, in grey-green camouflage, had stood their ground during the air-raids. Now, they looked down

on an army of riveters, welders and painters working around the clock, to send more fighting-ships down the slipways into the fray. The machine-gun-like sound of riveting, broken every so often by a passing merchant ship, came bouncing over the water to where the boys were standing,

Looking west, the widest part of the river was alive with shipping, a vast floating forest of masts, funnels and rigging, rising and falling with the tide. Tim had seen it all, close up.

"Let's find the docks!" he yelled, pointing, "There's bound to be some fighting ships there, perhaps an MTB - that's a Motor Torpedo Boat - and a Sub or two."

They hoped he was right, this time, gulped down their sandwiches and trudged back to the Dingle and the Dock Road.

They had been walking for ten minutes and came to a high wall topped with rolls of barbed-wire.

"This must be a dock-wall," said Sid, hopefully.

They followed the wall for what seemed like miles and, at last reached a gateway with a sign saying HERCULANEUM DOCK. At one side of the gate a soldier with rifle and fixed-bayonet stood 'At Ease' outside a little hut. As the boys approached, he snapped to attention, shouldered his rifle, marched smartly across the open gate-way, about-turned, and returned to his hut and 'At Ease'. It was all perfectly choreographed. The boys were impressed and, to avoid distracting their new hero, they found a position to one side of the gate with a good view into the dock.

Not more than fifty yards away in the calm waters, an enormous cargo ship, flying the Stars and Stripes of America, had tied up, and an army of dockers swarmed about on the dock-side, busily off-loading crates.

"Good old America coming all this way to help us!" said Billy.

"My Dad says they're not in the war," said Ken. "That's why the German subs leave them alone."

As they watched, a crate with the letters JEEP stencilled on the side was lowered onto the dock-side and unpacked.

Sid gasped. "What a dinky car! It hasn't even got a roof... or proper doors. Even I could drive that!"

Billy laughed.

"Straight into the dock, you mean!"

At that moment, a soldier climbed aboard, started up the engine and accelerated, in a cloud of smoke, past the admiring watchers, and out onto the Dock Road.

Now the boys watched closely as more crates were dumped on the dockside, loaded onto trucks and carted away. Perhaps that was all the action there was going to be. After the impressive drill, it was another disappointment, but then, just as they were thinking of moving on, a group of sailors trotted down a gang-plank, chatting, heading towards the gate.

Ken plucked up courage and stepped forward.

"'Scuse me, mister," he called out to one of the sailors. "We saw the Jeep. What else is your ship carrying?"

The sailor stopped.

"H'ya, boys! Well, we've got maize - tons of it, so you British kids can have your Corn Flakes! We've brought you a few things to help you to fight Adolf, too...tanks, armoured cars, aeroplanes, that sort of thing! But don't spread it around!" He put a finger to his lips, and glanced over his shoulder. "You never know who's listening!"

He grinned, and pulled a small package from a pocket.

"Oh yeah! ...and we brought lots of this, too. I guess it's more interesting to you kids than maize!"

He lobbed it in their direction.

"There you go, buddies...some chewing gum all the way from the United States of America!"

All four buddies made a grab for it, but it was Sid who held it up.

"Thanks, mister!"

"That's OK!" The sailor replied. "But I gotta go now, boys. See ya!" He waved and ran to catch up with his friends.

"See ya!" they yelled back. They hoped so. They were all in

favour of the United States of America, and gathered around, as Sid tore the cover off the package and handed out four sticks of the gum.

"There's one left over," said Sid, "but we need a ruler! We'll have to split it when we get home."

They waved 'Cheerio' to the sentry, who stared straight ahead, and set off past another high wall.

They were in dockland now and Tim recognised names, Harrington, and Toxteth, which he had heard his Dad mention. Wherever they looked, there was the same feverish activity - swarms of dockers unloading cargo from Canada, New Zealand, Australia, and the West Indies, all members of Britain's Empire and now her war-time allies.

As they reached a dock gate, they hung around for a few minutes, glanced inside, then moved on. If there were any MTBs and Submarines around, they weren't supposed to be seen.

It was late afternoon, and the sun was dropping into the orange haze which, on warm, summer days, hung over the water-front buildings. The chewing gum had lost its flavour, their feet were tired and hot, and progress had slowed from a walk to a trudge. They were losing interest in dockland and thinking of home and tea. The tram back to Wavertree seemed a long way off and Ken was falling behind. On the overhead railway, a train rumbled past. What they needed was some transport of their own, Tim thought, something like a Jeep, with enough room for four, a cooling breeze in their faces and himself at the wheel! The road was very busy now, with motor- trucks and horse-drawn carts coming and going.

They had almost reached Brunswick Dock, and a cart, pulled by an elderly horse, driven by an elderly gentleman puffing at a cigarette, emerged from the gate at a slow trot. Straightaway, Tim noticed the lip along the back-end of the cart. It was just like the one on the cart at Crab Mill Farm, easy to hang on to, and good news for people with sore feet! It wasn't a Jeep, but, as his Mum would have said, 'Beggars can't be choosers!'

"Come on, you lot!" he said in a loud whisper, dashing out onto the road, "this one's going our way!" In a few quick strides he had reached the cart, grabbed hold of the lip, and swung his feet forward to rest them on a metal rail underneath. Billy and Sid were quickly on board, but Ken was struggling to catch up.

"Hurry up, slow coach!" Billy whispered, and, in a despairing, half-dive, half-leap, Ken caught hold of the lip and came alongside, red in the face and out of breath. The driver, with no load to keep an eye on and no rear-view mirror to consult, wasn't interested in what was going on behind him.

They passed Queens Dock and as they approached the gate to Wapping Dock a group of sailors spotted them and cheered. The driver, not realising that his cart was being hi-jacked, smiled and waved back. The boys giggled quietly; but by now, with the uneven movement of the cart on the cobbles, their fingers were aching and Ken was in trouble.

"I can't hold on much longer," he grunted.

Tim glanced at Billy. If Ken let go, they would all be in trouble.

"You've got to, Ken," muttered Billy. "Grit your teeth!" To make matters worse, the driver was calling for more speed from his faithful nag and it had gone up a gear. They were travelling quickly, now, and Tim was thinking it was time to jump ship; but how? They needed the driver to slow down, perhaps to let an old person cross the road or, better still, to stop at traffic lights. But there didn't seem to be any old persons or traffic lights on this stretch of the Dock Road.

He gulped. This was an emergency, calling for clear thinking. If he and Billy could join hands behind Ken to give him some support, he might survive. He had seen it done by the Lone Ranger and a chum. Or was it a stunt man? Either way, it must be possible, he guessed. But he would need to get to the other side of Ken first, and that wouldn't be easy. Ken was very stocky.

Fortunately, before his desperate plan could be tried out, help came from a totally unexpected source. They had just passed the gate to Brunswick Dock, and above the sound of the traffic they heard a loud shout.

"Oi there!" Tim glanced over his shoulder. The dock-yard policeman had spotted them. "Where d'you think you're goin'?"

Now the driver looked back and noticed his unauthorised passengers.

"Whoo! Betsy!" he shouted.

Betsy, probably glad of a reason to slow down after the recent burst of speed, did her best to dig her hooves into the cobbles and slid to a halt, about a hundred yards past the dock gate.

Gratefully, the boys dropped off and regrouped on the pavement. The policeman was already striding quickly towards them.

"Do we run?" said Tim.

"What's the use?" said Billy. "If he blows his whistle we'll have everybody after us...and, anyway, Ken couldn't keep up!"

"And we can't leave him behind, can we?" said Sid. Tim was in two minds. In this kind of situation, his first thought would be to run, but he hadn't thought about Ken, who was smiling gratefully at them. How could they leave him behind, to be nabbed by the law and taken to the nearest cell for the night? It would be like abandoning a wounded comrade on the battle-field. They had to stop and face the music, together. They stood in line, rubbing their hands.

"Try to look sorry, everyone!" muttered Sid.

The policeman now arrived at the scene of the crime, helmet in hand and out of breath, and joined the driver, who had dismounted and was glaring at the four offenders.

"A'right, then!" The policeman had taken his notebook and pencil out. They were in trouble!

"Do you realise 'ow dangerous that was?" He paused to let the seriousness of the situation sink in. "If you was my kids, I'd tan the 'ide off the lot of you!"

"Me too!" added the driver, grinding his cigarette-end emphatically into the pavement with his heel, putting his foot down, as it were, to express solidarity with the officer of the law.

The boys stood, shoulder to shoulder, trying to look sorry. Sid was studying the pavement. Ken was thinking about what would happen when the police turned up on the doorstep to confront his Mum. She would probably faint. Tim was visualising a conversation with his Dad about the high-jacking of a cart on the Dock Road, in broad daylight. Only Billy seemed to be taking things in his stride. He was frowning, as if to ask 'What's all the fuss about?'

The policeman was about to tell them. Like most policemen, he enjoyed an opportunity to lecture young delinquents about right and wrong. He was determined to impress on them the seriousness of their crime, but seemed to be struggling to think of a suitable punishment. Having no success at that, he had obviously decided that a good dose of shame would have to do. He pointed through the gate.

"In this 'ere dock there's ships from Canada and America, come all that way to bring us food, riskin' bein' sunk by 'itler's U-Boats... and losin' all them young lives... and 'ere you are, young scallywags, riskin' breakin' yer necks, playin' games on this 'ere gentleman's cart." The driver nodded and muttered a quiet "'Ere, 'ere", to keep up the pressure. Billy was frowning, trying to work out the connection between being torpedoed in mid-Atlantic and hitching a ride on the Dock Road. He wasn't going to go down without a fight.

"We were only having a bit of fun!" he muttered, loud enough for the policeman to hear.

"A bit of fun! A BIT OF FUN!" repeated the he officer, for emphasis, as policemen do.

With pencil poised, he went on..."A'right. What's yer names, then?"

"Sid Shaw, sir," "Tim Oliver, sir," "Kenneth Cox, sir," "Billy Thompson...SIR!"

"And where d'you live?"

"Wavertree, sir", said Ken.

"Well, now," the Bobby continued, "Sid, Ken, Tim and Billy, by the way, I don't like your attitude, sonny! I've got yer names - they're down in me book, and I want you to promise that, when you get home, you'll own up to your mums and dads about the trouble you've caused, and promise you won't do it again. A'right? D'you promise?"

"Promise, sir!"

"And what are you goin' to say to this 'ere gentleman?" He pointed to the driver.

"Very sorry, sir," came the reply, in unison.

"But thanks for the lift all the same," Billy added, grinning.

"That's alright," said the driver, unsure how to react to Billy's vote of thanks. "Just don't forget yer promises!"

He climbed back to his seat, lit up another cigarette, and with a jerk on the reins, cajoled the waiting Betsy into action. The policeman pocketed his note-book and strode back to his post inside the dock gate. The boys watched as the cart rattled on its way, then set off, at a thoughtful pace, for the Pier Head and the tram home, as Ken poured out heartfelt thanks that they hadn't left him to face the full force of the law all by himself.

****

"I've told you before, Tim...when you get into trouble, you let the whole family down! Why you have to do these things, I cannot understand. The Dock Road isn't a public playground."

At number 6, the evening meal was over, and Dad was summing up for the prosecution. Tim had kept his promise and had given a reasonably accurate account of the happenings on the Dock Road, pleading, in their defence, that they were 'fagged-out', their feet were sore and, well, 'it was only a bit of fun', after all. But after a long, hard day at the office, Dad couldn't see what was funny about it. After all, the docks were part of his business territory.

There could be only one verdict - Guilty, as charged by the absent policeman. All that remained was the sentencing.

"That was a dangerous thing to do," said Mum, "and you must learn your lesson, Tim. So you may not have next week's sweet ration. You can explain to Mr Wattleworth, and he won't be pleased. But your father and I are glad that you have owned up, so you may keep this week's Rover."

The defendant grinned slightly. He was feeling rather pleased with himself, considering that he had toyed with the idea of not owning up. He decided to go and see if Shirley might like to hear the story of his run-in with the law, and cheer her up with an impersonation of the Bobby.

"A'right, a'right! What's yer names then?"

That would be one good deed in a disastrous day.

****

The four convicts met at the Den the next morning, to compare notes. They had all owned up and had been sentenced accordingly. Billy had lost a week's pocket money. Ken would be deprived of the week's edition of the Hotspur, and had to listen to a long lecture from his Mum about being too easily led into trouble by his 'unruly friends'. Like Tim, Sid had lost a week's sweet ration. But he had brought a ruler and his pen-knife, and the others watched closely as he divided up the last stick of gum into four. It was a small consolation, as they sat in silence, chewing and reflecting on life's injustices.

On Monday it would be back to school.

CHAPTER SEVEN

BACK TO SCHOOL

Tim wandered through the gates, pulled up, and gaped. It was the first day of the new school year, most of the evacuees were back and the chatter in the playground was deafening. He caught a glimpse of his class-teacher. The luckless Mr Donaldson was on playground duty, as hard-pressed as ever, hemmed-in by a little crowd, all asking questions at the same time.

The whistle sounded, the chatter stopped and Mr Donaldson cleared his voice to take command. It was business as usual at Dovedale Road Juniors, and, back in their old class room, it felt as if nothing had changed. There was the tell-tale smell of ink-wells, and sticky tape all over the windows. Even the art-work which they had been doing before the bombing started, was still there. Tim spotted his own effort at capturing THE SCOT in full flight.

Mr Donaldson had been evacuated to Wales with the class, and now gave a short, off-the-cuff reunion speech about being 'good to be back in the old classroom...never forgetting the kindness of the people of Wales who took us in at a time of peril', and so forth. The speech ended with a warning that gas masks must not be thrown away, 'in case Herr Hitler changes his mind! and the Luftwaffe come calling again!'

"Which is most unlikely of course," he added quickly, noticing some anxious looks.

"Now, 5B," he continued, "quite soon you will be taking a most important test, which will help us to decide who will take the Grammar School entrance examination next year. So we will all be putting in a special effort between now and then, to make sure that we are confident and ready to give a good account of ourselves in the examination room." Mr Donaldson liked to talk as if he was one of them. He smiled, and some smiled back, as if to say 'Leave that to us, Sir!' They were the clever, confident ones, Tim noticed.

At home, there had been talk about him gaining a place at his Dad's old School, the Collegiate. But he knew he wasn't ready for the important test. For one thing he was a long way behind at arithmetic. He had never liked arithmetic. But then, he had never liked school. He wasn't the kind of pupil who wakes with the local larks, leaps out of bed, washes and dresses in double-quick time, gulps his breakfast down, and can be found at the front door, dinner money in hand, waiting to be escorted to school. Tim could usually find a reason for delaying setting out for school. If he had to be there, he would make the stay as short as possible.

Perhaps it was unfortunate that his very first school, Bridge Road Infants, lay directly over the road from Mossley Hill Station where the main line expresses pounded through regularly, reminding pupils that life outside the school was much more interesting than inside. In Tim's opinion it was the best thing about the school and it wasn't long before he had found a seat on the castellated, sandstone wall running alongside the railway embankment, not too near the school, where he could squeeze into one of the dips, to enjoy a ringside view of the latest rolling stock.

But when incriminating crosses began to appear opposite his name in the daily register, the Attendance Officer had called at number 6 to ask how a pupil could be at school on certain mornings, chasing a football about the playground, but was nowhere to be seen after lunch.

"He obviously wasn't ill, so he should have been at school!"

Then Mum remembered that he sometimes took his Train Spotters book to school, saying that he might do 'a bit of spotting' on his way home.

"You might try the railway embankment," she said, and that was where he was discovered, one sunny afternoon, happily whiling away the time between the comings and goings of the trains.

He was hauled up before the Headmaster, together with his mother, and warned that taking an afternoon off school was against the law and would hinder his progress. Mum said it wouldn't happen again, and set a fast pace on the way home.

"Just wait until your father gets home!"

According to Mum, father had had an impeccable, truant-free school career. In fact, it seemed that he had actually enjoyed school, and found it hard to understand why his son and heir should be so different.

Tim's school career had got off to a bad start, and when war broke out and he arrived as an evacuee at Lyneal village school, where education was taken very seriously, things got worse.

Mrs Low, the Headmistress didn't want city kids, especially boys, at her little school. The sudden arrival of evacuees meant that the school was overcrowded, and Tim found himself in a class of noisy five, six and seven year olds. Worse still he was terrified of the Headmistress. Everything about her sent waves of fear and confusion crashing around his mind, scrambling her words of wisdom, especially the arithmetical ones. So he had given up, preferring to day-dream about trains or football or life back at the farm, and had spent a lot of time standing on a stool looking at the wall.

At Dovedale Road, his Mum had already explained to Mr Wilkins, the Headmaster, that, while he was an evacuee, Tim had made little progress, especially in arithmetic, at which he had evidently made none. Mr Wilkins had assured her that, if anyone could turn her son into a mathematician, it would be Mr Donaldson, who was keen on football, which should help!

Away from the classroom, Tim's worst fears about the football pitch were about to be realised. Each class had been allocated one of the boxes, and a new subject on the curriculum, VEGECULTURE, had been thought-up by the enthusiastic Headmaster. In a stirring speech to the assembled school, he said how sorry he was to deprive the footballers of their prized stretch of grass, but pointed out that, 'in the struggle for right against wrong,' it is sometimes necessary to sacrifice something close to one's heart'.

"Girls and boys, this is our school's chance to carry the fight to the enemy! So I hope that each class will make the most of its opportunity to dig for victory."

Mr Donaldson, who wasn't a keen digger himself, had consulted a hand-book and noted that autumn is the best time for turning over the soil in preparation for sowing in the spring which, he said, would be hard work, as the ground had been pounded hard by the feet of so many dedicated footballers down the years. There was also a shortage of spades, so a rota was drawn up for two teams taking turns. Tim and Billy were in team B, and looked on, sadly, as Gladys Jones and Brian Richards of team A cut the first sods in 5B's little patch of England.

Football practices were now held on the playground where the ball did bounce about more than usual, as Tim had pointed out to Mr Spinks, and, to their surprise, they found that they were becoming better at ball control, as Mr Spinks had pointed out to Tim. The caretaker knew more about football than he had given him credit for!

A match had been arranged against Rose Lane Juniors and, every morning, Tim searched the notice-board. At last the team-sheet was pinned up and 'Tim Oliver, Outside Right' seemed to leap off the board to meet him. He grinned. He might be a flop at arithmetic, but he could shine at outside right!

The match was played on the Mystery which, as already noted, was close to Welbeck Avenue, and they were about to kick off when Tim noticed that his Mum had arrived with Billy's Mum, and they had taken up positions near the halfway line, where, Mum said, they could be more involved.

He gulped. Parents, especially mothers, can be embarrassing at football matches, and Mrs Thompson was worse than most. For example, if Billy was pushed over or kicked in the shins, she would accuse the teacher in charge of the opposition of using 'bullying tactics'. But his own Mum wasn't much better. She had a habit of calling out instructions, such as 'Look out, he's behind you!' Or, worse still...

'Pull your socks up, Tim!'

It was the one drawback with playing their matches near to home.

"I hope they behave themselves!" Billy muttered.

"Me too!" said Tim.

And, on this occasion, both mums were perfectly behaved, smiling sympathetically at the group of Rose Lane mums, when Dovedale Road scored the winning goal. In victory, it was easy to think kindly of the opposition.

Meanwhile, there was no sign of victory in the war, or an end to sweet rationing. At the TUCK SHOP, the paltry four ounces seemed to buy less than ever, and Mr W observed, gloomily, that the ration 'probably wouldn't be increased for some time'. This news wasn't well received in The Den. Did the government have any idea what hardships they had to put up with, they wanted to ask. Did anyone understand? Did anyone care?

Half-term finally arrived, and they had just taken their places in The Den, when the cheerful face of Mrs Cox appeared at ground level. She had seen a notice in the window of Peagram's Grocers, announcing that A SMALL QUANTITY OF BROKEN BISCUITS would be on sale the next morning, A PENNY A BAG - RATION BOOKS NOT NEEDED - FIRST COME - FIRST SERVED. She had queued for over an hour and, despite quite a lot of jostling, had been able to claim a penny-worth.

"Here's a little half-term treat!" she said, passing it over. They grinned. In days of hardship such as these, a biscuit, even a broken one, was almost as good as a sweet, and good old Ken's Mum had run the gauntlet of a Peagram's queue on their behalf, to get her hands on a bag full! Ken's Mum understood and cared!

With great care the contents were emptied onto the table, and each piece, however insignificant, scrutinised, as an archaeologist would examine a precious fragment of pottery, then allocated to one of three categories - the 'perfect', the 'badly damaged but recognisable', and 'the almost unrecognisable', which had only just survived the trip from Crawford's factory.

To thank her for all the trouble she had gone to on their behalf, they voted that two category-one Bourbon Creams, her favourites, should be handed back for Ken's Dad and herself to enjoy with their afternoon tea. Mr Cox, however, declined the gift, muttering discreetly to his wife that he 'wouldn't stoop to eat sub-standard biscuits, even in wartime!'

"The wolves can keep the lot!"

But the wolves agreed with Mrs Cox, that a biscuit, even a broken one, is still a biscuit. They would happily stoop, and for the next ten minutes the only sound was that of munching.

The last crumbs had just been cleared-up when Billy, grim-faced, broke the news. According to his Uncle Chris, who knew almost everything there was to know about trains, Billy's Boys Book of Steam was out of date!

"The Mallard has just been timed at a hundred and twenty-five miles an hour," said Billy. "That's ten faster than THE SCOT!"

They stared at each other in disbelief. There must be some mistake! Had anyone checked the watch? Was the course level? Was there a following wind? They were clutching at straws. But it was no good. Uncle Chris had made enquiries. Two watches had been used and carefully checked; so had the stretch of line. It was true!

It was a mournful group which assembled on the wall in a light drizzle the next morning and, as THE SCOT rushed past, it was hard to keep the tears back. An era had ended. But to cheer them up, Uncle Chris had sent a message. With a bit of luck, the foot-plate men on THE SCOT might find some more speed from somewhere and win the record back.

"It's probably nothing that an extra shovel or two of top-quality coal can't put right, he said."

They could live in hope.

CHAPTER EIGHT

TIM AND BILLY ARE INSPIRED

Back at school after the holiday, everyone was talking about 'THE FOUR FEATHERS', the latest adventure film, which was showing at the GRAND. The action was set in the Sudan region of North Africa, then a part of the British Empire, around the year 1882. The local leader, the powerful Mahdi wanted to put an end to British rule, and a regiment was to be sent out to put him in his place. It sounded just the kind of action that would have Tim on the edge of his seat and, after school, he made straight for the cinema to do a reconnaissance. The poster outside showed a scarlet-coated British officer in hand-to-hand combat with a Dervish warrior, one of the Mahdi's crack troops. That was enough to get his pulse racing. Underneath, it said NOT TO BE MISSED, and he was determined not to. But he had to act quickly. It was Tuesday, and the film was showing until Friday.

Back at home, he talked excitedly about 'the brilliant, patriotic film' showing at the GRAND, but his Mum didn't take the hint. Instead she took the opportunity to remind him that a visit to the cinema, other than a Saturday matinee, was a treat which had to be earned by extra-good behaviour, and that he hadn't yet made up for the Dock Road incident!

A less determined person than Tim might have given up, but, at Crab Mill Farm, he had been learning the art of diplomacy from Joe who was particularly good at thinking up clever ways of getting into his Mum's good books at a time of great need. For example he would offer to polish everyone's shoes before church, or, as a last resort, to keep his bedroom extra tidy. But time was short. Tim had to come up with something special.

It happened that Grandpa and Grandma Dodd were due to come

to tea the next afternoon, and he remembered Joe saying that one of his most successful, 'last ditch' strategies for impressing a reluctant parent, was being extra attentive to an elderly relative.

"It's quite easy, if you plan carefully."

Mum's parents duly turned up. The Impitts, next door, had also been invited and, when Tim got home from school, they were already on their second cup of tea. He had planned carefully. His eyes shone attentively, he had combed his hair and rehearsed his lines. Now all he needed was an accomplice, and Grandpa Dodd should be ideal. He had been a stretcher-bearer in the 'Great War', often venturing out into no-man's land to rescue lots of wounded soldiers, Tim felt sure. He had been a casualty of the gassing, although he would never talk about it. Would he talk about the present war? Tim was banking on it.

There was a brief lull in the conversation, and the young enquirer asked, earnestly, "Grandpa, do you think we'll win the war?"

Grandpa took the bait and launched into a quite passionate speech on 'why the powers of evil will never prevail against the powers of good'. Grandpa believed that, since God is always on the side of right against wrong, and, therefore, on Britain's side against Germany, there could be only one conclusion to the war. Hitler and his cronies would be beaten and disgraced, the Nasties would get a dose of their own medicine, etc., etc., and WE WILL WIN! He finished with a line or two of Rule Britannia, Grandma singing along.

Everyone felt better for this exercise in patriotism, and Mr Impitt, the expert on modern warfare, complimented Tim for asking a surprisingly sensible question. Tim smiled modestly and handed out the scones. Everything was going to plan. Mum had taken note, and was in a good mood. She was playing into his hands and said that he might attend the early Friday evening showing of the patriotic film at THE GRAND, on condition that Billy could go with him. There was just one possible snag.

"It's an A rated film, all the violence and bloodshed, that kind of thing, so they won't let you in by yourselves. I can't leave Shirley at home by herself, and Dad won't be home from work in time. Mrs Thompson's working late at the factory these days. So you'll have to ask a grown-up, perhaps two, to take you in."

He nodded. Having come this far, that wouldn't be a problem. A few seconds later he was knocking, joyfully, at number 7.

Billy's Mum said he could go, and when Friday finally arrived, having spent the week dreaming about Dervishes struggling with British infantrymen, Tim had been ready for half an hour, hair combed and stockings pulled up, when Billy came over. He had also passed an in-depth inspection. They were surely the kind of boys any kindly grown-up would be happy to adopt for a couple of hours.

They reached THE GRAND in time to take up a good position near the ticket office, but not too close to the Colonel, who recognised them instantly, despite their unusual smartness, and scowled, as if to ask 'Haven't you got a mother of your own?' A life-size picture of the beautiful Miss Duprez, one of the stars, smiled down on the two hopefuls, as if to say 'Take no notice of him!' The boys took

no notice. They focussed their attention on the latest arrivals, and when a promising candidate came along, took it in turns to ask 'Will you take us in, please?' But they were having no luck. Some smiled sympathetically, but shook their heads. Some just shook their heads, and the seconds were ticking by. A notice over the ticket Kiosk said PROGRAMMME STARTS AT 6PM, and the clock nearby said 5.48pm. They had twelve minutes to secure two precious seats.

"If Mrs Duprez was here," said Tim, "I bet she would take us in!"

About fifty yards away, a tram pulled up, a lady got off and walked towards the cinema. It was Billy's turn to ask and he stepped forward.

"Will you take us in, please, missus?"

"I can't take both of you," she said. "It's not allowed."

"But we've got to stay together," said Billy. "Our mums said so."

"Sorry," she said, sadly, and walked to the kiosk.

"That was bad luck!" Tim muttered, as the Colonel continued to scowl.

More children arrived, confidently attached to grown-ups, and disappeared happily through the swing-doors to where the action would soon be starting.

"Smile, Billy," said Tim, "and try to look polite!" Billy responded with his best grin; but it wasn't doing any good, and the hands of the clock moved on to 5.56pm. The projectionist would be warming up.

"We're never going to get in," Billy muttered.

Tim was desperate.

Then Billy pointed down the road to where someone they recognised was striding briskly in their direction.

Mr Donaldson spotted them and quickly summed up the situation.

"Hello, boys. You having no luck?" They nodded. "Well, you can be my kids for the evening." He grinned. "But in return, I'll be expecting great efforts at school, next week, especially you, Tim!" They grinned. Sir to the rescue in the nick of time, with an offer they weren't going to refuse. Tim would have agreed to anything.

But would the Colonel agree? He was looking uneasy. After all, rules are rules!

The teacher glanced across and smiled.

"It's alright, Colonel. They're my pupils at Dovedale Road... studying British Colonial history!"

The Colonel was impressed. "Right you are, Sir!" He touched

his cap in salute, and turned away. The boys glanced at each other. That was quick thinking by Sir!

They handed over their money, and passed through into the cinema just as the lights were being dimmed. An usherette shone a torch to show them to their seats. They squeezed and 'scused their way to reach them and, as they sat down, Billy whispered....

"Just wait 'til we tell the others who took us to the pictures!" Tim nodded, but said nothing. The projectionist had swung into action with a cartoon, and he was already concentrating. The Pathé Newsreel followed, showing German tanks racing towards Moscow and the Russians in full retreat. Now the cinema was very quiet, except for the rattle of tank caterpillar-treads.

Next on the screen, a gentleman reminded everyone, in grave tones, that careless talk costs lives! Billy grinned at Tim. As if we didn't know! The grave gentleman was followed by an elderly lady tearfully digging up a favourite flower-bed.

"Women of Britain," said the commentary, "Let Mrs Briggs of Fazakerley be your example! Remember! FOOD BEFORE FLOWERS! DIG FOR VICTORY!"

The lights now came on for the interval, and the lady with the torch reappeared as a sales person, with a tray of soft drinks and peanuts.

Billy thought he would make the most of having their teacher all to themselves.

"Mr Donaldson, why did Germany attack Russia?"

"Well," said the teacher, "there's a saying.....'There's no honour among thieves', and I guess it's the same with bullies. Hitler's probably worried that, while his armies are busy keeping an eye on his ill-gotten gains, such as Belgium and France in the West, Stalin might attack him from the East. He's guarding his back! And there's another reason. Russia's got a lot of things that Hitler would like to get his hands on...oil and coal and lots of land! He's going to need them for his Thousand Year Reich, as he calls it."

Billy winked at Tim. A history lesson in three parts, and just for them!

The lights were being dimmed as the drinks lady retreated, backwards, through the swing doors, the talking stopped, and the boys settled down in the well-worn seats. It was time for the Big Picture.

THE FOUR FEATHERS begins with Harry Faversham, a bit older than Billy and Tim, making his way up a staircase past portraits of famous ancestors, all in splendid military uniforms. An elderly family friend is describing their achievements and then turns to Harry.

"We all hope you will follow their steps, one day!"

Harry nods, but says nothing. He isn't sure that he can live up to such hopes, but, in due course he joins the army and becomes an officer in his father's old regiment, the one which was being sent to deal with the troublesome Mahdi. Then, on the day before the regiment sails for the Sudan, everyone is shocked to learn that he had resigned his commission. Instead of going to fight the Mahdi's hordes he would stay at home, marry Miss Duprez and look after the family estate. But when three fellow officers and his fiancée each send him a white feather, accusing him of cowardice, he sets out to prove them wrong.

He follows the regiment to the Sudan, but to reach it, he must cross the Mahdi's territory. To avoid having to speak the language and give himself away, he has a brand burnt on his forehead, to disguise himself as a member of an Arab tribe of deaf-mutes. As smoke rises from the branded forehead, the boys are firmly on the side of Lieutenant Faversham, as their new hero sets about rescuing his fellow officers who, by this time, had been taken prisoner. Together they liberate the rest of the British prisoners, recapture Omdurman, the Mahdi's capital city, and raise the Union Jack.

Back in England, as Lieutenant Faversham's heroic exploits are spread over the newspapers, the three friends take back their feathers, with apologies. Ms Duprez takes hers back, with kisses, as the two boys looked away.

That was the end of the programme, and everyone moved out, blinking, into the bright, evening sunshine. The boys were the very last to leave, glancing enviously at the queue waiting to go in to the second performance, and heading home with heads full of brave thoughts.

Back at school, Mr Donaldson spun the globe and pointed to Malta, Britain's rocky naval base in the Mediterranean, holding out against constant attack by the Luftwaffe, to ensure that provisions reached the 8th Army in its fight against the Africa Korps. It was more inspiring food for brave thoughts, and all next week they kept their part of Mr Donaldson's bargain. Tim had rarely made such great efforts, and now he had decided that he would like to become a soldier.

CHAPTER NINE

AN IMPORTANT FOOTBALL MATCH

It was early December and, in the Den, the four friends huddled together. Even with the door shut and an old blanket hanging across the entrance, the temperature wasn't much higher than outside. It was almost too cold for chat. The Saturday morning meeting was going to be brief. Ken was puzzled.

"At the Kiosk it says STAB IN THE BACK. I wonder what it means?"

"Well," said Sid, "my Dad says Japan's air force attacked America's fleet, without any warning, last Sunday morning, and sank a lot of their battleships. It was at a place called Pearl Harbour."

"Why did they do that?" asked Billy.

"Dad says he thinks the Japs are out to grab territory in the Far East, and they had to put the American fleet out of action, so there'd be no one to stop them. They dropped torpedoes to hit the ships below the water-line so they would go down and stay down. Some of them just toppled over and sank. Lots of sailors were trapped inside."

"That must have been horrible!" said Ken.

They all nodded, sadly, and sat thinking, as the icy, muddy, water lapped over the duckboards.

Sid went on...

"Mum says the Japs probably chose a Sunday morning 'cos that's when people are relaxing, playing tennis, going to church and that kind of thing, so they wouldn't be able to fight back."

"That was a stab in the back, like Mr Erskine says!" said Tim.

"Anyway," Sid went on, "Dad says they've made a big mistake, 'cos America's got too much muscle, and now they've declared war on Japan."

"But they're on Hitler's side," said Billy, "so doesn't that mean America's on our side...against Hitler, I mean?"

"I s'pose so!"

"Yippee!" said Ken, and suddenly the Den didn't feel so cold.

At school, it was nearly the end of term, as usual a time for noughts and crosses, doodling and general messing about, when the teachers can't be bothered to teach anything, and pupils don't want them to bother - a kind of educational stalemate. Just one important event remained on the calendar. The football match between staff and boys was meant to be a fun way of ending the year. The netball match between the girls and lady teachers had ended in an honourable draw. The boys were keen to go one better, and teach the teachers a thing or two.

It was a bright, chilly afternoon, and the whole school crowded the touch-line, as the staff team, led by the Headmaster, emerged shyly from the changing room. The Head, built stockily, not for leaping about, would be in goal where, he said, he couldn't get in the way. Tim was surprised to see Mr Spinks. He was a 'guest' member of staff for the afternoon. At left back, he would be marking Tim, and as the teams lined up, Tim thought he winked. Was it a sign of friendship, or a challenge to all-out combat? Tim grinned back. The caretaker must be almost as old as his Dad. He would run rings around him!

At first there was a general scramble, as usually happens on such occasions, everyone, except the Head, being keen to get an early touch of the ball, and, for most of the first half, the play was scrappy.

Tim was surprised to find that Mr Spinks wasn't as slow and easy to dribble past as he had expected. In fact, on at least two occasions, the caretaker dribbled past him, much to his annoyance and 5B's amusement. He was wishing he had asked to play on the other wing. Meanwhile, on the staff right wing, Mr Donaldson, all elbows and knees, was distinguishing himself by arriving at the scene of the action just after it had moved somewhere else.

The half-time whistle came just in time for most of the staff-team, and an extra five minutes was added, unofficially, to the interval.

The second half started with the boys swarming forward and the staff defending courageously. Mr Spinks in particular was making spectacular tackles, and the Head, helped by several large slices of luck, was performing miracles in goal. Then, against the run of play, fortune favoured the elderly as well as the brave. With only four minutes left, the Head punted the ball high into the boys' penalty area, where Mr Donaldson suddenly found himself, by accident, and managed to get a toe onto it and prod it into the boys' net. A loud cry of appreciation, mixed with surprise, went up from the crowd. The Sirs were in the lead! The boys continued to swarm, but the staff defence held out somehow, until the referee signalled full time. The teachers had won against all the odds, and back in school after the Christmas holiday, when met in the corridors, they would be treated with more than usual respect.

As the teams trooped off the yard Mr Spinks shook Tim's hand.

"Well played, Tim Oliver! It's all that ball-control practice! I told you so."

"Thanks, Mr Spinks," Tim grinned. "You played well, too!"

The teams headed for the dining room where the cook was

complaining, wistfully, that after-match teas were 'a bit of a luxury' in time of war, and apologising that the sandwiches weren't 'what they used to be!' Tim understood perfectly. It wasn't his fault...just one more thing Adolf Hitler should have on his conscience. The sandwiches on offer were mainly fish paste, although no one was sure what kind of fish was involved. Perhaps the odd perch poached from Sefton Park lake during the Park Keeper's lunch break.

To the boys it was fun jostling with the teachers for access to the Madeira cake, which didn't quite live up to its exotic name, but was available in generous quantities.

Mr Donaldson, with an eye on the cake, had positioned himself next to Tim who had just helped himself to a second slice.

"I thought you were doing well on the wing, Tim, considering who was marking you," whispered the teacher. Tim frowned.

"You mean the caretaker?"

"Yes...Mr Spinks mightn't look much of a footballer when he's pushing his trolley around, but in his younger days, he was quite a star. He played inside left for Aigburth Peoples' Hall, I believe, and he hasn't lost his touch, as you discovered today! It's a good lesson to learn, Tim. You can't always judge a book by its cover!"

"So that's why he winked!"

****

The news that America had come into the war on Britain's side cheered everyone up, but, for the Olivers, there was worrying news from the Far East.

A few days before Christmas, a letter arrived by airmail, post-marked HONG KONG, Britain's island colony off the coast of Southern China. It was from Joe Quie, one of Dad's closest school friends. Joe was from Hong Kong, and after leaving school he had gone back to build a railway running up the mountain at the centre of the island. With the latest news in mind, Dad feared the worst, and read the letter out loud.

Hong Kong

11th December 1941

Dear Tom and family,

I am writing at a difficult, dangerous time. You will know all about the Japanese attack on Pearl Harbour, and now they have invaded the Philippine Islands. Their navy has sunk HMS Prince of Wales and HMS Repulse which were our only protection, apart from our small British garrison and, unless they can be stopped, they'll be knocking on our door very shortly.

Tom, do you remember that wintry day at school when we had a snowball battle against the SFX boys from over the road? We were outnumbered, so we pulled back inside the West yard and closed the gates, accidentally leaving little George May outside in the street, all by himself. He stood there, like Horatius holding the bridge, with a snowball in each hand, showing his teeth, and they beat a hasty retreat! We cheered and pulled him back inside the yard! George could look pretty fierce when he wanted to!

Well, here in Hong Kong we need some George May courage now, although it will take more than a show of bravado to stop the Japanese.

We hope that Shirley is getting over her illness. She is a very brave girl. And how is young Tim getting on? Will he gain a place at the old school? We hope so.

This will probably be one of the last letters to leave the island. We will try to keep in touch.

Yours, affectionately,

Joe Quie

****

Christmas morning arrived at last, and the bad news from Hong Kong couldn't dampen the excitement of exploring stockings and pillowcases. For Tim there was a new football. The old one, Dad said, had 'almost given up the ghost.' Tim was overjoyed.

"It's the best Christmas present ever!"

The BIGGLES ANNUAL 1942 was second favourite. It would come in very useful on a visit to Grandma and Grandpa's home, where quietness must reign.

The family had been invited to Christmas lunch.

CHAPTER TEN

'SIXTY-FIVE'

Outside it was chilly, bright and very quiet. The railways had closed down for the Festive Season, only a few trams and buses were operating, and the Olivers' chosen transport to Grandpa's house was by taxi. Shirley, well muffled-up, squeezed in between Mum and Dad, and Tim sat facing them on a little tip-up seat, Biggles Annual in hand. Dad had pointed out that the new football wouldn't be welcome at Grandma's house.

Number Sixty-five, Kremlin Drive, or 'Sixty-Five', as it was known to family and friends, was a tall, three-story residence on the northern edge of the city. The imposing front door was reached via three steps, and, once inside, a vestibule opened onto the spacious hall from which a sweeping circular staircase led to the upstairs floors.

The visitors were ushered into the drawing room, where a log-fire crackled. Sprigs of holly and mistletoe, strategically balanced over pictures, were almost the only festive decorations on show. Perhaps to compensate, a particularly grand specimen of Christmas tree took centre-stage, topped by an extra large star.

Grandma and Grandpa were waiting to greet them; a peck on the cheek from Grandma and a rather tired pat on the head from Grandpa. To his grandson, the latter, white-haired with matching moustache, always seemed rather distant; not unfriendly, but probably of the opinion that, in general, children should be seen and not heard. He had retired from the wine trade, and spent much of his time poring over his valuable collection of British Colonial postage stamps and pottering about in the back garden with its pergolas and fruit trees.

Grandma was in a different mould. She had been used to running the household in the manner of a Regimental Sergeant

Major, although her regiment had dwindled drastically in numbers since the outbreak of war. Her word was law. It was Grandma who had laid down the one about quietness.

Tim had already come to terms with this and, on previous visits, he had adapted his lifestyle accordingly. His policy was to be not only unheard but as unseen as possible. Fortunately, the geography of Sixty-Five made temporary invisibility quite achievable. There were the cellars, well-stocked in pre-war days, from Grandpa's business trips to northern France. Now the wine had gone and the shelves gathered dust; but a young fugitive could stay holed-up, underground and unnoticed, for hours, passing the time with a pile of comics or a game of skittles played with empty bottles and a tennis ball, always remembering to surface in time for tea.

There were four rooms on the top floor. One housed reminders of the days when two lively schoolboys, Tom, Tim's Dad, his brother Bill, and their sporty sister, May, had been in residence - a Slazenger tennis racquet, slightly warped with a few missing strings; a clock-golf set, awaiting reinstatement on the back-garden lawn; and a football shirt, distictly musty, with what had once been royal blue and black halves, (now grey and lighter grey), and an embroidered shield. It was his Dad's school First Eleven football shirt, Grandma said. Tim had made a note. Two other rooms were out of bounds. The fourth was notable only for a sea of baking apples, claimed from the trees in the garden, laid out on the floor in neat rows, shrivelled, but priceless in days of fruit-rationing. This room was visited only when something like apple-pie was on the menu, and Gertie, the daily help, was sent up to reclaim some. It was the most fragrant of the attics, where the grandson might be found during a family visit, surrounded by apples, head in a comic, hoping that the world of grown-ups had forgotten about him. Gertie was a lady of late middle-age, who might have been called a 'skivvy - according to the Oxford Dictionary, an 'ordinary low-ranking domestic servant', but, to Tim she was extraordinary. Although no beauty, having unusually protruding front teeth, she had permanently rosy cheeks and a beaming smile, often aimed in his direction, as if she understood that he had a problem with grown-ups. She was wise, and he could talk to her. In his estimation, Gertie ranked higher than most people in the world of the grown-up.

A third optional bolt-hole, known as the Breakfast Room, was on the first floor at the rear, overlooking the back garden. Before the war, a maid would have been seen at breakfast time on her way up the staircase, bearing Indian tea and hot, buttered toast, to where the senior Olivers waited. Now that the war had arrived and the maids had departed to play their part in the war effort, breakfast was more a help-yourself arrangement on the ground floor, so the room was usually deserted, and ideal for a bit of privacy.

Downstairs the chatter was well under way, the coast was clear, and he slipped out, Biggles in hand, heading upstairs. As he had guessed, the Breakfast Room was unoccupied. Closing the door noiselessly, he pulled a chair over to the window and was soon lost in the frantic world of the ace fighter-pilot taking on the Luftwaffe, almost single-handed.

He sat, riveted, for half an hour, then glanced into the garden where the lawn was covered with a thin coat of frost. Over the tops of the trees he could just make out the spire of St James's Church, where the Christmas Morning Service was coming to an end with an enthusiastic rendering of *O come, all ye faithful*. At any moment, the congregation would be emerging and heading briskly homewards with lunch on their minds. It was time to leave his bolt-hole, but, as he turned away from the window, there was a movement down below, where Grandpa had appeared on the garden path, walking very slowly, bent forward slightly, resting his chin in his hand. It reminded Tim of painful dental visits to the heartless Mr Catley, who didn't seem to understand why his young patient wasn't enjoying his time in the chair. Was Grandpa's trouble serious? He would soon find out.

Lunch was a great success, and compliments flew in Grandma's direction... 'a magnificent spread, making a little go a long way', 'against all the odds, no thanks to Herr Hitler!' and so on.

Back in the drawing-room it was almost time for the King's Christmas speech. During the blitz, he and the Queen had walked around the London dockland, picking their way past gaping craters and mountains of rubble, smiling, sympathising, shaking hands and patting heads. Now, almost everyone was looking forward to the Christmas Day message. Only Tim was thinking of going missing.

"You'd better stay, Tim," a voice whispered. Dad had read his mind. "We should all listen to the King's speech. At a time like this, when we're faced with a powerful enemy, it's a way of showing loyalty to the royal family, and solidarity with everyone."

There was no escape. He had to sit it out, and try to show solidarity, whatever that was.

At five to three, Grandpa switched on the wireless. There was the usual mixture of crackling and high-pitched humming, then a drum roll, followed by a BBC-type voice.

'His Majesty, King George the Sixth.'

Everyone stared intently at the wireless, as if expecting to see the royal face. Instead, it was the royal voice, quiet but determined, speaking about the courage of the people of Hong Kong in resisting the new enemy, and calling on everyone not to lose heart and to play their part in the war effort.

The drum rolled again and everyone stood for the National Anthem, after which Grandpa was ready with a little impromptu speech of his own.

"Yes indeed...we have a gracious, noble, King, a great example to us all, of courage, faith and determination!" He raised his glass.

"THE KING!" Glasses of lemonade and assorted, stronger drinks were raised enthusiastically.

"THE KING!"

Now everyone sat down, except Grandma. Not to be left out, and while she was 'on her feet', as she put it, she wanted to add 'a few personal words of appreciation'!

"I think we should sing 'God save our Noble Queen,' too! I'm sure He will. I mean, there she was, walking around the mess the Luftwaffe had left behind, shaking all those hands ...some of them pretty grubby, I should think... chatting with everyone and smiling all the time...she's got a lovely smile ...and staying close to us all in the midst of the danger. After all, she could have taken the Princesses to safety in Canada or somewhere!" Everyone nodded, as she raised her glass.

"THE QUEEN!"

"THE QUEEN!"

Grandma and Grandpa now disappeared for a nap, and Mum and Dad set off for a brisk walk around the block. Shirley reclaimed her seat near the fire, and Tim retreated again, this time to the attics. To save electricity, Grandma had laid it down that lights might be switched on only after dusk. Until then, she insisted, 'daylight will have to do!' and as the last dilute rays of the winter sun were still filtering through the sky-light, there was just enough light for a chapter of Biggles versus Von Schonbeck, Captain of the deadly U-517 submarine.

Then, as if to call 'time' on the festivities, the door-bell rang. The taxi had arrived. The family squeezed aboard to head back to Welbeck Avenue, and Tim was deep in thought.

"I saw Grandpa in the garden, Dad. He was holding his chin as if it was hurting. Is he alright?"

"No, Tim. He's got an illness of the jaw, called cancer. It's serious...and very painful."

Dusk had merged into darkness and Tim stared sadly out of the window as the taxi ran on through the quiet, blacked-out streets. It reminded him of the carol about the little town of Bethlehem on the night that Jesus was born.

Yet in thy dark streets shineth the everlasting Light,
The hopes and fears of all the years are met in Thee tonight.

That cheered him up a bit.

Later that evening, Dad switched on the wireless for the news bulletin. The situation in the Far East was even worse than he had feared, and Hong Kong Island had been seized by the Japanese.

He shook his head. On this of all days, when people everywhere were thinking about 'peace and good will to men'! And what had happened to Joe Quie and his family? The Japanese troops were not well-known for being kind to prisoners.

CHAPTER ELEVEN

A MOMENT OF TRUTH FOR TIM

Back at Dovedale Road, the spring term was under way, the big test loomed up ever closer, and 5B classroom was unusually quiet. Mr Donaldson had written out some challenging, arithmetical exercises on the blackboard, the kind they were likely to get in the test, he said, and everyone seemed to be scribbling away, more or less confidently, with one exception. Tim gnawed at the end of his pencil, and stared at the meaningless hieroglyphics.

The teacher moved slowly up and down the rows, peering over shoulders and pausing now and again. He drew alongside Tim and looked down at a blank sheet of paper.

"Mm. I see we're still having trouble with long division, Tim."

"Yes. It's figuring out where the dot goes…and things like that."

Mr Donaldson nodded.

"Let's start again."

Tim sighed. Only recently he had spent what seemed like hours after school, struggling with the teacher's patient working on the blackboard, and still hadn't fathomed the mysteries of long division. He glanced across at Grace Vernon who had already finished. He sighed. Some kids are destined to shine at arithmetic!

The teacher and pupil went over the ground they had already covered several times, then Mr Donaldson moved on down the row. Tim continued to gnaw, and hope for a flash of inspiration or, better still, that the bell would ring for morning break.

There had been an election for the important post of milk-monitor, and, in an impromptu election speech he had impressed everyone with accounts of early morning milk runs through the Shropshire woods. It was his bit of war effort, he explained. The only other person interested in the job was Cynthia Milligan. She was keen, and pretty, but those were her only qualifications, whereas this was a job where previous experience counted. So he had won, with a clear majority, and hoped that, while he was a disappointment to Sir at arithmetic, he might at least impress him as a servant of the people.

Mr Donaldson was duly impressed by Tim's dedication to milk-distribution, but with the vital test looming up, he wished that he was equally dedicated to arithmetic. He had tried every strategy in the book to inspire him, but had drawn a blank. At last, knowing what was the nearest thing to his pupil's heart, he had decided to talk 'football'. It was a final, desperate throw of the dice, but time was running out quickly, and he was willing to try anything.

"Studying arithmetic's a bit like playing football, Tim, in a way. It's all very well having star forwards in the team, but if your defenders aren't much good, you'll let in as many goals as you score …perhaps more, and then you'll lose. Think of arithmetic as your defence, and you need to strengthen it!"

Tim sighed. If only arithmetic was as easy as football.

****

CAUGHT NAPPING!

Tim had gone to pick up the week's edition of the Rover, and couldn't miss Mr Erskine's latest headline.

"What does it mean, Mr Erskine?" he asked.

"Singapore has fallen, Tim. It's our main base in the Far East and our defences let us down! Didn't expect the Japs to reach us so quickly, I suppose. The Echo says the city lights were left on, so their dive-bombers had an easy target. And that's not all. Our guns were pointing the wrong way...out to sea, 'cos that's where the Japs were expected to come from. But they came by land...straight through the jungle! How they found the way, goodness only knows. Have you any idea what they use for maps?" Tim shook his head.

"Atlases! Like the ones you use at school! That must be a scale of about a millionth of an inch to a mile. I worked it out! And they've got the secret of moving fast through the jungle. They go by bike! Ordinary bikes! Tanks and armoured cars are no good in the jungle with all that mud. But travelling by bike, if they can't ride it, they just put it on their shoulders and carry it. Then when they come to a path or road, they jump on and start pedalling again. Clever, isn't it?"

"It sounds like it. But what happens if they get a puncture?"

"If they can't mend it, they ride on the rims! That's true! Our chaps say that when a detachment of Jap soldiers is riding along, it sounds as if the tanks have arrived! It's scary, they say. They're much better in the jungle than our troops. That's the big difference between them and us. We Brits don't like the jungle...all the creepy crawlies and the mud; but to them it's like fighting in their back garden, and they must be pretty good at it, 'cos they've taken a hundred and thirty thousand of our troops prisoner - including quite a few Aussies. Mr Churchill says it's the worst defeat in British military history!" He shook his head, sadly. "But, I must get back to my work. Nice to talk, Tim!"

Good old Mr Erskine, a mine of vital information. There would be plenty to talk about in the Den.

****

The test was held just after Easter and, in spite of Mr Donaldson's inspired strategy, Tim's defence had let him down. He had failed, and wouldn't be allowed to take the Grammar School entrance exam. It was an end to his slim hopes for a place at Dad's old school.

Billy had passed, and on their way home after school, he was doing his best to cheer his friend up.

"You should have been evacuated with the rest of us, Tim, and Mr Donaldson would have been your teacher. Then you'd have passed."

Tim nodded ruefully, as Billy went in to celebrate with his Mum.

Instead of crossing to Number 6, Tim headed for the park, to be alone with his thoughts and his football. The swings were deserted, apart from one little girl who was enjoying having the playground all to herself, like a butterfly fluttering from one interesting flower to another. He perched himself on a swing and settled down to a time of gloomy reflection. He had let everyone down! Mr Donaldson, who had tried so hard to turn him into a mathematician...Auntie May, who had generously set aside a large quantity of sweets 'as a reward for success'; would she hand it over for extra effort without success? ...Dear old Gertie who had wished him 'All the best!' If only!... Shirley, who badly wanted him to win a place at his Dad's old school, for Dad's sake as much as Tim's, and Grandma. Both of her sons had been pupils at the Collegiate. She would be disappointed. And how would he tell Mum and Dad? What would they say?

He glanced across at Ken's house, just over the road from the swings. Like Billy, Ken had passed the test and was probably being showered with praise and rewards at that very moment. And yet, if it hadn't been for the war, he might be celebrating, himself. He pushed the swing into slow-motion and reflected, then considered doing some dribbling practice; but his new football seemed to have lost some of its glow and, in any case, he couldn't stay there forever. He dismounted and headed home.

As he turned into Welbeck Avenue he could tell that they were still celebrating Billy's success at number 7. Even from that distance he could hear Mrs Thompson singing, which was always a sign that she was in a good mood. He crossed the road to Number 6, took a deep breath and knocked. After a few moments, the familiar figure of his Mum appeared through the stained-glass panels. The door opened and she stood looking down at him, smiling gently, as if she knew what he was going to say.

"I failed, Mum." It was more a mutter than a statement.

She said nothing, but leaned forward to take his hand, and pulled him gently up the front step and into the hallway. She closed the door and put her arms around him.

"You're not a failure, Tim. You were just unlucky that you had such a strict teacher, and you couldn't help that!" He nodded. "But you were safe! That's what really mattered. There'll be lots more tests, and you'll be ready for them, just you wait and see! So cheer up, and come and do a bit of nursing! Shirley's tea-tray's ready."

He followed her into the kitchen, picked up the tray and trudged upstairs. Shirley's bedroom door was slightly open. He tapped, then peeped in. Shirley was in bed, propped-up on pillows. She spotted him and smiled.

"Hello, Tim!"

"Hello, Shirley. How're you feeling?"

"A bit better, thanks. Just fed up with having to stay in bed!"

He put the tray on the eiderdown and stood back, biting his lip.

"I failed the test." The words came out quietly.

"Oh...I'm sorry, Tim." She frowned. "If you hadn't been evacuated, I'm sure you'd have passed!"

Tim nodded. It was comforting to know that everyone else seemed sure that he would have passed, if it hadn't been for the war. He picked up the nursing cup and pointed the spout towards her mouth. She drank slowly, then shook her head to say 'that's enough'.

"Dad'll be disappointed," she said.

"Yes." He didn't need to be reminded, and, at that moment, there was the sound of a key turning in the front door lock. Dad had come home early, hoping to hear good news. There was a murmur of voices as Mum met him in the hallway, then footsteps on the stairs. Shirley was always his first port of call when he got home. She brightened up. Tim bit his lip.

A head looked round the open door.

"How's our patient today?"

"Fine, thanks, Dad." It was her usual reply, and he knew it wasn't entirely true, but smiled. Then he looked at Tim who was hovering, cup in hand.

"Mum has told me the bad news, Tim. It's very disappointing."

"I tried my best, Dad. Mr Donaldson says it was probably the arithmetic."

"Well, I wasn't very good at arithmetic myself." That wasn't

true, either. It was his way of letting Tim down lightly. He smiled.
"Just remember, Tim, when us Olivers are knocked down, we pick
ourselves up, dust ourselves off and carry on!"

The nurse said nothing. He tried to muster a smile, nodded,
picked up the tray and went downstairs.

At school the next morning it wasn't easy to hold his head up.
Quite a few of the others had failed, too, but to Tim it felt as if he was
the only one. He was glad that Cynthia didn't look across, and it was
good to have Billy in the next desk.

But the term would be ending soon. Then he could forget about
school and tests. The summer holidays would be a great chance to
pick himself up and dust himself off. Six weeks of freedom couldn't
have come at a better time.

****

For millions all over Northern Europe, under the heel of the German invader, freedom was only a precious memory. But Britain was still free to send waves of bombers - Lancasters, Halifaxes and American Flying Fortresses - on raids, night and day, deep into Germany, to attack munitions factories. In the safety of his bunker, deep underground, the Fuhrer raved. Those impudent Englanders! Only Germany has the right to drop bombs on other people!

Meanwhile, in their Wavertree bunker, the boys were laying plans for the usual holiday round of train-spotting, matinées at The GRAND and Cops and Robbers or cricket in the park. Ken would be away for a week, with bucket and spade, changing the shape of Southport beach. Billy would be doing something similar at Colwyn Bay on a compulsory visit to ageing Aunt Dot, short for Dorothy. Sid's family would be going on day-trips to places in North Wales with unpronounceable names like Penmaenmawr and Ffestiniog. Tim had promised to go back to Colemere and the farm, to visit his country family.

CHAPTER TWELVE

COLEMERE REVISITED

The 11.35a.m, from Wrexham to Ellesmere, shimmered in the hot July sunshine, motionless, and the wild poppies at the track-side wilted. Elson Halt was living up to its name.

Sitting in his compartment, waiting for some action, Tim was thinking about his Mum. She had made this trek dozens of times, to visit them - sixty slow, tedious miles, on and off buses, ferries and trains, and the last bit on foot. Sometimes she had made it there and back on the same day, risking being caught in the black-out or, even worse, an air-raid. He bit his lip, hoping he had said 'Thank you!'

He was glad to have the compartment all to himself, except for an elderly gentleman on the seat opposite, who also seemed to be wilting. He stared at the gloomy, sepia photographs under the luggage rack on the opposite wall. The caption said 'Scenes on the Welsh borders' and he had already decided that he wouldn't bother going there.

Considering his enthusiasm for the world of steam, on previous trips, this was the part of the journey that he had enjoyed least. In particular the long, unexplained delays. The buses and ferries always seemed to operate on time. Why not the trains?

Take Elson Halt, for example. They had arrived approximately on time, but didn't seem to be interested in departing, even though the station clock indicated that they should have left already. The driver had left the engine ticking-over, judging by a jet of steam escaping now and then; but he had disappeared into the station master's office with the guard, probably for a cup of tea. Tim frowned. Had they forgotten that there was such a thing as a time-table?

And yet no one else seemed to have noticed. Why weren't

heads sticking out of carriage windows, angry voices raised, and fingers pointing at the clock? His Dad would call it the 'stiff upper lip' - putting-up with things like queues, hold-ups and unexplained stops, as one's contribution to the war-effort. Thoughtfully, he helped himself to another gob-stopper. Good old Auntie May, true to form, had handed over the sweets she had promised as a reward for passing the test. She hoped it would make up for the disappointment, and help to shorten the journey.

The silence, broken by a solitary fly on a tour of the compartment, seemed to underline the general lack of activity. Looking around for the umpteenth time, through the open window he spotted a faded poster showing a gentleman with a finger to his lips and, underneath, a caption said **LOOK OUT, THERE'S A SPY ABOUT!** He stifled a chuckled. If only! That would be something to tell the others back at the Den. But, what self-respecting Nazi spy would be found snooping around Elson Halt? Further down the platform, another poster reminded everyone to Dig for Victory! There was no getting away from the war! The fly, having completed its tour, opened up its throttle and exited through the open window, as the silence returned.

His fellow-passenger had finally given in to the sunshine and was sound asleep, chin on chest. Tim thought of stretching his legs, but decided not to. This wasn't THE SCOT! There was no corridor, and he daren't get off, in case the driver suddenly decided to come back to work. He would just have to sit it out. He made himself as comfortable as possible on the well-worn seat, glanced again at the Spy notice and began to day-dream.

Suppose the Nasties took over at Elson Halt. Of course, it was very unlikely, now that America and Russia were on Britain's side; but just supposing. What would it be like? He had seen that sort of thing in films about the Resistance. The tiny ticket office would be engulfed by a huge swastika, to let everyone know who was in charge; a podgy, elderly soldier would strut up and down, hot and perspiring, but happy to be at Elson Halt rather than somewhere on the Russian Front; sinister-looking chaps in long, black coats and floppy hats would be scrutinising identity cards and asking awkward questions. There would be heel-clicking, saluting, shouts of 'Heil Hitler!' and probably a lot of sore throats. Why did the Gerries need to shout so much? Was it to convince themselves that they were right, or to stop anyone else getting a word in? Local resistance heroes would be rounded up, put against the station wall and shot, although their names would live forever, in stone, outside the village hall.

He was jolted back to life by the guard's whistle. The driver had at last put in an appearance. There was an explosion of steam up-front, the clinking of coupling chains, and a sudden lurch forward. The old gentleman jerked upright, and looked at Tim as if to ask 'Are we there yet?' No such luck! Tim smiled back. But at last they were leaving, and three stops and twenty minutes later, they pulled into Ellesmere Station. Now he could flee the train and head for the Town Square and the Shrewsbury bus.

The turn-off to Colemere village was only a few minutes' ride on the Shrewsbury road. Joe was waiting to meet him, and they talked and joked their way along narrow lanes between high banks to Crab Mill farm.

In the still, hot air, Joe's Dad had heard them coming long before they reached the top of the lane to the farm. He had left the dairy and was waiting at the garden gate, as the boys walked up.

"So our evacuee has come back to see us!" He held out a rough hand to shake Tim's. "Welcome, Tim! Crab Mill Farm's been a bit quiet since you left us, and I've been wondrin', now you're back in the big city, do you still want to be a farmer, like you said?" He half-smiled and looked Tim in the eye.

"You 'anna changed your mind?"

The city boy had to admit, to himself at least, that he had. To tell the truth, farming had now dropped to number four on his list of possible careers; but how could he disappoint his country Dad? Instead, he would use delaying tactics, and tell a little lie. After all, he might change his mind.

"I'm not sure."

"Well, you've got plenty of time to make up your mind. Come on. Your country Mum's waiting to see you!"

Mrs Everson was in the kitchen, ready to pounce, and he braced himself for a big hug. They sat down to tea and scones, with Crab Mill damson jam, and swapped news. It was twelve months since the evacuees had gone back home, and the Eversons were anxious to hear about Shirley.

"The doctor says she's very ill and needs a lot of attention, so we've all got to play our part in looking after her...I've done quite a bit myself," he added, to everyone's surprise. It was hard to imagine Tim as a nursing sister.

He described the Mersey Armada, the ruined Corn Exchange, the Den, anything but school, and the talking went on until quite late.

The next morning after breakfast, while Joe was doing his jobs about the farm, Tim set out to catch up with old farmyard friends.

Shep the sheep dog, moving slower than ever and, according to Joe, still hopeless at chasing rabbits; just a kind of elderly, family retainer with free board and lodging, in return for being around to announce the occasional visitor. He recognised his evacuee friend straightaway and somehow found the energy to bound across the yard, in an elderly kind of way, for a warm reunion.

Tim jogged up to the top yard, where he had spent a lot of time as the farm egg-collector, and soon located his team, happily scratching about in the mud, in no particular hurry, oblivious of their vital role as the nation's egg-producers.

He found the cows in the top field - Friesian black and whites - the stars of the Crab Mill scene, just as he had left them, wandering about the top field, tails working overtime, swatting flies, heads down and munching non-stop. Soon it would be time to report to the milking sheds, to do their bit for the war effort.

Then there was good old Sheriff, the Crab Mill cart-horse, casually observing the farmyard activity over his stable door, as if he hadn't heard that there was a war on, a symbol of stability in a very unstable world. Tim thought about the times he had carried him and Joe home after a hard day at the Mrs Low Academy for Unwanted Evacuees, legs astride his broad, muscular back, high up, level with the tops of the hedges. Sheriff wasn't choosy! The city boy was as welcome as the farmer's son.

He strolled back to the lower-yard, perched himself on an old milk-churn and looked around at the main farmhouse with its garden and orchard, and just outside the front door a large circular stone let into the ground, a reminder of the days when it had been part of a mill. At the other end there was a cobbled yard and, along two sides, a row of sheds, the cowhouses (pronounced 'cowuses') where the cows were milked, and the dairy, where the milk was processed before being sent to the collection centre at Ellesmere. Beyond that lay the upper yard with hay stack, hen house and machinery, a mixture of old and not so old.

All this had been 'home' to the two evacuees while the Luftwaffe was trying to knock theirs down. True, he missed his Mum and Dad, especially at bed-time; Mum's prayers and Dad's stories; but if they couldn't be there to look after them, Joe's Mum and Dad had played the part well. Joe's Dad wasn't as strict as his. Perhaps he made allowances because Tim was away from his home and family; but he would tell him off if he forgot to do his bit around the farm, and remind him that, at Crab Mill, he was a country lad and must try to act like one! Their country Mum was kind, not fussy; but he was expected to keep his bed-space tidy and get up in time to do his milk run.

Muriel, Joe's sister was the same age as Shirley and understood why she worried so much. She and Shirley had been like sisters. It was the same with Joe and Tim. Joe was a year or so older than Tim, and treated him like a younger brother. He had stood by him when the village lads poked fun at the 'city kid', and especially when the headmistress was giving him a hard time.

Like Joe, Tim had little jobs to do around the farm. Joe had shown him how to roll a churn over the cobbled yard and brush Sherriff down. But his main job was egg-collecting, sniffing out places where the cleverer chickens had hidden their eggs, for instance, among nettles and brambles, where they knew humans don't like to go. He had taken them on at their own version of Hide and Seek, and knew where to look. There was the excitement of uncovering a cunningly hidden nest, and the satisfaction of doing his bit for the war effort. Mr Churchill would have been pleased.

But for someone who loved to run, there was nothing like 'running the rabbits' at harvest time, following the tractor and cutter, waiting for the driver to point to one as it crouched at the edge of the wheat, preparing to make a dash for freedom. Then the shout, "Here he comes!", and the chase, in and out of stooks, over sheaves, and the final, hopeful dive to grab it before it reached its burrow. Then, when all the wheat was cut, cooling down with a mug of cool cider,

the runner's perk. The happy memories came flooding back.

Yes. He had been happy at Crab Mill Farm.

The next morning, with a head full of messages, a bag of apples and damsons, and half a dozen new-laid eggs, by courtesy of his team, Tim said a sad 'Goodbye', promising to come again. Joe walked with him to the bus stop and waved until it disappeared around a bend, and he braced himself for the long trek home.

****

The holidays were almost over, the friends were all back from family excursions and keen to catch up with the action on the river. They could take a tram to the Pier Head for a ferry trip. Better still, if they had enough money, an Overhead Railway ride would take them to Seaforth Sands, near the mouth of the river. They could witness fighting ships - an MTB or Destroyer in grey, brown and green camouflage, returning to port after an engagement with the enemy, sometimes with great gashes in their hulls. It was a perfect place to get close to the action without having to dodge bullets. Troop ships, packed to overflowing, steamed in the opposite direction, and when

the troops saw them and waved, the boys waved back until their arms ached. If they were lucky they would spot a submarine slipping into port with its crew on deck enjoying the fresh Mersey air. Hospital ships headed for a dock where a row of ambulances would be waiting to transport casualties to one or other of the city's hospitals. Bulky merchantmen, bringing food for the hungry nation and low in the water, headed for one or other of the docks or the Ship Canal. They had survived the dangerous waters of the Atlantic and a nervy, life-and-death game of Cat and Mouse with the U-boat packs. Now the skippers and crews could breathe again, until it was time for the return trip and more peril on the sea.

For the watchers, the hours flew by, until the Liver Clock warned them that it was time for the return trip on the railway, squeezing in among businessmen and dockers, listening to the latest dockland talk.

Otherwise, it was one thing or another in the park, an hour on the end wall, paying homage to THE SCOT, or muscling-in with the Saturday matinée mob at THE GRAND, to annoy the Colonel and claim a noisy seat near the front. So, by the end of the holidays, penniless, it was almost a pleasure to be thinking of going back to school. It would be their last year at Dovedale. Billy, Sid and Ken would have their heads down, focussing on the Grammar School test in June. Tim had already decided that there wouldn't be much worth focusing on. He would run for re-election as milk-monitor and concentrate on football.

CHAPTER THIRTEEN

A SPECIAL BIRTHDAY

Back at Dovedale for the first day of the new school year, 5B had become 6B. They had arrived! Nobody could boss them about, except the teachers, of course, and they liked to treat Year Sixers more as chums than pupils. They were excused allotment duties, at lunch they would be first in the queue for 'seconds', and, in assembly, they could sit right at the back. They were the favoured few!

The first assembly of the year followed the usual pattern, starting with the school hymn, *He who would valiant be*, by John Bunyan. It was Tim's favourite, about the hero, Pilgrim, fighting with giants, hobgoblins and foul fiends, Bunyan's way of describing the forces of evil in the world. The Headmaster would then remind everyone that all of life is 'a kind of pilgrimage, a journey on the side of good or evil', and stress the importance of being on the right side. Year Six had heard it all before and had already switched off, as the Head continued...

"Girls and boys, our sixth year pupils here this morning can remember the dark day when our nation declared war against Germany, and they became evacuees."

Suddenly the favoured few were listening. The Head was talking about them! He went on...

"Uprooted from their homes and mums and dads, they were sent far away, where the bombers couldn't harm them. It was sad to wave them goodbye, but, when they came back to us, they were braver, more confident and, how shall I put it...more enthusiastic."

The sixth years looked at each other.

'Were we really?'

The Head smiled down at Year 4, the new pupils, squatting at his feet.

"So you see, girls and boys, that is what hardship and adversity can do for us!" He waved a hand towards the back, where the heroes were enjoying this surprising pat on the back. After all, being evacuated hadn't been as hard and adverse as the Head seemed to think, what with extra sweets from home, no parental supervision and hardly any homework. For the lucky ones, who had shared a dormitory, there had been pillow-fights, ghost stories and even the occasional 'midnight feast', with bread and jam smuggled upstairs after tea.

The Head soldiered on, with the famous Pilgrim in mind...

"But today, powerful giants are roaming our world. In the Far East, the Japanese are gobbling up one country after another." He smiled towards the staff. Had they noticed the pun? "The German fiends have grabbed most of Europe and they're even trying to get their hands on North Africa, although goodness knows what they can do with all that sand! But our brave 8th Army are holding them up, and although we can't be there to fight alongside them, we can do our bit with our prayers, can't we? Let us pray!"

The Head now embarked on a long prayer, ranging over continents and islands, 'for all our brave servicemen and women, especially the 8th Army 'in the desert heat and sand,' and, 'a speedy victory, if possible!" All joined in an enthusiastic 'Amen', and a speedy exit.

****

September 23rd 1942 - another birthday.

"Happy birthday, Tim, and many happy returns!" Dad had delayed setting out for his office.

The birthday boy grinned. He was glad he had reached double figures, and there were presents to be opened before school. A model of the new four-engined Lancaster bomber, built to scale, with full camouflage, nose-guns and twin revolving tail-guns. Unlike the flimsy, balsa wood Spitfire and Hurricane fighters hanging over his bed, it was solid timber, salvaged from the base of an old armchair.

Dad had worked on it secretly for weeks, in the backyard shed.

"The Spits and Hurricanes have been getting all the glory so far," he said. "Now it's the turn of these chaps, and they deserve it. The German defences are giving them a hard time."

Tim was overjoyed.

"It's amazing, Dad! It'll look great in between my Spitfire and Hurricane. They can be its escort!"

"A brainwave, Tim!"

At that moment Shirley came downstairs

"Many happy returns, Tim!" She handed over a neatly-wrapped parcel.

"I couldn't go to the shops, as you know, but I've got lots of time to spare, so I thought I'd knit you something." She smiled eagerly. "They're to keep your hands warm on those draughty football pitches!" She paused, biting her lip. "I hope they're not too bright, Tim. Mum unravelled an old cardigan. It was the only wool she could find. There's none in the shops."

"Thank you, Shirley." He conjured up a weak smile, but feared the worst.

Prising the parcel open, he stifled a groan. How could he possibly be seen playing football in a pair of bright purple gloves? But his poorly sister had gone to a lot of trouble, and she was peering into his eyes, as she tended to do on such occasions, hoping that he would be overcome with joy. He must try to sound grateful. After all, it was nothing that a bit of mud wouldn't put right.

"Oh thanks Shirley...very much, they're just what I needed." It was true. Eighty minutes on the wide-open spaces of the Mystery, with a wind coming straight from Central Russia, was enough to freeze the fingers of the toughest outside right.

In school, the time passed very slowly, but, back at home, everything was ready for a party, with places for seven. Taking centre spot on the table was the cake, topped with white icing, and depicting THE SCOT, in full flight.

Sid, Ken, and Billy had been invited. The guest-list was shorter than Tim would have liked, but, as Mum explained, 'Birthday parties suffer like everything else, in wartime.'

"After I'd made the cake there was just enough margarine for sandwiches. Mrs Impitt kindly lent me a cup of sugar, and Mrs Thompson saved the tops of the milk for a whole week to give us some cream to go with the jelly. It won't be a feast, but with your friends to share it, I hope it will seem like one!"

The friends arrived early, as young guests tend to do at parties, especially in times of rationing, and what with the lively chatter and boyish jokes, seconds of jelly and cream and generous slices of cake washed down with TIZER, the latest fizzy drink, they all agreed that it was as good as a feast.

The rest of the evening was spent scaling ladders, sliding down snakes and playing AIR-SEA RESCUE, a present from Billy, Sid and Ken. It was the latest board-game, about air-crew members, shot down and adrift in a dinghy, having to survive dangers such as discovery by a German ship, lack of water and food, and the attention of hungry sharks. The winner would be the one who was spotted and picked up first by a Sunderland Flying Boat, and everyone hoped that the throw of the dice would favour the birthday boy. But it was Sid, down to his last glucose tablet, badly dehydrated and baling desperately, who was the first to be rescued. That was the cue for a last round of Tizer and the end of the party.

The trees in the parks had started to change colour, and Mum was becoming very plump around the middle. Tim wasn't sure what to think about the 'happy event' everyone seemed to be talking about. A baby was due to be born sometime around Christmas. He hoped it would be a boy - someone he could teach to kick and trap and shoot. If it was a girl...well, even girls can be quite good at football. He wouldn't rule a sister out.

****

THE END OF THE BEGINNING!

Billy and Tim were passing the newspaper Kiosk on the way to the Den and spotted Mr Erskine's latest headline.

"What does that mean?" Billy frowned.

"Why don't we stop and ask?"

They liked Mr Erskine. Their comics were always ready for collection on Saturdays, and it was nice to think that they helped to keep him in business. He smiled down from his elevated seat as they walked up.

"Good morning, boys. What can I do for you?"

"Will you explain your headline, please, My Erskine?" said Billy.

"Well, our Monty and his 8th Army have walloped the German Afrika Korps at El Alamein."

"Does that mean the war will be ending soon?" asked Tim.

"I'm afraid not, boys. Mr Churchill says it isn't even the beginning of the end. More like the end of the beginning; but it's an important victory, all the same, so we've got something to shout about at last, and the church bells can ring this Sunday."

"It's a clever headline!" said Billy.

"Well, Mr Churchill wrote it for me, in a way!"

****

As Christmas approached, all the excitement about the new family member was overshadowed.

After school one afternoon, Tim picked up Shirley's tea-tray and headed upstairs. He could tell straightaway that she had been crying. Her eyes were red and her usual brave smile was missing.

"Is something wrong, Shirley?"

"It's Grandpa Oliver, Tim. He's very ill. Mum told me this morning."

"Poor Grandpa!"

"and poor Grandma!"

"…and poor Dad!"

It seemed more a time for thinking than talking. He thought he'd better leave the tray and retreat.

****

December 19th 1942 was a bitter-sweet day for the family. Grandpa died in hospital that morning, and later in the afternoon Roger, a brother for Shirley and Tim, was born.

Dad spent most of the morning at Sixty-Five, where Auntie May had come to be with Grandma. After lunch, he took Tim and Shirley to visit Mum and their baby brother, and Tim had been thinking

"Did God arrange it, Dad...I mean baby Roger taking Grandpa's place, in a way?"

Dad smiled. "Well, I think it's just a happy coincidence, Tim. I'm sure it's comforting to Grandma, losing her husband but gaining another grandson! There's Uncle Bill's three, Robert, Jim, and Richard, you...and now Roger."

"That's five in all!" Tim brightened up. "Mm... almost half a football team!"

The nursing home was a large, private house just inside Newsham Park gates, and Dad led the way into a room which Mum was sharing with two others. There was a cot alongside each bed, and flowers everywhere.

Shirley lost no time in making a beeline for her new brother and launched into baby-talk. She had been practising for hours. For Tim, this was unfamiliar territory, and he decided to stand his ground, not far from the door. A nurse pottered about, serving tea and checking pulses. More visitors arrived with more flowers. Apart from that, nothing much seemed to be happening. Tim looked around. So this was how babies arrive in the world! Where were the squads of nurses, the doctors and horror-scopes or whatever they were called?

Mum looked very tired. She was resting on a large pile of pillows and beckoned.

"Tim. Come over and say 'hello' to your brother!"

He gulped, and made his way over, as instructed. Edging cautiously around the end of the cot, he peeped in, smiled down at the pink little face and, taking advantage of a brief break in Shirley's monologue, whispered quietly...

"Hello, Roger! I'm your big brother, Tim!" and baby Roger seemed to smile back. Tim grinned. He had made contact!

****

Grandpa's funeral took place at St James's, just after Christmas. Tim and Shirley didn't attend the service, but were at Sixty-Five when a large group of mourners, led by Grandma, arrived for a solemn tea-party. Tim spotted Gertie, wearing her best smile and floral pinafore, to cheer everyone up, threading her way through the crowd with plates of what looked promisingly like éclairs. Someone's chocolate ration had been sacrificed! And, with any luck, there would be a few left over when people had run out of sympathetic things to say, and had gone home. Until then, he decided, he would make himself scarce, and headed for the breakfast room with the week's issue of The Wizard. Leaving the door slightly ajar, so that he could monitor the comings and, especially, the goings, down below, he was soon lost in the world of the Amazing Wilson.

William Wilson was the reason why Tim had given up the Rover for the Wizard. According to legend, he had learnt the secret of something like eternal youth from an old hermit, and in an amazingly long career, he had broken almost every world record at running, throwing, lifting and jumping. Tim couldn't convince himself that it wasn't all just made up; but, to someone who loved to run, there was something inspiring in the pictures of the hero's twelve-foot stride eating up the ground. One just had to use one's imagination.

By four o'clock, the last of the mourners had torn themselves away from the éclairs. Tim now broke cover and made his way, hopefully, down to the kitchen, where his friend had secreted two, one for Shirley and one for him. She had read his mind! It was a happy ending to a sad day. But now there was another cloud on the horizon.

During the taxi-journey home, half tuned-in to Dad's quiet conversation with Shirley, it crossed his mind that something unpleasant might be about to happen and, later that evening, squatting at the top of the stairs when he should have been in bed, he strained his ears trying to unscramble the murmur of voices coming from the kitchen. He noticed that the familiar words 'Sixty-Five' kept cropping up, and was doing some calculating. Grandma would be all alone in her big house now, and Six, Welbeck Avenue had suddenly become very small. Were they going to move? He hoped not.

It wasn't that he didn't like Sixty-Five. After all, it was where Dad had been a boy, there was a big garden and lots of space, not to mention all those optional bolt-holes, which were bound to come in useful in a house-share with Grandma. But there were so many things he would miss - his friends, the SCOT, the Tuck Shop, The GRAND, even Dovedale Road Juniors, where life at the top, with all the privileges and no pressure, was quite enjoyable. It would be a lot to give up. On balance, he hoped they would be staying.

Then one January evening, his hopes were dashed.

Supper was over, and the seven o'clock news was just starting.

With Uncle Joe Quie in mind, they were anxious to hear what was happening in the Far East. The Japanese were swarming everywhere, as the Headmaster had said, but now the Americans were hitting back.

Dad switched off. It was time for a special bulletin on the home front.

"Now that Grandma's all by herself, with lots of space to spare, she has invited us to go and live with her at Sixty-Five."

So they were moving!

"We know you'll be disappointed, leaving your friends." Mum had spotted Tim's frown. "But you'll soon make new ones. You're good at that, Tim. I've made enquiries at Lister Drive School. It's close to Grandma's, and has a very good name. We hope they can fit you in."

He frowned again. Not another school!

At break-time the following morning, he reported to the others.

"We're going to live with my Grandma, 'cos our house is too small."

There were long faces all round and, at first, nobody spoke. Then, as usually happens at such times, everyone tried to sound cheerful. 'We can still be friends', 'we've had a lot of fun,' and so on. No handshakes. Just sad grins.

At the end of lessons, Mr Donaldson spoke to Tim.

"So this is your last day at Dovedale Road, Tim. I'm sorry you're leaving. You and I haven't broken the long division code yet, and the football team will lose a key player. Now...a bit of advice for when you start at your new school. Try to learn the art of paying attention. It helps a lot, in lessons!" He smiled. "You've got a lot of catching up to do, and you can't blame it all on your strict country teacher! Now, off you go, and show the lads at Lister Drive how to play football!"

"I'll try my best, Mr Donaldson...and thank you for all your help."

At ten o'clock the next morning he climbed on the end wall

to wave a sad 'Cheerio' to THE SCOT. It might be only the second fastest express in the world, but, to him, it was still the best. His eyes followed the guard's van sadly, until it was a dot in the distance, then he dropped down off the wall and trudged home.

The removals van was loaded and driven away, the taxi arrived, and the Welbeck committee came out to wave 'Goodbye!' It seemed hardly any time since they were standing in the same spot, wet-eyed, seeing the kids from Number 6 off to Shropshire.

"After all," Mrs Ferguson said to Mrs Impitt, "the little lad was just a toddler, really!"

Of course, the little lad wasn't a toddler anymore, and she had already complained to his Mum several times about his football landing in her front garden, disturbing the Nasturtiums, and upsetting Henry. But now he was going away again, and she was feeling quite sad. She would miss him, she said. She was standing in a little group with Mrs Simpson, Mrs Impitt and Billy's mum. There was a sad chorus of 'God bless!' and 'Come back and see us sometime', then a flourish of hankies, as the taxi headed north towards Kremlin Drive.

CHAPTER FOURTEEN

TIM HEARS GOOD NEWS

At Sixty-Five, the old order was changing quickly. Sadly, Grandpa had gone, but Grandma was still in charge. After all, it was her home, where she had ruled for thirty or so years. She had moved her headquarters upstairs to a 'bed-sit' on the first floor at the front, where she could check on the traffic to and from the front door and keep an eye on things in general, without being too involved. All she wanted now was peace and quiet.

Dad had already impressed upon Tim that, now they were living with Grandma, he must try to move about more quietly, which he was finding difficult. He wasn't a quiet kind of boy. For one thing, the circular staircase was an unmissable challenge to reach the ground floor quickly. One couldn't just saunter down such stairs. Grandma had noticed, and had already had a word with Dad.

"Must Timothy move about the house like an express train?"

Co-existing with Grandma wasn't going to be easy.

As for Grandma, she seemed unsure what to make of her grandson. Their paths didn't often cross, so opportunities to get to know each other better were few, and both seemed quite happy for matters to stay that way, because neither could think what they might have in common to talk about. Grandma wasn't a fan of the Amazing Wilson or a football enthusiast, and grandson wasn't exactly an authority on gardening or education. So when it happened that they did meet, any conversation was usually brief and to the point.

"Hello, Grandma!'

"Good morning, Timothy."

Then, one afternoon not long after their arrival, Tim was returning from Shirley's tea-run, as Grandma was leaving her bathroom and they almost collided. On this occasion, Grandma was ready for some dialogue.

"Good afternoon, Timothy. Your father was telling me that you haven't qualified for a place at the Collegiate School. I know he's disappointed. I am myself. We were all hoping to see another Oliver wearing blue and black on the football field."

He nodded and smiled sadly. "Yes, Grandma."

****

Lister Drive Junior School was situated in the shadow of the Newsham Power Station, a huge, box-like edifice covered with grey and brown, jig-saw-like camouflage, on the edge of the park. When war broke out it was considered a likely target for the Luftwaffe, so the school was closed down and the teachers and pupils were evacuated to North Wales. But now they were back. The school was open for business again, and as he followed his Mum across the vast, empty playground, Tim wasn't impressed. It reminded him of a Dock Road warehouse, a grimy mountain of brick and glass, badly in need of some camouflage of its own, and, once inside, things weren't much better - just a large, rectangular open space with classrooms on the two long sides, a stage at one end and dark-brown, glazed tiles everywhere, an unsuccessful attempt to improve on the boring brickwork. A staircase led up from the ground floor to a walkway, the kind one would find in a prison, with more classrooms and tiles.

'Lister Drive', as it was known, had been built at a time when schools were meant to make it clear to a new pupil that education is about such things as graft, diligence and hard work, and the designer had succeeded. However it had got its very good name, Tim reflected, could have had little to do with its architecture.

A notice directed the newcomers to a door saying 'ENQUIRIES'. They stepped inside and sat down to wait. After a few minutes a secretary came to escort them to the Headmaster's room.

Mr Ogilvie the large, enthusiastic Headmaster smiled

sympathetically across his desk, as Mum explained that Tim's education had been badly interrupted by the war.

"But he's very good at games and things like running."

"Well, Lister Drive School has a name for bringing the best out of its pupils," the Headmaster enthused, "especially the weaker ones!' Tim frowned. He was only weaker at arithmetic!

"As for running…" Mr Ogilvie continued, waving a hand at photographs of past pupils striding impressively across the playground, "Tim has come to the right place, and at the right time! We may not have a running track or even a field of our own, but we have had many promising athletes here down the years, and Sports Day will be coming soon. I look forward to seeing him in action!"

The new pupil sighed. Another school without a playing field! But Mum seemed to be reassured, and departed.

Tim now followed the Headmaster across the hall to a door stating that this was Class 6B's room and that Mrs Walker was in charge. He ushered Tim inside and 6B lost interest in what they had been doing. Mrs Walker, a small, thin lady with red hair, rose from her desk to meet them.

"I have brought you a new pupil, Mrs Walker," said the Head. "His name is Tim Oliver, and he's especially good at sport." He turned to the class.

"Now, 6B, Tim here was an evacuee, as most of you were, so you have a lot in common. I'm depending on you to show him what a friendly school ours is!" He beamed down at them, then at Tim, and left, as 6B focussed on the new boy.

The teacher pointed to a vacant desk at the back of the class.

"That will be your desk, Timothy." Mrs Walker seemed to disapprove of the use of shortened names in the classroom. Tim nodded and found his desk, as she rooted among some papers.

"Now, let me see…you're good at sport, the Headmaster says, and Shaftesbury House needs one or two good sportsmen. So, for games, that will be your house. You've heard about Lord Shaftesbury, have you?"

Timothy had to admit that he hadn't, which seemed to disappoint his new teacher, but, undeterred, she seized the opportunity for a bit of general revision.

"Well now, who can tell Timothy about the kindly Lord Shaftesbury?"

The answer was that most of them could. They had beavered away for hours, producing reams about the Earl who had dedicated his life to doing away with such things as child-labour, with graphic illustrations of hollow-cheeked, shoeless children shinning up chimneys and under factory machinery. It was old hat to 6B. A sea of hands was raised, more or less enthusiastically, and, when Daisy Wilson was chosen to answer on behalf of the rest, she launched into an impressive account of the Earl's kind achievements, all from memory. Mrs Walker nodded approvingly.

"So there you are, Timothy. I hope you will be proud to wear the green braid of Shaftesbury House!"

Tim nodded. If Shaftesbury House needed him, he was ready; and green had suddenly become his favourite colour, after blue, He couldn't wait to slip a braid over his shoulder and go into action.

Mrs Walker explained that there were three other boys' houses, all named after 'great heroes of by-gone days...William Wilberforce, who fought against the slave trade, Doctor Barnardo, who founded homes for orphans, and David Livingstone, a missionary doctor in darkest Africa'.

At break in the playground, he was surrounded, and bombarded with questions.

"Where were you evacuated to?" "Have you got any shrapnel?" "Are you any good at footie?" "What position do you play?" And a more difficult one - "Which school will you be going to when you leave Lister Drive?" He hadn't thought about it.

He discovered that 6A would soon be sitting the Grammar School entrance exam.

"They want to be College puddins," said one boy with a squeaky voice, called Trev. "We don't want to be like them, always reading books and wearing those funny caps!"

Tim frowned. Was that true? Or was Trev just disappointed that he wouldn't be a College pudding himself? And what about the others in 6B? Some of them seemed clever enough. Daisy, for instance, with her inspiring talk about Lord Shaftesbury. Perhaps she just wasn't very good at arithmetic, like him. It seemed a pity that they couldn't all be going to a Grammar school. Trev said that the entrance exam would be held just after half-term.

"After that, everyone can concentrate on Sports Day."

Half-term was an opportunity for a trip on the overhead railway, to keep in touch with the action on the river. He hoped he might even bump into Billy, Sid and Ken. It would be much more fun. But there was no sign of them. Of course, they would probably be revising. He had found the local recreation ground and joined in a game with some local lads, and now he was looking forward to being back at school. It would soon be Sports Day.

He had been chosen to run the hundred yards. Mr Stott the Shaftesbury House Master, called it 'The Blue Riband of the track', and it was during a break in practice that he heard about Brian Williams, who was in 6A. He would be running for Livingstone and, according to Trev, he wasn't just clever.

"He's fast, Tim!" Tim took note.

On the morning of Sports Day he woke early, too excited to over-sleep. He washed, dressed and ate his breakfast in a hurry, and was one of the first through the school gates. It was twenty to nine. The Sports Day programme would be starting at ten o'clock, and butterflies in his stomach were already warming up. Then in assembly, during the prayers, he noticed that his socks seemed to be different colours. He looked again. There was no doubt. One was grey, the other blue. He had got dressed too quickly! There was no time to go home and change them and, soon, the whole school would be lining the track to witness one of the great Lord Shaftesbury's representatives running the Sixth Year boys' Blue Riband race in odd socks!

Then he remembered Mr Allan, the sports teacher, saying that 'the faster your arms move, the faster your legs will move'. It was 'simple cause and effect', he said, and Tim decided it would be worth trying. If Mr Allan was correct, he would move his arms extra fast, his feet would hardly touch the ground, and the crowd would see just a grey and blue blur as he went past.

At ten o'clock the whole school poured out onto the playground, together with the Head and Mrs Ogilvie, the teachers, the dinner ladies and cleaners. The fun races - the sack race, egg and spoon and three-legged - came first, followed by the foot-races.

In the Sixth Year Girls hundred yards , Daisy, the historian, won for Nightingale House. The boys' race was next, the last event on the programme.

Tim pressed his stockings down as far as they would go, slipped his braid over his shoulder and jogged over to the start. Brian was there already, muscular, calm and confident, unlike Tim. His mouth was dry and the butterflies were falling over themselves.

The crowd, three or four deep, leaned forward to look down the track, as Mr Allan, the starter, raised his flag.

"On your marks...SET!...GO!"

The flag fell and a great shout went up...

"BARNARDO!"..."WILBERFORCE!"..."LIVINGSTONE!" ..." SHAFTESBURY!" four great names mixed together, as the runners sprinted across the yard. By half-way, Brian was a yard or so ahead, with Tim in second place, arms and legs moving faster than ever, but not fast enough. Gritting his teeth, he was clawing back Brian's lead, but, at the finish, it was Brian first and Tim second, a couple of feet behind. It was disappointing, although coming second, behind the great Brian was hardly a disgrace. Then he thought about his socks and glanced at the spectators. Nobody was pointing or laughing! They hadn't been noticed.

So far, so good. But there was still the prize-giving to come. He would have to go forward to receive his certificate in front of

the whole school, and the limelight was the last thing he wanted. He
decided that he would wait until attention was focussed on the popular
Brian receiving his certificate, perhaps posing for a photograph. Then
he would go up to receive his certificate, retreat quickly and mix with
the crowd. He pressed his socks down again. The announcer went
into action for the last time.

"The One hundred yards, sixth year boys... first Brian Williams,
Livingstone." The Livingstone pupils cheered wildly, as Brian
stepped forward, with a smile and a modestly-raised hand, to receive
his certificate. It was all in a day's work for Brian.

"Second, Tim Oliver, Shaftesbury." The Shaftesbury pupils did
their best to equal the Livingstone cheers, as Tim walked forward
smartly.

"Well done, Tim Oliver!" said the Head, beaming as usual.
"Your Mum's right. You can run!"

"That was a good race," said Mrs Ogilvie, as she presented him
with the Runner-up certificate. She smiled. "And what interesting
socks you're wearing!"

So someone had noticed, after all! How many others?

"Thank you, Miss." He wouldn't try to explain. He took the certificate and mingled quickly with the crowd heading for the gate and home and sanctuary.

****

The next Saturday morning he was laying out the clock-golf course and trying to decide where IX should be, when Mum and Dad came into the garden.

"We've got some wonderful news, Tim!" said Mum. "A very good friend of the family has offered to pay for a place for you at the Collegiate Preparatory School.

"Yippee!" Now he was jumping up and down. Then the jumping stopped.

"Which friend is it?"

"We're not allowed to say," said Dad.

"But... how can I say 'Thank you,' if I don't know who it is?"

"It'll be sufficient thanks for him, or her, to know that you'll be going to my old school," said Dad.

"Well, whoever it is, please say 'Thank you VERY much' for me!"

"We already have!" said Mum, and they retreated to the house, leaving him to finish the clock-face, and very excited. He had got a place at Dad's old school, and at the eleventh hour! But who was the mysterious 'very good friend'?

He finished the clock-face and went in to break the news to Shirley. She was in the Breakfast Room. With its view over the garden it had been taken over as a sanatorium.

"I can go to the Collegiate after all, Shirley. Mum says a very good friend of the family will pay for a place for me at The Prep."

"Oh, that's wonderful, Tim! But who's the friend?"

"That's what I wanted to know, but I'm not allowed to. Dad said 'him or her', which doesn't help much!"

"Mmm" she frowned. "It could be almost anyone! Let's see... we know it's a friend... a very good friend of the family...someone who must think a lot of Dad and his old school...someone who seems to like you, Tim, although I can't think who...only joking!.. someone who knows that Mum and Dad can't afford to pay for a place at the Prep, and must be quite well-off. That narrows the list of possibles down quite a lot. I'll think about it!"

Later the same afternoon Tim met Grandma as he was going up to his bedroom. She smiled.

"So you'll be going to your father's old school, after all, Timothy! I'm very pleased. I can already see you in your cap with those blue stripes!"

"Yes, Grandma. A friend of the family's paying for me, although I'm not allowed to know who." He paused. "I just wish I could say 'Thank you'."

"Well I'm sure the person, whoever it is, doesn't need you to, dear boy!" She turned away quickly, smiling slightly, and at that moment he felt sure he knew who the mysterious 'friend of the family' was.

Back in the sanatorium the two detectives discussed the latest developments in the mystery, and Tim's hunch.

"She smiled at you, Tim! That's a good clue. And we know she's keen on the Collegiate, 'cos both her sons went there. She must be quite well off, too, living in such a big house. The pieces are beginning to fit together. Tell me again what she said."

"Something like...' So you'll be going to your father's old school, after all.'"

"Well, if Grandma isn't the person we're looking for, I think she'd have said something like 'I hear that you'll be going to your father's school.' We can't be sure, Tim, and we can't ask Dad. But I think we might have identified our 'very good friend of the family'!"

"Yes, and in case we're right, I'll try to be quieter in future!"

"And you can start getting ready to be a Collegiate boy!"

****

At Lister Drive, the news was around the 6B classroom in seconds.

"So you're going to be one of those College puddins, Tim!" Trev grinned. "Just think. All that homework!"

Tim frowned. In the excitement, he hadn't thought about that.

"Good luck, anyway, especially with your running! But don't forget to check your socks!"

"Thanks, Trev, I won't! And good luck to you in your new school."

Mrs Walker smiled. "I hear that you'll be going to the Collegiate School, Timothy. That will be a great incentive to shine...a big challenge, too, I imagine! I wish you success!"

As he reached the school gates he turned to glance back at the dingy building and thought about the day he had arrived and the gloomy first impressions. He had been at Lister Drive for only a few months, but, looking back, he had been happy with Mrs Walker and his 6B friends, among all the brown tiles. He nodded, as if to agree with his final judgement. He wouldn't make the same mistake on his last day. Lister Drive School was one book that shouldn't be judged by its cover.

CHAPTER FIFTEEN

THE PREP

The Collegiate School Preparatory Department, 'The Prep', for short, could be found on the top floor or, to be more exact, among the attics of Sandheys, once a large, private residence on the northern edge of the city, whose grounds ran alongside the Collegiate School playing fields. It had been taken over by Holly Lodge High School for Girls, and when the need for a 'prep' department for the Collegiate arose, the governors of the girls' school had generously offered some roof space, strictly on the understanding that the girls and boys wouldn't have to use the same entrances, staircases and corridors, where squeezing past each other would not be desirable. For that reason, the way in and out of The Prep was via a cast-iron fire-escape attached to the north side of the house, involving a stiff climb up five short flights to reach the entrance leading to several small rooms, with low ceilings at odd angles.

It was the first day of the new school year, and the pupils had gathered at the bottom of the fire-escape, preparing for the ascent. The new boys led the way, shoes and faces shining, listing heavily to one side on account of satchels stuffed by conscientious mums with everything they might possibly need and some they almost certainly wouldn't. The gaggle of mums down below followed each step with anxious eyes, as if they might never see their offspring again, hoping desperately to be rewarded with a wave, a nervous, downward grin or, at least, a hand raised in resignation. Then, as the climbers reached the summit and disappeared from sight, the devoted watchers turned away, to head for home and a consoling cup of tea or something stronger, and while-away the fretful hours before returning, at least half an hour early, for letting-out time.

At assembly, Tim stood in line next to another new boy who said his name was Yozzer.

"That's my nickname. My real name's Hughes."

Mrs Taylor, a Scottish lady, who seemed to be in charge, read a passage from the Bible about making the most of one's talents, followed by a prayer about not giving up when facing a big challenge in life. It was written by 'the Great Sir Francis Drake', she explained, brightly, 'so we should all be inspired!' Then Miss Sterland, a tall, stately teacher, launched into a long prayer about the importance of such things as diligence, politeness, using one's talents and keeping the school rules.

Mrs Taylor welcomed the new boys and congratulated them on making the ascent successfully! It was her little joke, to get the school year off to a good start, and she went on to explain about the perils and temptations of life at the top of a fire- escape.

"Now boys, at The Prep we have two very important rules. Up here, level with the tree tops and the flight paths of the pigeons may seem a perfect place for launching paper aeroplanes and such-like projectiles. Well, it can be most distracting to the girls below, especially any who may be interested in aero-dynamics. It is forbidden! Secondly, on your way up and down the stairs you may be tempted, out of curiosity, to glance into the girls' class-rooms, or even wave, especially if they wave first, as sometimes happens, unfortunately. You must resist!"

"Those are our rules. In life, as on the sports field, there must be rules, if there is to be order and happiness. That's why God gave us ten in the first place, to get us started! We also believe that a busy school is a happy school. We do not set homework. Instead we want you to work hard at your lessons, so that you can spend the evening with your family, your hobby or your friends, have a good night's sleep and rise refreshed for another challenging day here at The Prep."

So far, so good. Tim was impressed. Pity about the ban on projectiles, but even the easy-going Mr Donaldson used to set a bit of homework! He thought he would like Mrs Taylor.

"However," she continued, as if to say 'Not so fast!' "...we do want you to exercise your minds in preparation for your move to the Big School, where you will be entering the world of conjugations, equations and such things. So, each term, we want you to learn a poem off by heart, and we look forward to hearing you recite the one of your choice."

A poem a term! Tim glanced at Yozzer and ginned. Life at The Prep was going to be a stroll!

And the Headmistress hadn't finished. "Now, here at the Prep we go by a wise Latin saying - *Mens sana in corpore sano*. It means 'a healthy mind in a healthy body'. It was written long ago, but it's just as important today. Our minds need exercise, and so do our bodies! We have a saying of our own, don't we, that 'all work and no play makes Jack a dull boy', and we don't want dull boys at The Prep, do we?"

Not if you say so, Miss. She went on...

"Some of us come from sporting families." To Tim's surprise she pointed at him. "Like Timothy here. His father was one of our Big School heroes many years ago." She smiled down at him.

"Wasn't he, Timothy?"

He gulped. "Erm, yes, Miss!"

"Of course," she continued, "we can't all be sports heroes, but we can all do our best to be fit and healthy, can't we, Timothy?" Timothy nodded, frowning. Why doesn't she ask someone else?

"So, here at The Prep," she continued, brightly, "Friday afternoon is Sport and Fitness afternoon, when we will be visiting the Big School playing fields, next door, to play football in the fresh air, taking care not to upset Mr Harris, the groundsman!"

Miss Sterland now stepped forward, looking grave, as if about to announce the end of the world.

"Now boys, at lunch we will be sharing the girl's dining room." She paused, to let the awful truth sink in. "Now, I know that girls sometimes behave strangely in the presence of boys, giggling and so on. Well, if that happens, you must take no notice! Show them that you are gentlemen! There will be a separate queue for you. Join the end, do not push in, and wait patiently until you are served ... and do remember that we are at war and food is scarce! So don't complain about what is on the menu!"

For instance, if it's cheese pie, as it often seems to be these days, try to remember that that very cheese may have been brought all the way from New Zealand, across dangerous seas. Courageous sailors may have risked their lives to bring it to us. Yes, I know, some might only have come over the Mersey from Cheshire." She had read their minds. "That is beside the point! Cheese is good for us! And another thing ... please do not complain if you consider that your portion is smaller than the next person's. That has been known to happen. The serving ladies have a difficult enough task, trying to make sure that everyone receives the same amount. And just one more thing..."

Why are teachers so keen on making long speeches, they wondered. Perhaps it goes with the job.

Miss continued...

"...if seconds are announced, do not scramble for them. Remember...we are gentlemen!"

On that note the assembly finally petered out, the gentlemen headed for their appointed classroom and, as Tim was passing her, the Headmistress stopped him.

"I've heard a lot about your father when he was a pupil at the Collegiate, Timothy, and I'm sure he's very pleased that his son will be following in his steps, although that won't be easy." She smiled, sympathetically. "So, when you go to the pavilion on Friday to get changed, be sure to look up! There's something there to inspire you! It will be a big challenge. Oh, and do try to remember, won't you, that I am MRS TAYLOR, not Miss!"

"Yes, Miss."

The rest of the morning slipped by pleasantly, with routine matters such as timetables, milk-break and an essay to write on 'What I would like to do when I leave school.'

Tim was still in several minds. As has been noted, farming had already slipped from second to fourth place. For instance, compared with having his feet firmly placed on the bridge of a big ship, the prospect of spending his days ankle-deep in mud wasn't very appealing. Soldiering was also losing ground. The difference between the elegant uniforms of Lieutenant Faversham's day and the drab khaki he had seen on the city streets had raised a serious question mark in his mind. He had mentioned these misgivings to his Mum, who said that perhaps he was looking for the wrong things in a career.

"I mean, you could hardly run a farm without encountering a lot of mud, Tim, and the colour of a uniform doesn't make a man a soldier!"

Even his third choice, life as a Naval Captain, wasn't as attractive as he had thought. From all accounts, the German U-Boat packs were having a field-day sinking Allied ships, and he had always thought that drowning must be a horrible way to die. He hoped the war would be over long before he would have to make up his mind. All of which left his favourite choice, footballer, unchallenged, in first place, much to Mrs Taylor's disappointment, as she glanced over his shoulder.

He had embarked on an illustrated account of Life at Everton Football Club...terraces alive with fans in caps and armed with rattles, ladies in blue and white showering the crowd with toffees, and a self-portrait in full Everton kit, holding a ball. It wasn't the kind of thing the Headmistress was hoping for from a Prep pupil, but before he could go into more detail, the bell rang for lunch.

Some of the boys had brought sandwiches, lovingly prepared and packed by doting mothers, and could wander, munching, among the rhododendrons. The rest, with Miss Sterland in the lead, descended the fire escape silently, 'as lambs led to the slaughter,' before turning, nervously, through a doorway into the girls' dining room. Hundreds of eyes turned to look at them, and hands went up to mouths to stifle giggles. Miss Sterland led the way across to the serving hatch.

"Remember!" she whispered. "We are gentlemen!"

In response, they concentrated on what was on offer, written in chalk over the serving hatch -

Sausage & Mash with peas
or
Fish pie with peas

Not even a hint of cheese. The ladies had made a special effort on their first day, to win them over. For pudding, the choice was Bakewell Tart with custard, or Tapioca. The gentlemen smiled politely, stifled muttered references to frog spawn, ate as speedily as possible, and made their escape.

The best thing, by far, about The Prep, Tim thought, was its location, right next to the Big School playing fields. At Sixty-Five, he had often heard talk about 'Holly Lodge', the arena where his Dad and his big brother, Uncle Bill, had performed heroics, once upon a time. Now, he was keen to see it for himself. He lost no time finding a gap in the boundary wall, and once through that, he had the playing fields all to himself.

For a few minutes he stood, motionless, taking everything in. On the far side were the cricket nets, although some had been sacrificed to make space for allotments, which was no surprise. To his right, a long, low ridge, topped by a row of firs, gave some cover from the northerly winds, and, in front of him lay acres and acres of playing fields, complete with goal posts of one sort or another. Paradise!

He grinned. This was where, against all the odds, he had dreamed of playing, one day, the very spot where generations of Collegiate boys had done battle with rival schools - The Institute, St Francis Xavier's, Quarry Bank, The Holt, and others - urged on from the touch-lines by chanting crowds. He had already learnt the words, off by heart...

'Boomeranga, boomeranga, boom, boom, boom,

Chicaraca, chicaraca, chow, chow, chow,

Oo – Ah – Oo-ah-ah, Coll, Coll, Collegiate!'

Whether the strange words actually meant anything, nobody seemed to know or care, but, coming in unison from hundreds of young throats, they could strike terror into the hearts of the most confident opposition.

Over to his left lay the Pavilion. It was built early in the century, and had lost most of its first glow, but still reeked of sporting history. It was here that Mr Harris, Irishman, groundsman and potentate, reigned from his favourite position in front of a row of football and rugby balls, like a mother hen guarding her eggs. 'Sam', as he was called by those who dared, was lord of all he surveyed, above all the first eleven football pitch. This stretch of lovingly-mown turf, seventy by one hundred yards, right in front of the pavilion, was reserved only for the feet of the school's elite and, albeit grudgingly, those of their opponents. No one else was considered worthy to set foot on it. No one else dared. Mr Harris was a perfectionist, whether behind a line-marker or mowing machine and, as often happens with perfectionists, he was easily annoyed.

The new boy knew nothing of this. He hadn't picked up Mrs Taylors's thinly-veiled warning. He would soon learn. Now he retraced his steps through the gap, past the rhododendrons to the fire-escape.

Friday afternoon, Football and Fitness time, couldn't come soon enough; and, because it followed lunch, a dedicated footballer could eat quickly, flee the dining room and be changed and ready, long before Miss Sterland would arrive, whistle in hand, to start the game.

Not surprisingly, then, who should arrive at the pavilion entrance well ahead of everyone else, but Tim. This was where his Dad used to get changed! He grinned. There was no sign of Mr Harris, but there could surely be no harm in looking around. He hesitated, then poked his head inside. A large space opened onto changing rooms and, in the centre, a stove burned, giving off a smoky haze. A row of footballs, blown up and waterproofed sat, invitingly, on a shelf.

A few minutes went by and still there was no sign of the groundsman. It was then that he thought about Mrs Taylor's words, and looked up to where there were rows of boards, high on the walls, inscribed with the names of the school's first teams down the years. His Dad's name must be there! He stepped inside for a closer look.

His father had left the school in 1921, so he knew where to start looking. One board, headed 1919-20 - FOOTBALL FIRST ELEVEN, read W.F.Oliver, Captain. That was Dad's brother, and below that - T.J.Oliver, Vice Captain, that was Dad. The next board, headed 1919-20 - CRICKET FIRST ELEVEN, read T.J.Oliver, Captain, and below that - W.F.Oliver, Vice-Captain. They had just changed places! No wonder the Headmistress said he should be inspired, and now he understood what she meant about it being 'a big challenge.' He thought of Lieutenant Faversham, expected to live up to the glorious achievements of his ancestors. In his front seat at THE GRAND he had felt sorry for him, even though he guessed that he would succeed in the end. Heroes always do! He returned to his place at the door, but hated to be wasting time, just hanging around. Surely he could get ready. He chose one of the changing rooms and soon emerged, wearing the treasured football shirt. Gertie had given it a lot of wash-tub treatment, and it had lost some of its mustiness.

He jogged up and down on the floor boards, eyeing the balls impatiently. Even if he couldn't borrow one for a kick-about, there could surely be no harm in testing his studs and, with that, he ran out onto the hallowed First Eleven pitch. It felt so springy under his feet, and to think that this was where Dad had once played! He jogged about for a few moments, and had just done a short sprint and a quick turn, when a loud shout came from the direction of the gap in the wall

"Oi! You there!" He glanced over to the gap, where an elderly gentleman was pointing to him in an agitated manner. This must be

Mr Harris, whom they should avoid upsetting. He had finally turned up, and seemed to be upset about something. Tim looked across to ask for further instructions.

"Yes, you!" the groundsman nodded. "Just you come over here!"

Tim ran across to where the groundsman stood, purple-faced, fists clenched as if about to throw a punch, glaring at him through thick lenses. Tim thought he should leave him to open the conversation.

"And what do you t'ink you were doin' on that pitch?"

Tim stepped back, out of range, and said nothing. After all, wasn't it obvious what he had been doing - just running up and down? Then, to his surprise, the groundsman leaned forward to take a close look at his shirt.

"And what's that shirt, you're wearing?"

"It's my Dad's school football shirt, sir, the one he used to wear when he played there." He pointed to the First Eleven pitch.

The groundsman looked closer, examining the crest.

"That's a Senior Shield team badge. And what would your

father's name be, then?"

"Oliver, sir. Tom Oliver."

"Well, oi never! He was at the school when I first came here."
He paused. "He was a foine all-rounder...footballer, cricketer and
quarter-miler... and scholar, too, so I heard. So you see, 'tis a high
standard you've got to live up to, and you haven't made a very good
start!"

"Yes Sir. I'm very sorry...about going on your pitch, I mean."

The groundsman almost smiled.

"That's alright. Just don't be doing it again, unless I say so.
Now away wit' you and play football!"

He waved an arm in the direction of the Prep boys who had
changed while the groundsman was lecturing Tim, and were being
divided into teams by Miss Sterland, in tweed skirt and pullover,
football stockings and boots, and a neat little cap. Tim ran across
to join them and, as they lined up to kick off, he looked around,
grinning. He was about to play football on Dad's school playing
fields in Dad's football shirt. History was repeating itself!

CHAPTER SIXTEEN

LIFE IN THE SLOW LANE

The day Shirley took her place at Blackburne House School in her smart, dark-green, uniform was a red-letter day. The doctor said that she would have to pace herself carefully, but should soon be 'dashing about on the hockey pitch'. As it happened, Shirley wasn't the dashing-about type, preferring more genteel activities, like hop-scotch and tennis. In any case, she had other priorities - almost two years' schooling to make up, and a lively little brother to keep an eye on.

Tim's nursing apprenticeship was over, and he considered that, as a beginner, he had done quite well, confiding to Gertie that he 'must have climbed thousands of steps' as Shirley's tea-boy, not to mention all those brotherly bedside chats. True, he had drawn a line at holding hands, but, looking back, he had 'spent hours' keeping Shirley up to date on how Flash Gordon and the Lone Ranger had been holding back the forces of evil in Outer Space and the Wild West respectively. She had listened patiently to whatever he had had to offer. Dr Minnitt said that his sister was a kind of war casualty, so perhaps his efforts counted as a kind of war-effort? And now she was almost her old self. The Fuhrer had done his worst, but she had won through. He was proud of her, and quite pleased with himself.

Meanwhile, life at the Prep was turning out to be even more leisurely than he had hoped. Of course, there was no escaping arithmetic, which might have spoilt everything; but, to his great surprise, it was here at the Prep that he finally made the break-through. Where the sporty Mr Donaldson had failed, the motherly Mrs Taylor triumphed. In just a few weeks the long-division penny had dropped. Now he could even free-wheel!

Form 3 seemed to spend a lot of time on 'Art and Craft'; sometimes it was painting, which Miss Sterland liked to call 'working with colour'; sometimes messing about with newspaper and glue, which she called 'Introductory Sculpture'.

For a whole hour each week there was 'French conversation' with Mademoiselle Flaubert, known as 'Mam'selle'. There wasn't a text-book in sight. Just informal chat about everyday life, such as *'Un jour au bord de la mer avec maman,* or *Un jeu dans le parc avec Koko le chien'.* It was 'ow you say 'a fun way' of starting to learn a new language, she explained; and, if anyone was going to set Form 3 on the road to fluency, it was Mam'selle, who was younger than the other teachers, and much prettier. French Conversation was very popular. Tim, unfortunately, couldn't see the fun or the point in learning to speak someone else's language. One language was enough to be going on with. He had decided that he would do as little conversing as possible.

Geography lessons with Mrs Taylor were even more leisurely, whiling away the hours producing a map of the world, colouring the territories of the British Empire in shocking pink, the only kind she could lay her hands on. It was to 'encourage a sense of imperial pride and solidarity, at a time of imperial danger,' she explained.

In History lessons, Miss Sterland was all enthusiasm. She was putting the official syllabus on 'hold', she said.

"After all, who wants to learn about the Wars of the Roses when there's a war-to-end-all wars going on at this very moment?"

She had dedicated herself to rising early to catch the first news bulletins and had pinned up a map of the world covering most of one wall of the room. She called it 'our very own Ops (for 'Operations') Room' and, as the weeks went by, stuck little flags here and there - the Union Jack, the Stars and Stripes, the Hammer and Sickle, the 'detestable' Rising Sun and 'even more detestable ' Swastika - with arrows to demonstrate, hopefully, that the war was 'flowing our way, at last!'

She had special names for the various 'warring parties'.

"Those brave Ruskies, that's the Russians, have saved Moscow and are holding out at Stalingrad. The Tommies, our boys, have been reinforced after the Singapore disaster, and joined the Yanks to hit back at the Japs, that's the Japanese, of course."

"The Allies have landed in Southern Italy," she announced, triumphantly, a few days later. "The Iti's, that's the Italians, have given in already. They don't have the stomach for war, which is strange, considering they're direct descendants of the Romans who were always looking for a fight!" She chuckled. "Mussolini, Hitler's stooge, has gone to ground! We won't be hearing much more from him, I think!"

They grinned. With Miss Sterland in charge, history lessons were going to be non-stop fun.

That was not so in the case of English lessons, which were spent in a non-stop study of poetry. At the very beginning, Mrs Taylor had explained that, to appreciate the English language fully, 'one must explore the world of the English poet'. That wasn't good news to Tim, who had never been keen on poetry, and certainly couldn't be bothered to explore it. But there was no avoiding the poem-per-term rule and, as the Autumn Term drifted slowly to its close, the hapless members of Form 3 were being called upon to recite the one of their choice.

Peter Galvin had just given a word-perfect rendering of one by William Wordsworth, about wandering around all by himself in a field of daffodils. Tim was in his favoured seat at the back, keeping his head down. Yozzer was waving a hand, volunteering to be next; but the teacher waved a hand in Tim's direction, smiling hopefully.

"Now let us hear your chosen poem, Timothy. Vitae Lampada, isn't it?"

Gulp! He had meant to work on it the previous evening, but was late getting back from football, and exhausted. This was going to be tricky.

"Yes, Miss."

He rose slowly, cleared his throat and began.

"Vitae lampada, by John Henry Newbolt."

'There's a breathless hush in the close tonight, ten to make and the match to win,

A bumping pitch and a blinding light, an hour to play and the last man in...' He paused slightly, perhaps for dramatic effect or wondering what came next...

'And it's not for the sake of a ribboned coat or the selfish hope of a season's fame, but his captain's hand on his shoulder smote,

'Play up! Play up! and play the game!'

"That was quite moving, Timothy," said the teacher, smiling slightly. "But I seem to remember that you gave us verse one last time and the time before that! May we hear verse two now, please... and verse three would be nice."

Now all eyes were on him, as he went on...

'The sand of the desert's sodden red, red with the wreck of a square that broke, the Gatling's jammed...' Again he paused, and closed his eyes, hoping to conjure up the words he knew were there, somewhere in the recesses of his mind.

The others noticed that his face had turned pale.

"Keep going, Tim!" whispered Yozzer; but it was the teacher

who came to the rescue.

"*...and the Colonel's dead,*" she said quietly, unsmiling now.

'*And the Colonel's dead,*' he repeated,'*...and the regiment blind with dust and smoke.*

'*The river of death has brimmed its banks,...*' He closed his eyes again. Was it to pray?

By now, a breathless hush had fallen on Form 3.

"*...and England far, and Honour a name,*" again the teacher prompted. He bit his lip. She knew it better than he did!

"*And England far, and Honour a name*", he repeated, "*...but the voice of a schoolboy rallies the ranks, 'Play up! Play up! and play the game!'*

Here he stopped. He had made it to the end of verse two, just. Wasn't that enough, or would he have to go on? If so, would the kindly Mrs Taylor come to his rescue yet again? He glanced at her.

The answer to all three questions was a silent frown. The kindliness had run out. There would be no reprieve. He was on his own. He must 'soldier on alone' as John Henry Newbolt might have put it. Now, how did verse three start?

'*This is the word...*' he began, then stopped. For a minute he looked out of the window, saying nothing. He had dried up, and Mrs Taylor knew. They all knew. There was a long silence before the teacher spoke.

"Well, I must say I'm very disappointed that you cannot recite your poem without my help, Timothy. After all it's nearly Christmas, and you've had a whole term to commit it to memory. There are only three verses. You made heavy weather of verse two, and we have heard only four words of verse three! I wonder why you chose it."

Now there was an extra long hush.

"Well...I really liked the first verse, Miss,...the cricket match, the ribboned coat, all the excitement..and the bit about playing the game was inspiring. But I didn't like verse two very much. "

"And why was that?"

"Well, it was the bits about the river of death and the sand soaked with blood. It's not very nice, Miss, especially in a poem. I told my Dad, and he said war isn't very nice. He says that every night now, a thousand bombers are raiding German cities. They drop incendiary bombs first, to start fires, then high explosives to fan the flames and make them spread quickly. Fire-storms, they're called, Miss, and sometimes people can't escape. I think that sounds cruel."

"And I think that's one reason why Mr Newbolt wrote his poem," she said. "Good poetry tells the truth about all of life, the ugly and cruel bits as well as the pleasant ones. This whole poem is what's called a metaphor. It's the poet's way of describing life as an arena - a cricket pitch or battlefield - in which our character, the kind of person we are, is shaped and tested. It's true that war is always ugly, but fine things, like self-sacrifice, courage and service can come out of it. That's what the poet calls 'playing the game', although it's much more than a game. It's worth living, even dying for, Mr Newbolt says, and handing on, like a flaming torch, to those who come after us,.....which is what verse three says, Timothy."

"Yes, Miss," he muttered, slumping down in his desk.

She had made her point.

"Now, please listen to verse three, everyone."

'This is the word that, year by year, while in her place the school is set,

Every one of her sons must hear, and none that hears it dares forget.

This they all, with a joyful mind, bear through life like a torch in flame

And, falling, fling to the host behind, 'Play up, Play up! and play the game!'

Now she smiled at Tim.

"So you see, Timothy, you chose a very moving poem!* She

---

* NOTE The whole text of Vitae Lampada was printed on the front page of the Times newspaper several times during the Great (1914-18) War, to inspire the spirit of service, courage and self-sacrifice. The school mentioned is Clifton School, Bristol, Newbolt's school.

sighed. "What a pity you couldn't recite it all for us. I'm sure your father would agree."

"Yes, Miss." He frowned. Going to Dad's old school had its drawbacks.

CHAPTER SEVENTEEN

ONE POTATO, TWO POTATO

At Sixty-Five, now that he had retired from nursing duties, Tim was available for what Mum called 'a bit of shopping' which, he complained, usually meant 'a lot', trailing her in and out of huge city stores, up and down endless aisles. In reply, Mum had pointed out that, considering that he could play football until he dropped, his stamina on a shopping outing ran out surprisingly quickly.

It happened, one Saturday morning, that they had run out of potatoes, and he was despatched, ration book and cash in-hand, to collect the week's quota. Waterworth's, the Greengrocer's, lay just around the corner from the end of Kremlin Drive and, arriving at speed, as usual, he pulled up, frowning. There was a queue as far as the door, and he hated queuing.

He had done this run once or twice before and had noticed that the person in charge never smiled, although her lapel badge said HILDA - MANAGERESS. It was puzzling. If you've got a nice job, in charge of dishing out vegetables to hungry people in war time, shouldn't you be smiling? The ladies throwing free toffees to the crowd at Goodison Park always smiled. But Hilda's face was set, like a mask, with a smear of rouge to brighten it up. She frowned down at him.

"Can I help you, Sonny?" He didn't like being called that, but, in the interest of the family potato ration, took no notice.

"I've come for some potatoes …please" He passed the ration book over, and the Manageress examined it carefully, as if it might be counterfeit. She detached one coupon, then strode across to a wooden, cupboard-like container with KING EDWARDS written in chalk, on the front, and began to rummage. Selecting one of the larger specimens, she placed it in the bowl on the scales, glancing at the dial, while chatting confidentially to the next customer. Retrieving the potato, she dropped it into a paper bag as Tim looked on.

"That'll be four pence," she said.

He frowned.

"Is that all we can have?"

"It's all you're entitled to!" she replied.

"One potato isn't very much!" he muttered, making for the door.

"Next!" snapped Hilda.

Back at home he put the potato in its bag on the kitchen table. A few moments later, Mum came in, spotted the bag and glanced inside.

"What's this, Tim?"

"It's our potato ration, Mum."

"THIS is our ration?" She took the potato out of the bag and held it up.

"THIS is our RATION! " she repeated.

Tim gulped. He had seen his Mum in a furious mood on numerous, uncomfortable occasions, and had noticed that, when a storm was about to break, it was usually preceded by a brief calm. On this occasion, however, the calm phase had already been by-passed. He feared for Hilda, and although, in his opinion, she didn't deserve much sympathy, he thought he should try to deflect the storm or, at least, slow its progress down.

"Hilda weighed it," he said, "and she said it's all we're entitled to."

"We'll see about that! And who is Hilda? I don't recognise the name."

"She's the one in charge."

"She must be new."

He bit his lip. Perhaps they should weigh the precious potato first? That wasn't necessary. Mum could recognise two pounds of potatoes when she saw them. She had had plenty of practice. This called for decisive action, and she wasn't going to be deflected or slowed down.

"Come with me!" Leaving her coat and hat behind, she picked up the bag and potato, grabbed his hand and stormed out.

Drat! Couldn't she leave him out of this? After all, he was only the messenger. On the contrary, he would be the chief witness for the prosecution! The vice-like grip on his hand tightened.

By the time they reached the shop, the queue had shrunk in size to just a small handful, and, as mother and son swept in, they stepped to one side, sensing trouble.

After the brief walk in the fresh air, Mum had calmed down enough to be able to choose her words. She would be brief and to the point.

"Which of you is Hilda?"

"I am, Madam!" replied the manageress, tight-lipped. "What can I do for you?"

Mum took the potato out of the bag, waved it in the manageress's direction, and dumped it on the counter.

"This is what you gave my son. It's supposed to be a potato ration for five! I have a baby and a daughter who has been very ill, and you have given me ONE POTATO!" Tim dropped back. Mum, on the attack, could be terrifying.

Hilda, however, wasn't easily terrified. She hadn't made it to the dizzy heights of Waterworth management by accident. She had been in this kind of situation before. She looked closely at the angry customer, trying to size her up. The mask cracked very slightly, in a forced imitation of a smile. She could handle this!

"That is your ration, Madam, as I pointed out to your son!" She cast a frown in Tim's direction.

He dropped back further.

"Well, we don't believe it, do we Tim?" She looked at the witness. Tim shook his head.

"The scales don't tell lies, Madam!" exclaimed Hilda, in a tired tone of voice, raising her eyes, as if to place her case before a heavenly tribunal. "But, to settle this, we will weigh the potato again!" Mistake, Hilda! She continued..."Now let me see... if I remember rightly, you are entitled to two pounds of potatoes."

With a confident sweep of the hand, as if to say 'We have

nothing to hide', she placed the potato in the bowl on the scales. In the silence, all eyes were glued to the spot on the dial where the finger had stopped quivering. It was pointing at one pound twelve ounces. The Tribunal had given its judgment. Four ounces of potato were missing! Under the rouge the mask had turned grey, and Hilda was squirming. She nudged the scales, but nothing changed, and the onlookers were nodding, in unison. They had closed ranks behind their fellow-customer. After all, if it could happen to her, it could happen to any of them.

The scales don't tell lies, Hilda, as you said yourself, and almost anyone else in your place would be sorry, even a little penitent. You might have said 'You are right, Madam. I gave your son short-weight.'

But with the Hildas of this world, it goes against the grain to admit that one is wrong, especially over something like a paltry King Edward. She would rather go down fighting. Seizing the bowl, she strode over to the bin, head held high, rooted about, and returned with a few small specimens which she dropped, one by one, into the bowl, while scrutinising the dial. Choosing one, she held it up between thumb and index finger, as if to demonstrate to everyone 'how insignificant!', then dropped it into the bag.

"There's your extra four ounces of potato, Madam," she said, "and I don't see what all the fuss is about!"

"Well, I'll tell you, Hilda!" Madam replied. "This is wartime, in case you hadn't noticed, and that one extra potato will give our baby a lot of extra nutrition to keep him strong." The jury nodded as one. Madam pressed home her case. "Please be more careful reading your scales in future!"

So saying, she picked up the bag, grabbed Tim's hand and swept out.

Hilda said nothing. She had met her match.

****

In the Ops Room, Miss Sterland excitedly plotted the advance of the Russian battalions all along the Eastern Front. She rubbed her hands gleefully. "The Fuhrer has met his match, this time, boys!"

****

LIVERPOOL COLLEGIATE PREPARATORY SCHOOL

MID-YEAR REPORT - FEBRUARY 1944
Pupil: Timothy Oliver
Form: 3

Timothy seems to regard life at the Prep as a pleasant pastime which, in one sense, pleases us. We want happy, willing pupils who come each day with a spring in their step. However, it would give us greater pleasure if Timothy showed some interest in what he is supposed to be doing once he arrives.

It has occurred to us that Timothy may be relying on the fact that his father won many laurels at the Collegiate School and that, for that reason, he need not exert himself. If so, he must learn that, in life, one must have laurels of one's own to rest on, and that they are won only with diligence and effort. Otherwise, in September, he will find that the Big School will come as a big shock.

E.J.Taylor
(Headmistress)

This report was not well received at Sixty-Five. Mum shed a few tears, and Dad was thinking of a drastic reduction in football time.

In the meantime, on a fact-finding visit to the local library, Tim discovered that, at the ancient Olympic Games, held in Greece, a small crown made up of sprigs of laurel was placed on the head of the victors. The Games had been discontinued in the third century AD, but started up again in 1896, and were due to be held in London later this year, if Herr Hitler hadn't spoilt things. It was one more item on Tim's list of complaints to present to the Fuhrer, should they ever meet.

****

By now Yozzer and Tim had become firm friends, even though Yozzer was hopeless at football and keen on poetry. Mrs Taylor said that, having a Welsh background like Yozzer's was 'a definite advantage' when it came to reciting poetry. It was something to do with what she called 'lilt'. She had raved about his recitation of Ode to Autumn, by John Keats, which Tim thought was soppy, especially the end bit about swallows twittering in the skies.

After the Vitae Lampada disaster, he had decided to play safe, and his choice of poem for the Easter term was Drake's Drum, a patriotic poem about the great Sir Francis himself. It was bound to impress Mrs Taylor. By coincidence, it was also by John Henry Newbolt, but the lines were shorter than those in Vitae Lampada, which was a bonus. In the poet's imagination, the great man is resting on his laurels in the port of heaven, long after his victory over the Spanish Armada, and gives his inspiring, last order, according to J.H.Newbolt...

Take my drum to England, hang it on the shore, strike it when your powder's running low.

If the Dons (Spaniards) sight Devon, I'll quit the port o' heaven, and drum them up the channel as we drummed them long ago.

Tim thought about the Admirals under the City streets, planning to drum the German U-Boat packs from the Atlantic, and Sir Francis himself coming out of retirement to inspire them. It was enough to make anyone dash down to the Pier Head and volunteer.

At the final recitation, just before Easter, if not exactly word-perfect, he reached the end, to earn one of Mrs Taylor's weaker smiles.

"Well, Timothy, we must congratulate you on giving us the whole of your poem this time! In future, do try to put more of a lilt into your recitation, like Roland." He sighed. If only he was Welsh!

Roland was also very clever with electrical things and, when he wasn't memorising poems, he had been putting together what he called a Crystal Set. Like Tim, he had a big sister, so he was usually last in the queue when it came to choosing a favourite programme on the family wireless. How much better would it be to have a wireless of his own? He had picked up the idea from a film about Resistance groups in German occupied countries, where wirelesses were banned. If they could do it, why couldn't he, without the risk of being put up against a wall and shot. His Dad had found a sheet of instructions in THE HANDYMAN manual.

"It was dead easy to put together!" he said. "First I had to find the parts, Tim... just bits and pieces - the cardboard inside of a toilet roll...a wire coat hanger...the lead from a pencil...a safety pin...a few tacks and screws, a rusty razor blade and a flat piece of wood to lay it all out on. The hardest thing to find was some copper wire. The iron-monger said it's all going to the war effort. So I had to do some scrounging. Anyway, my Granddad rooted around in his shed and found some in an old electric motor. Then I just needed head-phones to pick up signals, and a friend of my Dad let me have an old set. Why don't you come around and have a go with it."

Tim didn't need a second invitation and, one afternoon soon after the start of the Easter holidays, he knocked on Yozzer's door in West Derby.

The crystal set had been given pride of place in Yozzer's bedroom among an assortment of Air-fix models and poetry books. Yozzer pointed to a stool.

"Sit there, Tim, and I'll show you how it works."

"Wireless signals from many radio stations come to the set from the aerial," he pointed, "go through this coil of copper wire and then to earth. Moving this slider along the coil, enables us to tune in to the signal we're looking for. The sound is picked up by the head-phones when the tip of this lead pencil, attached to the coil, finds a sensitive spot on the razor blade.

Tim looked mystified.

"It sounds complicated, but it's simple really and easy to operate. You have a go, Tim. Just move the slider along, but very slowly, and listen for a clear signal."

Tim put the headphones on and did as instructed. For a few minutes, nothing happened, and then a smile spread across his face.

"That sounds like the Home Service!"

"Yes. We can listen to the news bulletins, and if we want Children's Hour or some music, that kind of thing, we can tune in to the Light Service. It's easy to find," he grinned. "So that's my wireless, Tim. Guess how much it cost!"

Tim shook his head. "No idea!"

"FIVE PENCE!" He grinned. "Just think of that, Tim! A wireless-set for less than a tanner. The soldiers in their foxholes use them to keep in touch with each other!"

Now Yozzer had a protégé and Tim was soon making his own way over the air-waves. The war seemed much nearer. They could imagine themselves hidden away in a cellar or attic, somewhere in German-occupied Europe, listening out for vital coded messages sent out by the BBC to an Allied agent or Resistance Group.

One message in particular - *Mathurin likes spinach* - was repeated several times, so they guessed it must be urgent. Who was Mathurin, and what did spinach mean? They were stumped, and decided to sleep on it.

The next morning, Yozzer thought he might have cracked the code.

"I think spinach is the key word, Tim. Miss Sterland says that, when the Allies cross the channel, they'll need help from the Resistance groups. Well, you remember how, when Popeye's in trouble with some bully or other, he grabs a can of SPINACH and gulps it all down...the spinach, I mean. Then his muscles grow bigger, and he sends the bully packing. Well, I think 'Mathurin' means the Allies and 'spinach' means the Resistance. So the message means "We're on the way, but we need your help. Get ready!"'

Tim glanced at his friend. What it is to be brainy! Yozzer, the next Sherlock Holmes!

"Good thinking, Yozzer. Let's hope you're right."

"Well, we'll soon know!"

The next Saturday morning Tim had the earphones on.

"I've noticed a little tune repeated at the end of news bulletins. It's just four notes played on bass drums. It's eerie! D'you think it means something important?"

"Yes, it does, Tim! My Granddad says those four notes, three short and one long, dum-dum-dum-d u m, are the letter V in Morse Code, and V stands for victory! It's a clever way of telling everyone listening, that victory over the Gerries is on the way. And what about this, Tim! They're the first four notes in a Symphony by Beethoven, Germany's greatest composer, my Dad says! How about that for a coincidence? The Gerries can't possibly miss it, and they'll know what it means!"

"They must be biting their nails!"

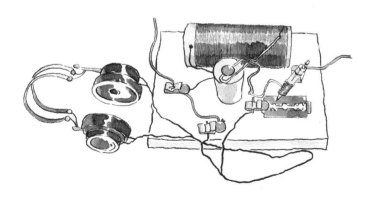

CHAPTER EIGHTEEN

HUGHES AND OLIVER,
SPECIAL CORRESPONDENTS

The start of the summer term came too soon, but if they had to report back at school just as the fine weather was arriving, the top floor of Sandheys was the place to be, with views over the pines, cedars and rhododendrons and beyond, to the Big School playing fields. The goal-posts had gone into storage, but there was the exciting smell of new-mown grass, as Mr Harris manoeuvred his mower up and down the cricket squares, humming Irish ditties. The versatile Miss Sterland, in her summer-term role as cricket coach, wiped the cobwebs off her Len Hutton bat and, when no one was looking, practised the square-cut and cover-drive in the staff-room mirror.

This would be Tim's last chance to shine at poetry, if reluctantly, and leave Sandheys with at least one laurel to his name. To be helpful, Mrs Taylor now hinted that he may have overdone poems with a war-time theme. Why not try something more peaceful and gentle, like Peter's first choice, pottering about among daffodils - 'bucolic' was the word she used. Or had he considered something with a love theme, such as 'My love is like a red, red rose' by the immortal Robbie Burns?

"Erm. Not really!" With due respect to the immortal Mr Burns, the prospect of delivering a love-poem in front of Form 3 was too gruesome to contemplate.

Instead he had chosen '*O to be in England, now that April's there*', by Robert Browning, according to Mrs Taylor, 'one of England's greatest poets'. As poems about nature go, it was one of the better ones, he thought - quite patriotic, in a soppy sort of way, and not a bad choice in time of war. It reminded him of the popular new song, 'There'll always be an England', although he thought that was a bit hard on Yozzer and his Welsh relatives. But a big advantage with this poem was that the lines rhymed. He had always thought that a proper poem should rhyme, in which case this one could probably be recited with a lilt. The great Mr Browning knew his stuff! Yozzer would give him some coaching and, with a bit of luck, Miss would take back her damning mid-year report, and send him on his way to the Big School with a glowing write-up in his hand.

At assembly, Mrs Taylor, true to form, got the term off to a challenging start.

"For some of us, this will be our last term at the Prep, so let us all remember that, as Sir Francis himself reminded us, when God gives us an important task, such as a final term at The Prep, what matters is that we reach the end successfully! That's what brings the true glory, boys, according to the great man himself, and he could talk!" They nodded. They had got the message the first time!

After the long break, the Ops Room was buzzing. Miss Sterland was quickly back into her stride, with updates from what she called the 'theatres of war', gleefully moving more flags and arrows around. 'THE HUN ON THE RUN!' was the theme, chalked up above the map.

"The Ruskies have broken through in the Balkans," she exclaimed excitedly. "That's well on the way to Berlin,...I think, and over here in Italy," she wafted the pointer about, "the allies are on their way to Rome. It's in the hands of the Gerries at the moment. Let's hope they leave the glorious Colosseum alone, after all it wouldn't take much to knock it down!" She chuckled; then with a flourish, swung the pointer North-West, across France to the English Channel.

"And now the Yanks are coming, as the song says, by the boatload! I bet they can't wait to cross the Channel, after coming all this way! Old Adolf must be worried! He knows it won't be long before we're knocking on his door; but he doesn't know where or when. We're keeping him guessing, and it jolly well serves him right!"

They nodded. Miss might not be very good at Geography, but she would have made a great military strategist!

"After all," she went on, "he didn't give any warning before his Luftwaffe made a mess of beautiful Warsaw, or our own lovely city, not to mention all those other places!" She waved the pointer randomly, here and there.

"Well, now we're going to have a Blitzkrieg of our own!"

She chuckled, then noticed that a hand had been raised.

"What is it, Roland?"

"Well, Miss, Tim and me've been listening to the war news on my crystal set, and we think the Allies will probably land near Calais."

Miss beamed.

"So we have some special correspondents in Form 3! Well done, boys! That's exactly what I was thinking! But are we bluffing... to put the Gerries off the scent, I mean? We know they'll be listening in to our wireless messages. So, for now, we'd better keep our little hunches to ourselves! Remember - Careless talk costs lives!" They nodded. How could they possibly forget? But it was fun being sworn to secrecy about such top-secret information!

As half-term approached, Mam'selle was all agog, trying to explain, in a torrent of French, that, on the Free French wireless, she had heard that, if all went well with the invasion, 'La France, her 'chère Patrie' would soon be 'libérée!' They didn't understand half of what she said, but picked up the gist, and smiled happily for her. And she hadn't finished. In an unashamed outburst of patriotic fervour, she scribbled the first verse of *La Marseillaise* on the blackboard, humming as she wrote, pausing only to wipe away a tear and add a rough, spoken translation in English. It was breaking the rules, and they noticed that she had particular difficulty with the letters 'h' and 'th'; but her pronunciation of their language was so enchanting, nobody noticed. It was all very touching, that so young, SO pretty a person should be in tears for her country. Arthur Evans was the only one lucky enough to have come to school with a handkerchief, which he now offered, blushing, to Mam'selle. The others could only look on, enviously. And still she wasn't finished.

"Ah mes petits, you 'ave understood 'ow I feel," she continued, sweetly, French conversation having gone out of the window. They frowned. They didn't like being called 'little ones', but would make allowances. Mam'selle went on.

"I 'ave remembered that, when my country surrendered to the vile 'uns, your 'andsome leader, Monsieur Winston, spoke to my people on the wireless. 'E 'as said 'Rest while it is night. The morning will come.'" More tears. Arthur's hanky was getting soaked.

"Et maintenant, mes petits, will you stand up and sing La Marseillaise wiz me? Just the chorus, et en anglais, s'il vous plaît?" 'Ow could they refuse? The next minute the little ones were on their feet, singing happily, if not all in tune, Mademoiselle waving the board-duster to keep time.

"March on, march on, all hearts resolved, to victory or death. "*Bravo!*" She dabbed her eyes. 'Their 'arts were broken.' Down below, Mrs Pennycuik paused momentarily in the middle of Holly Lodge 4B History, and smiled at the thought of Prep Form 3, in full voice, off to man the barricades.

Meanwhile in Art and Craft lessons, the ever-inventive Miss Sterland had brought in some back copies of the Echo, with paint and brushes and a bucket of homemade glue.

"Today, in sculpting!" she announced, grandly, "let us be bold, and have a go at modelling the human form. Who knows, we may have a budding Michelangelo in our midst?" They looked doubtful. She went on "Well, even he had to start somewhere, I suppose!" She chuckled.

Most of them had never heard of the great Michel, but guessed that, if Miss rated him highly, he must have been pretty good in his day. Undaunted, they set to, after a glance at the Sports page, tearing the newspapers into strips, dunking them in the glue and stirring from time to time. When it had almost dried, the mix would be perfect for modelling, Miss said.

"Now," she continued, "all we need is a model. Who will volunteer?"

In the long silence which followed, everyone was doing a rough mental calculation. To sculpt or be sculpted; or, to put it another way - to have ones fingers covered with glue, possibly for days, or sit gazing at the ceiling all afternoon, at the mercy of one's form-mates. There could surely be only one sensible response. In time, glue can be removed from fingers, but the prospect of having ones features, horribly distorted, exhibited to future generations of Prep kids, was unthinkable. Still the silence continued and Miss was looking glum, désolée, as Mam'selle would say.

Then, when all seemed lost, a hesitant hand was raised. It was Peter Galvin's. He would make the ultimate sacrifice, and the others could breathe again. Pete would be ideal, with his unusually large feet, and they had been spared. Now to face the glue.

Miss beamed and played her trump card.

"Now, what better pose should we ask our model to take up, than one of our very own, brave Red Berets?" A great idea, Miss! As things turned out, it wasn't, but how were they to know? How was Miss to know?

Peter now mounted the teacher's dais, as one would ascend the scaffold, perched himself on the edge of her chair, arms raised and bent at the elbows, as if dangling from a parachute harness, eyes turned skyward, and by the end of the afternoon, fourteen miniature paratroopers in battle-dress and red berets sat on fourteen desk-tops, more or less ready for action.

Miss was thrilled.

"Can't you imagine them, boys, dropping out of the sky behind enemy lines...dislocating communications... dynamiting railway lines... setting up bridge-heads, and that kind of thing? I'm sure it won't be long now. And well done, Peter! You must be exhausted! Next week you can do some sculpting yourself. I thought we might have a go at making tanks. That should be fun!"

Peter smiled weakly. In fact, he was more bored than exhausted. But his sacrifice had paid off. The others would probably be scraping glue off their fingers for days, whereas, apart from a stiff neck, he was unscathed, and, with final reports only a month or so away, he thought his self-sacrifice was bound to have gone down well.

Meanwhile, at the end of the lesson, a squad of paratroopers stood, propped up below the map, with hands raised. They would be staying there, Miss Sterland announced, "Until our chaps drop in on Berlin!" They grinned.

In such ways, life at Sandheys drifted pleasantly towards half-term and, at last, the two war correspondents were free for a whole week of uninterrupted listening-in to whatever was on the airwaves. According to Yozzer's Granddad, it wouldn't be long before the balloon would be going up. The allies would be crossing the Channel to invade Fortress Europe.

****

Early on the Tuesday of half-term, perhaps sensing that something history-making was in the air, Yozzer resisted the temptation to lie-in, rolled out of bed, rubbed the sleep out of his eyes, and picked up the slider. The reception was a bit crackly, but he caught the odd word or phrase... 'This morning... Tuesday the 6th of June... Allied forces....Red Berets...Gliders...Normandy coast'.

"I think the balloon's gone up!" he yelled.

Pulling off the headphones, he changed into shorts, shirt and plimsolls, and shot out of the front door, heading for Kremlin Drive. Tim came to the door in his pyjamas.

"You've gotta come...quickly, Tim." He gasped. "The balloon's gone up!"

"You're kidding!"

"Why would I do that? I just heard it on the wireless! The Red Berets were the first to go in...by glider, probably so the Gerries wouldn't hear them coming! Clever, wasn't it? But hurry up and get changed!"

Ten minutes later they were back at Yozzer's place, side by side. The reception was clearer. Over 300,000 allied troops, mainly American, Canadian, British and French had landed on the Normandy coast of France, while Allied air-power kept the skies clear. Some of the invasion forces had been pinned down by heavy fire from the Atlantic Wall, the massive German defences, and were having difficulty getting off the beaches; but some had already broken through and were heading for Paris.

The bulletin continued; but that was enough news to be going on with, and they went downstairs to share the excitement with Yozzer's Mum and sister Myfanwy, who was also on half-term. It was the first time Tim had met Myfanwy and he noticed that she was very pretty.

"Hello, Tim!" She smiled. "Isn't the news exciting?"

"Er, yes...very," he gulped. Why did pretty girls have such a strange effect on him? Now he wasn't sure whether to stay and discuss the war or leave; but, being unsure how to pronounce her name, he decided to play safe and headed home.

That evening, outside Lewis's Newsagents, the headline declared WE GO IN! and the next morning it read - GREATEST SEABORNE INVASION IN HISTORY. The writer was working overtime, and, over the next few days, the story emerged in the news-print. A mock army had been assembled on the South East coast, with dummy camps, fake radio nets and newspapers, so the Germans were taken by surprise.

Back at Sandheys, a jubilant Miss Sterland could be seen bounding up the fire-escape two, if not three steps at a time, clutching a copy of the day's edition of the ECHO. History lessons were going to be livelier than ever! In the Ops Room, most of the arrows, like the teeth of a huge man-trap, were now pointing at Germany and Berlin.

"We fooled them, boys, didn't we? They fell for the bogus camps! Now they're on the run - on all fronts!" She waved the pointer about excitedly. "The Ruskies are closing in from the North and East, the Allies from the South and West, as we all know from our very own special correspondents". She beamed at Yozzer and Tim in the front row. The correspondents grinned modestly.

"It's the Gerries who've got their backs to the wall now. They're fighting for the Fatherland, and that's the time they'll be hardest to beat. But there'll be no stopping our boys! Adolf's days are numbered!" She rubbed her hands together gleefully. They nodded, and hoped she was right.

Mam'selle was in two minds. The new French leader, 'Le courageux General de Gaulle,' also known, disrespectfully, as 'Le Gros Nez,' had called upon the Resistance fighters of France to 'rise up and make life difficult for the 'uns', as they retreated.

"If only I could be wiz zem," she said, wistfully. "Mes chers parents are too old to be blowing up bridges." They all nodded, sadly. They understood 'ow she felt, and thought she would look even prettier in a Free French beret, with a stick of dynamite à la main. All the same, they were glad that she had opted to stay in England to converse wiz zem instead.

Friday afternoons on the playing fields were bliss, as long as no one ruffled Mr Harris's feathers. On visits to the pavilion, Tim would glance up at the Honours Boards and feel proud. Once or twice he mentioned them to his Dad, who muttered something about 'ancient history', and changed the subject.

Now they were on the run-in towards the end of the term and Tim thought that his report was bound to be an improvement on the previous one. He had avoided major confrontations with the authorities and had tried hard to give the impression that he was coming to school for the right reasons. It wasn't that difficult, after all. Waving a hand in a question-and-answer session, more or less enthusiastically, seemed to win an approving smile. If he happened to know the correct answer to a question, that was a bonus. If he got it wrong, it really didn't matter very much. At least he would appear to be trying. Anything to avoid yet another incriminating 'Could do better', which, as everyone knows, is a cleverly coded way of saying 'Could hardly do worse'. Anything to win a laurel of one's own.

One last cloud loomed up on the horizon - the final trial by poetry. Mrs Taylor would be writing his Final Report at any time. Could he do well enough to overturn her previous judgment; even make her eat her words? A good recitation might do the trick, and he had been practising his lilt.

The day and moment of truth arrived and, to play safe, he had written down the first word or two of each line on a small scrap of paper which he placed out of sight from the teacher's desk. It wasn't exactly cheating, he thought, and he was sure he wouldn't need it; but on previous attempts he had dried up at certain points, and he didn't want to risk that happening this time. Fortunately he would be on his feet before Yozzer, Peter and Norman, who would be hard to follow. The others were keeping their fingers crossed, as he began.

"O to be in England now that April's there, by Robert Browning." He was up and lilting, sounding, if anything, more Welsh than Yozzer, and made it to the end with not so much as a downward glance, just the odd 'um' or 'erm', and ending with a flourish...

"...and though the fields look rough with hoary dew,
all will be gay when noontide wakes anew
the buttercups, the little children's dower -
far brighter than this gaudy melon-flower!'

So the great man must have written it when he was on his hols, probably in the Bahamas, or wherever they grow melons, and feeling homesick.

The Headmistress appeared to smile approvingly. Was it in recognition of a surprisingly good recitation...or a great poet?

CHAPTER NINETEEN

FORM THREE STAGES A MOCK INVASION

At break-time the following afternoon, the teachers were enjoying their cup of tea in the little staff-room, while the boys roamed about at large. It was very warm and, down below, the girls of form 4B were struggling with Latin. Even Mrs Pennycuik was flagging and glancing at her watch. She wasn't in a good mood. Priscilla Dykes had just made a hash of the perfect tense of the verb 'video' and, as often seems to happen in Latin lessons, a kind of torpor had settled on the room.

It was as Priscilla slumped down in her desk, that what looked like a very small soldier, in full battle dress, attached by strings to the corners of a well-used handkerchief, floated down past the window. Mrs Pennycuik was the first to notice and, as the feet of a second figure came into view, this one with a blue-fringed, white canopy, she rose to her feet. By now 4B had been alerted and sprang to life. This was better than Latin; although almost anything would be better than Latin. But what would Miss do?

Mrs Pennycuik had already decided. She walked steadfastly to the door.

"It would appear that we are being invaded, girls! I will be back soon. Please keep your eyes on video!" Half-smiling at her little joke, she left the room and headed for the stairs, as the girls rushed over to the window. The teacher descended the stairs surprisingly quickly for someone of her not inconsiderable weight, and left the building by a door near the bottom of the fire-escape, as another figure touched down. As she watched, three more, with canopies of varied hue, floated down to land on the grass verge, while two more drifted on the breeze into the rhododendrons. Mrs Pennycuik shaded

her eyes, peering up towards the top landing of the fire-escape, which was now deserted. She had been spotted, and the afternoon drop had been called off, or at least suspended, she decided, smiling to herself at another accidental pun. Still smiling, she rescued all seven figures and ascended to the 4B classroom, where the torpor had already re-settled.

In the Ops Room, the following morning, Miss Sterland, who hadn't noticed that some of the paratroopers had gone 'absent without leave', was in the middle of the daily war-briefing, pointer in hand. The Gerries were putting up stiff resistance, she said, especially at Calais, Dunkirk and Caen.

"It's backs to the wall for them!" she said, and at that point there was a knock on the door and the Headmistress entered with the missing paratroopers and chutes draped over her arm. Miss Sterland gaped, as Mrs Taylor took the floor. The Head wasn't the autocratic type; but firm action had to be taken. It was important to appear seriously annoyed.

"Yesterday afternoon, these effigies" - she held the models up - "were seen descending from the top of the fire-escape, right past 4B classroom window, causing quite a disturbance. Stand up, those who were responsible!"

There was a brief, awkward pause. Then Frank Wilson got to his feet followed, at various intervals, by Peter, Yozzer, Tim, Arthur Evans, Harry Noble, and George Bates. The rest breathed a sigh of relief. They had all brought a handkerchief into school, and if Mrs Pennycuik hadn't interrupted the drop, they would all have been in trouble.

"I'm very disappointed, boys," the Head began, hoping to appeal to their better natures, and looked sadly at Tim in his usual position at the back. "You in particular, Timothy! I would expect better from someone whose father was such a model of good behaviour in every way." Tim nodded. He had to agree.

The Headmistress continued.

"As you all know very well, our rules at the Prep state clearly that the launching of projectiles from the fire escape is strictly forbidden. What have you to say for yourselves?" There was another, longer pause, as the seven offenders stared at the floor or the ceiling. What was there to say? They were guilty as charged. Then George spoke up.

"We thought it would be a good way to celebrate D Day, Miss, and Miss Sterland would be pleased, 'cos the paras were her idea."

Now the others cheered up. Good thinking, George, making Miss Sterland an accomplice before the fact, although she was looking anything but pleased. In the first place, she didn't like her boys' sculptures being referred to as 'effigies', which made her think of a Guy Fawkes look-alike. Furthermore, although she was actually rather pleased that some of the paras had done a successful maiden-drop, she had no intention of sharing the blame for causing the interruption to Mrs Pennycuik's lesson.

The Head frowned. She wasn't expecting a defence to be mounted.

"Well, Miss Sterland might have been pleased with your celebrations, although I very much doubt it; but I'm sure Mrs

Pennycuik was far from entertained!" As it happened, Mrs Pennycuik, like many older ladies, had a soft spot for the Red Berets. She, too, had been enjoying the manoeuvres, and was sorry that it was her fault that they had been called off. But in the interests of teacher solidarity, she hadn't said so to Mrs Taylor.

"But the fact is..." the Headmistress continued, now digging her heels in, "you know the rule, and you were almost, if not actually, caught in the act of breaking it!" A slightly smug smile crossed her face, as if to say 'Get out of that!'

There was an awkward silence, and then, just when George's defence had been knocked on the head, a voice spoke up out of the blue, paratrooper-like, as it were.

"But a parachute isn't really a projectile, Miss, is it?"

Everyone turned to look at the speaker. It was Harry Noble - quiet, humble Harry, blushing slightly. Noble Harry, one of the accused, to the rescue!

"What I mean is," he went on, "you don't project parachutes, Miss, not like you would project an aeroplane or glider. They just drop, don't they?"

A good point, Harry! The others rallied.

The Head's face fell.

"Oh! I hadn't thought of a parachute in quite that way," she muttered

She was stumped, but only briefly. Re-grouping quickly, she remembered the fail-safe rule in the Schoolteachers Little Emergency Book of Do's and Don'ts, that '*in the unlikely event of being up-staged by a pupil, be sure to have the last word*.'

"Nevertheless"- always a good first word, when needing to have the last, she continued, "we cannot have aerial objects, whether projected or just dropped, floating about past Mrs Pennycuik's classroom window. I must remind you once again that we are guests at Sandheys! So you must each write a note to Mrs Pennycuik and her girls, apologising." She turned to her colleague. "Miss Sterland, please remind me to write an amendment to the school rules...about projectiles and things." And with that, she dumped the effigies on the teacher's table and exited.

The seven offenders had an emergency, ad hoc discussion. They wouldn't grovel. They would be brief and to the point, like Frank, who wrote...

> Dear Mrs Pennycook and 4B,
> I'm very sorry about the paras.
> Yours sincerely,
> Frank Wilson Form 3

"Just think," said George, over a break-time bottle of milk "She might have frog-marched us down to 4B, to say sorry, face to face!"

They had been saved from a fate worse than death! The notes were duly delivered, and the next morning a reply came back, addressed to 'The sculptors of form Three.' Miss Sterland read it out.

> Dear sculptors of Form 3.
> We, accept your apologies. We would also like to thank you for sharing your D Day celebrations with us, and congratulate you on your sculpting!'
> Mrs Pennycuik and form 4B.

"I think it will be best if the Headmistress doesn't read this!" said Miss Sterland, smiling, as she dropped it into the waste bin.

****

The following Saturday morning, Yozzer was adding the finishing touches to a model of the Mustang, the new American fighter plane. Tim had found the Home Service and was listening to the news. He looked up.

"The Gerries have got a new projectile. It's a rocket called V 1...the V's for Vengeance. They're low-flying, pilotless missiles, launched from somewhere near Calais, but don't have a particular target. They seem to be programmed to cut-out somewhere, anywhere, over London."

"That's a nasty trick!"

"Yes. And another nasty thing ...they don't explode like a normal bomb, making a crater. The damage is done by the debris... glass, wood, bricks...anything that'll fly. So, if you hear the engine cut out, you've got to get down on the ground, fast!"

"Sounds scary!"

"Yes. The news reader said it's a kind of terror weapon, and now the London kids are being evacuated again."

"Why don't our Spits just shoot them down?"

"They can't fly that fast. Ack-Ack guns and barrage balloons are bringing some down, but a lot are still getting through."

"Can they fly this far?"

"I don't think so."

"So we won't have to be evacuated again?"

"Probably not!"

"Perhaps Hitler still thinks he can frighten us into giving in."

"Miss will tell us!"

****

"Adolf's death throes! That's what they are, boys."

Back at the Ops Room, Miss Sterland was quickly into her stride.

"Another crime to add to all the others! Just lob lots of bombs over the Channel! Who cares where they land? A hospital, a school, an old folks' home, a church. It's a tantrum, like throwing a stone and running away!" Miss could read the Fuhrer like a book.

She went on..." Except that Adolf's got nowhere to run now! Nobody loves him any more!" She chuckled. "And what's all this about vengeance? As if we were the ones who started it all! Ask the poor Poles who threw the first stone! And now he's trying to frighten us with his doodle-bugs! Well, he won't, will he, boys?"

"No fear, Miss!" Miss Sterland on the attack was worth listening to. What a pity that they would be leaving her behind when the term ended.

****

For Tim, the last day of term arrived with mixed feelings. It was sad having to leave the Sandheys holiday-camp and the teachers who had been more like indulgent aunties. In Tim's case, Mam'selle had been more like a chum, although she said that she wished he was more interested in speaking her language. 'He seems to have nothing to say', she wrote in his final report, 'although he does wave his hands about a lot, 'comme tous les Francais!'

Obviously, his efforts in question-and-answer sessions had been misinterpreted. Or had they been seen through? On the plus side, Miss Sterland praised his contribution to history lessons, 'as an unofficial war correspondent', and as Mistress in charge of Sport and Health she wrote that his dedication to football was 'quite remarkable!' which turned out to be the cause of his final undoing, as Mrs Taylor wrote...

> In conclusion, there is nothing much in this report to wave ones hands about. If only Timothy was as enthusiastic about his lessons as he is about football, we would be sending him up to the Big School with high hopes. As it is, we have grave misgivings. He has an outstanding name to live up to and we wish him well.
>
> Elspeth Taylor (Headmistress)

So that was that! Not a laurel in sight, and after all that extra effort! Mum read the report out aloud and had a good cry. Dad shook his head. He couldn't tell Grandma. But why couldn't they keep his name out of it?

Tim now retreated to his bedroom to wrestle with tough questions, such as 'how can I enthuse when there's nothing to be enthusiastic about, and how can I possibly live up to Dad's name?'

He had all the holidays to wrestle.

No one would miss the Ops Room more than Tim and Yozzer. Miss Sterland's enthusiasm was contagious, and they had caught it. But Yozzer would be away in Snowdonia for most of the holidays, shinning up mountains and practising his lilt, so the crystal-set wouldn't be operational just when it looked as if the beginning of the end had been reached. This wasn't the time to lose touch, so he decided that he would keep a kind of diary. Then he could bring Yozzer up to date when he was back in circulation. What he needed were headlines, and the billboard outside Lewis's newsagents should be an easy, shorthand way of keeping up-to-date.

The headline writer didn't disappoint, and all through August, Tim jotted down the most interesting one-liners, adding a personal observation or two. PLOT ON HITLER'S LIFE FAILS. That's bad luck! Pity the brave plotters if they're caught! DOODLE-BUG LANDS ON THE KING'S TENNIS COURT! They've got a nerve, as Miss would say. RED ARMY NEAR WARSAW. That's where it all started. JET PILOT DISARMS V1 ROCKET. That was really clever, and brave! FRENCH TROOPS FIRST TO REACH PARIS. Mam'selle will be extatique. PARIS LIBERATED! Mam'selle ditto. SNIPER IN CATHEDRAL MISSES GENERAL DE GAULLE. Mam'selle ditto encore. ALLIES OPEN SECOND FRONT ON FRENCH RIVIERA. Lucky allies! AVIGNON TAKEN BY ALLIES! Mam'selle will be dancing! And so on.

It would all be down in writing. Yozzer would be impressed. Perhaps even Myfanwy. Some hope!

Otherwise there was plenty to fill the days - football on the recreation ground; the Saturday morning scrum, elbow to elbow, with the hordes at the CARLTON where 'Tarzan of the Apes' had taken over from 'Hopalong Cassidy' as the kids' favourite; overhead railway outings to Seaforth Sands or ferry trips to Birkenhead and Seacombe for a close-up of the comings and goings of fighting ships; and as a climax, a day-trip to the Southport beach to introduce Roger to the joys of tide-fighting, and splash out some of his meagre ration on a stick of seaside rock. There was still no sign of an increase in the sweet ration. The torture goes on!

Finally, as the holidays ran out, the unavoidable, exhausting trek around the shops looking for such exciting items as nibs, blotting paper etc.

The Big School beckoned.

CHAPTER TWENTY

THE BIG SHOCK

The face of Charlie Chaplin smiled down from a hoarding at the passengers on the number 12 as it rattled past the Hippodrome Cinema, where The GREAT DICTATOR, Hollywood's brilliant send-up of Adolf Hitler, was showing, and swung left, up Low Hill. Upstairs was full and noisy, downstairs, it was standing-room only for Tim, who was strap-hanging, sandwiched between a portly gentleman in pin-striped suit and a lady who seemed distinctly unhappy at being treated like a sardine. He had arrived late at the tram stop, and was lucky to get on this one. As he hung, he frowned and reflected. So this was the shape of things to come - at least five, perhaps six, even seven years, squeezing in with the city's office workers, for the privilege of getting to school!

At the top of the rise, they performed a sharp right turn into Erskine Street, wheels squealing. The conductor shouted "Hold tight!" and they began a brisk descent past a terrace of elegant Georgian residences, minus one where an open space, brightened by clumps of wild flowers, marked the spot where a bomb had done its worst, another reminder of Luftwaffe inaccuracy.

At the bottom of the hill the tram ground to a halt, feet clattered down the metal stairs and a stream of boys in black blazers with the letters LCS in royal blue interwoven on the breast pocket and black caps with vertical blue stripes, disembarked. The Number 12, now much quieter, rattled on its way towards the city centre.

The stream merged with a wave moving briskly along Shaw Street with Tim somewhere towards the back, wondering what was the hurry. The answer, 'The Collegiate', as it was known - mountainous, grimy-pink against the grey early-autumn sky - loomed up ahead. It was the first day of the new school year, not a time to drag feet. He quickened his step.

****

The Collegiate School was founded in 1840, as the official brochure explained, 'to provide a quality education for the sons of merchants, bankers and professional men, based on Christian principles.' Built on four floors from the sandstone on which the city stands, with a grand, eye-catching, castellated frontage, matching turrets and towering arch over the main entrance, the impression was as much that of a castle as a school. Stretching for almost a hundred yards along Shaw Street, the Collegiate School was meant to impress. Officially declared open by William Gladstone, the future Prime Minister... it was the first of its kind in the city.

The black and blue wave veered right, into a side-road, past the point where the main building - and the grandeur - ended, and the wall of the schoolyard, every bit of ten feet high, began. Was it to keep a reluctant pupil in, or an intruder out, the new boy wondered. But who in his right senses would want to break into a school?

The wave, now more a flood, moved towards a gate in the wall and, through that, into the school-yard. Once inside Tim pulled up quickly and blinked. So this was what a thousand College puddings, all in one place, looked and sounded like!

Suddenly he felt very small and lonely. Where were Yozzer, Peter, Frank and the others? They had promised to look out for one another. He began to weave his way slowly through the crowds, scanning faces. Then, from close behind, a voice whispered.

"Mathurin likes spinach!"

He spun round to find his fellow wireless-operator.

"The time has come, Tim Oliver!"

"Yozzer! Am I glad to see you!"

"Me too! Come on. Let's go and look for the others."

But there was no time. The sound of a gong rang out, and vast doors swung open to swallow up most of the waiting multitude, leaving the new boys, stranded and nervous, in the vast, almost empty space. A prefect, with the beginnings of a moustache, emerged and began to read out lists. Tim crossed his fingers, listening for friendly names.

"Bates G, Form 3D...Galvin P, Form 3D...Harrison N, Form 3C...Hughes R, Form 3A...Oliver T, Form 3D...Wilson F, Form 3D... Turner A, Form 3C."

So he and Yozzer wouldn't be together. He had guessed as much. 3A must be the cleverest ones. Tim would settle for 3D, so Frank, Peter, George and he would be together. Room 21, their form room, another prefect explained, with an autocratic wave of an arm and pointed finger, was on the first floor at the south end, round to the left. He would show them.

The new 3D now fell in behind the prefect and trooped, in silence, up a wide staircase, with banisters topped at regular intervals by metallic, recumbent lions, to discourage sliding, they guessed. Reaching the first floor, they arrived at Room 21.

Richard Cave Esquire, their form-master, tall and athletic, with register in hand and friendly smile was waiting to allocate desks.

Tim's was situated ideally, he thought, towards the back next to a window, and over the aisle from Frank.

Mr Cave began to call the roll as Tim peered through the latticed window. An hour ago the street below was seething. Now it was deserted. He began to day-dream.

"Oliver. OLIVER!" Mr Cave glanced across.

"Are you with us, or aren't you, Oliver? "

"Oh, er, present, Sir!"

So, now he would be known as 'Oliver'. After the chummy, first-name days at The Prep, it came as a bit of a shock. At the Big School, teachers and pupils keep their distance! Food for thought! But this wasn't a time for thinking! There was the weekly time-table to copy out.

A quick glance confirmed that all the inescapable items were there. His heart sank as he reached for his pen, checked the nib and dipped it in the inkwell. How he hated the smell of ink!

Geography would be with the elderly Mr Hall. According to someone's older brother, as well as imparting such vital information as the names of the cotton towns of Lancashire, the rivers of Yorkshire and the location of the South Lanarkshire coalfields, he would bring his stamp collection to lessons, to foster interest in far-off lands and stamp-collecting. If they had a collection of their own, they would be encouraged to bring it into lessons, and there would be time for what he called 'swaps' at the end.

English lessons would be with Mr Riddle, also known, impolitely, as 'Jimmy', who, according to another reliable source of information, wasn't a poetry enthusiast like Mrs Taylor, preferring to concentrate on the joys of punctuation and grammar.

History, they would discover, ceased to be fun the day they left the Ops Room and the easy-going Miss Sterland. Mr Kneen, their new history teacher, was anything but easy-going. They could wave good-bye to the daily briefing. Instead they would be studying road construction in Early Roman Britain. Does he know there's a war on they wondered?

Teaching them French would be Mr Griffiths, who, according to rumour, had no time for the 'conversational' method of teaching, as popularised by Mam'selle.

"How can you learn a foreign language just by chatting? You've got to get the foundations, things like verbs, in place, first!" It was good enough for him in his day, so it should be good enough for them, in theirs! They must learn to imitate parrots. Je suis, tu es, il est, elle est, and so on, ad infinitum. Mam'selle, où es-tu?

Mr Cave, their form master, would be teaching them maths. He was rumoured to be a keen cricketer, and liked to use cricketing terminology to make his point, which should make life more bearable, Tim thought. Sporty teachers tended to be more easy-going than the rest.

For Physics, they would be in the hands of Miss Hill, a name passed down, in awe, from generation to generation; whispered along the stony, resonating corridors, around the dining room, even as far as the cycle-sheds. 'Ma' Hill', as she was known, a diminutive Scottish lady of awful temper, unerring eye and razor-sharp knuckles, would be waiting for them.

Finally there would be Latin, a language which was last spoken on Merseyside in the third century, when the Romans set up camp there. To Tim, even the name had a sinister ring about it. But, according to his Mum, Dad had done well at Latin, and people would expect his offspring to do the same. Mr Evans, a kindly, if excitable Welshman, would have the privilege of trying to knock it into their heads.

There were a few extras, a feeble attempt to sweeten the rest. In woodwork with Major Chalk, they would slave away at producing a letter-rack or coat-hanger, to be taken home with pride, and probably never seen again. Music lessons would be with the humourless Dr Wallace - forty minutes per week singing out-of-date songs, such as Men of Harlech and D'you ken John Peel. Physical Training, known as P.T, with the jolly Mr Handley, would be unashamed fun, ignoring the pommel horse, box and beam, in favour of wild chasing games, known as 'Pirates'.

That would surely be enough to be going on with. But, lest a single waking moment be lost to the Great Cause, it had been ordained by the powers-that-be, that there shall also be homework - three lots, thirty minutes each, ninety minutes per evening, etc., to ensure that what they had been studying in class would be the last thing on their young minds as their heads touched the pillow. Tim picked up his pen to copy the list down. It felt heavy in his hand. Monday - Maths, Physics and Geography, Tuesday - French, English and Latin, etc. It was like writing one's own prison sentence.

Tim had never agreed with homework. In his opinion, seven hours a day slogging away in class was a big enough imposition, without having to work overtime. It was twisting the knife in the wound. How was it, he wanted to ask, that such an iniquitous practice had gone on, unchallenged, down the ages; or had it been challenged and the challengers put down with the cane?

He had worked it out. The teachers had had to put up with it as kids, so why shouldn't today's kids? And now they had the power. This was their revenge! And parents had gone along with it. What easier way could there be to ensure peace and quiet for dad after a hard day at the office, a chance to put his feet up, light a pipe and read the paper, while son is despatched elsewhere to sweat over equations and verbs? And if challenged to explain why, the answer would be the same. 'If it did me good, it'll do you good!' But can they prove it? They say the same about that other odious imposition, the daily dose of cod liver oil. But has anyone ever seen a parent taking a daily dose? As usual, it was one rule for the few and another for everyone else.

To sum up - homework is not only valuable-time-consuming, it's unfair, and should be banned.

Not that everyone shared his opinions. In Shirley's case, homework wasn't a problem, and he looked on, mystified, as she beavered away eagerly into the late evening. Of course, she was making up for lost time. Then there was Yozzer. Next to whiling away the evening hours on the crystal set, he seemed to be at his happiest, wrestling with some knotty, mathematical equation or memorising a poem. Frank Wilson was another who seemed to have nothing better to do in the evenings, so there shouldn't have been a problem; but as a precaution, it was his Mum's practice to sweeten the drudgery with the offer of a substantial increase in pocket money, a reward for time spent at what she called 'the coal face'. Rightly or wrongly, Frank was deemed to be conscientious, a model of keenness and dedication, which reflected badly on Tim in the next desk. He was surrounded by homework enthusiasts!

Tim always had something better to do - football with the local lads on the recreation ground until dark; the latest exploits of the Amazing Wilson to wonder at; a chapter or two of nerve-tingling action with Biggles, taking on the might of the Third Reich, all by himself, or an hour on the crystal set and the chance of a glimpse of Myfanwy. It was hardly surprising, then, that, from the very start, his homework was presented poorly, late, or not at all.

He had discovered that being a 'middle' child had its advantages. When Mum and Dad weren't monitoring Shirley's progress at school, they had a full-time infant on their hands. Baby Roger wasn't a baby any more. He wasn't a boisterous child, but, like all nearly-two-year-olds, he knew how to demand attention. So Mum and Dad didn't have the time to look over big brother's shoulder. As far as homework was concerned, he could come and go under the parental radar, undetected.

That was not the case in the world of the Collegiate, however. One morning, not long after the start of the term, Mr Cave called him over to his desk.

"I understand that your father did rather well at the Collegiate, Oliver. A hard act to follow!"

DRAT! The vigilant form-master must have read Mrs Taylor's uncomplimentary report and picked up the glowing bit about his Dad. The term was only a few weeks old and already his cover had been blown. He nodded and bit his lip. He could guess what was coming.

"And you haven't made a very good start," Mr Cave went on,

grimly. "I myself have noticed that you lose concentration...take your eye off the ball, rather easily. Your other masters say the same. They complain that you don't seem to bother with your homework. 'Half-baked'...'sloppy'....'sketchy', and so on! That's what I hear!"

The school's radar was in perfect working order!

"Well," he continued, "to flourish at the Collegiate School, one must play a straight bat! That's what wins the day! Concentration!" Sir must have read John Henry Newbolt's stuff!

"As in batting," he went on, "sloppy stroke-play leads to disaster. I'm told your father always played a straight bat...captain of the School Eleven, and so on. Well, one can learn a lot from cricket and, in future, we will be expecting more of that...concentration, I mean. Otherwise you will find yourself in the nets!"

"Yes, Sir." Why couldn't he leave Dad out of it? And what did he mean by 'the nets'?

Frank explained.

"It's detention. An hour or two in Room Thirty-Five, after school."

Gertie found him on the clock-golf course, at six o'clock to be exact, the following Saturday morning. The putter and ball were still in the box. His old friend put her washing-basket down and walked over.

"Not practising your putting, Tim?"

"I don't feel like it, Gertie."

"Dear me! That's not like you! What's wrong?"

"Almost everything. My form master knows that Dad did well at the Collegiate, and wanted to know why I'm not doing the same. He says I don't concentrate. But it's always been the same, Gertie. At Lyneal school - that's where Shirley and me were evacuated - we were all thrown in together. It was so noisy. The teacher was really horrible, so I didn't learn much. Then when we came back home I couldn't even qualify to take the Grammar School entrance test." He frowned. "It was all her fault! After that it didn't matter whether I concentrated or not."

"But you did get a place at the Collegiate."

"That's because a friend of the family paid for me to attend the Prep, and, anyway, it was fun there. Now it isn't even fun."

"But does everything have to be fun? Things we find dull when we're young can become quite interesting as we get older, and useful, too. And after all, you're at your Dad's old school now. I'd bet he had to put up with plenty of dull bits when he was your age, and he did very well! You should talk to him, Tim. If I know your father, he's the right person to give you some advice."

"I'll think about it."

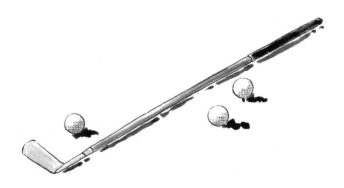

CHAPTER TWENTY-ONE

FORM 3D DOES ITS BIT

The trials for the first year football team, known as THE CHICKS, had been held, and Tim had been picked in his favourite position. There would be Saturday morning matches against other schools to look forward to. He had been elected form football captain, too, and his fragile morale was holding up, if against all the odds.

In Maths, for example, Algebra was a total mystery. It was one googly after another. Even Mr Cave couldn't get through.

Latin was no better. On the very first day, Mr Evans had noted a lack of enthusiasm, even before they opened their text books, and had appealed to their youthful sense of optimism.

"NIL DESPERANDUM!" He scrawled the words on the blackboard.

"There you are, boys. A bit of Latin to get you started. No despairing! That's what it means! Remember that, especially when you're flagging, thinking it's all mumbo jumbo! I know it's not easy. I was a boy myself, once! Try to think of it as a challenge!" Mr Evans would have made a good preacher!

He continued...

"And remember - it's closer to our language than to any of the others! For example, take any word ending in ant, ent, ify and ity; or starting with con, ad, diff, and inst. They'll be pure Latin, and there are lots more where they came from! We were quick learners, us Anglo-Saxons - quicker than the Germans and the French...even the Italians, and they had a head start! When it comes to learning Latin, boys, being English is a big advantage! So it shouldn't be too difficult, should it?" They shook their heads. They would take his word for it.

Sadly for Tim, after only a few weeks of declensions, tenses and conjugations, any hope which may have lingered had all but evaporated. Despair had already set in. His Dad might have been spellbound, learning that Gaul had been divided into three parts and that kind of thing, but, in Tim's case, despite Mr Evans's unusual teaching methods, Latin didn't make sense.

In the Physics lab, Ma Hill was living up to her billing. She seemed to take it for granted that all schoolboys are idle by nature, and need to be motivated by a continuous reign of terror. She would know about the whip and carrot, and had ruled the carrot out. Ma' Hill, when annoyed, which happened frequently and at the slightest provocation, became a kind of human V1, zooming in, unannounced, at low altitude, from any direction, primed and ready to explode on impact. In Physics lessons, apart from the clink of a pipette or the hiss of a bunsen burner, silence reigned. The key to survival lay in appearing to be concentrating.

French lessons were usually spent grinding out verbs.

"Never mind pronunciation! That's not much use if you haven't got the verbs to pronounce, is it?" Mr Griffiths would say, and seemed to find that amusing.

In History lessons, they seemed to be avoiding all the really interesting bits - the poisonings, assassinations, rebellions and conspiracies which they knew were there, somewhere. Instead, they slaved away, investigating everyday life in the Roman Empire, with freehand illustrations of stone columns, armless statues and extremely straight, cobbled roads.

Geography was doomed from the start, at least to those who, like Tim, couldn't produce a decent stamp collection. Mr Hall might wax eloquent about 'the sheer beauty' of the Penny Black, but it was lost on Tim, and an educational visit to Cronton Colliery to marvel at the slag-heap, didn't make up for the drudgery of mapping the route of the Wigan to Liverpool Canal.

In English lessons, Mr Riddle almost saved the day by continuing to ignore poetry altogether. They would leave 3D as masters of punctuation and grammar, if nothing else. It was the lesser of two evils.

Music lessons were a lost cause before they had sung a note. They all agreed that singing is for girls. For one thing their voices don't break, whereas most of 3D's were already half-way there. It added to the misery. Doctor Wallace might threaten dire punishments for non-cooperation, but Tim, for one, had decided to withdraw his labour. There were some things that, in all conscience, couldn't be done.

To sum up. Since Mr Cave's words of advice, as half-term approached, in the world of Oliver T 3D, nothing had changed. In his opinion, most lessons were uninspired and uninspiring. Often he didn't see the point of the topic being studied, and couldn't be bothered to enquire further. Playing a straight bat wasn't as easy as Mr Cave seemed to think.

Happily, away from school, there was inspiration from the crystal set. Hitler's Thousand Year Reich was running out of time and space. The allies had clawed back half of Belgium, the Americans were driving through north east France and northern Italy. Further East, the Russians were advancing through Hungary and into Poland. The pincers were closing. Miss Sterland would be having a field day! But the same old posters still urged everyone to Dig for Victory.

****

"Next Monday you'll all be having the day off school," said Mr Cave one Friday afternoon, smiling broadly, as if it was his idea. "But before you start throwing your caps around, I'd better tell you what you'll be doing. With food in short supply, the government has asked the farmers to grow a bigger than usual crop of potatoes this year, and now they need extra help to harvest them. That's where you come in! You've been given the job of saving the nation from starvation. You'll be potato-pickers for the day and, in return, you'll each receive the princely sum of two shillings. Report to school by a quarter to nine in some old clothes and shoes, and bring some sandwiches for

lunch. Anyone who misses the transport will stay behind in school!
So don't be late"

As if they would! This was a deadline no one was going to miss.

At 8.35 am, Tim ran along Shaw Street to where the First Forms
were gathering in front of the School, but there was no transport in
sight. At a quarter to nine they were facing the prospect of another
day at the coalface. Mr Cave was glancing at his watch. He had been
banking on having the day off. Then there was a cheer, as a column
of trucks was spotted approaching along Shaw Street.

Major Chalk now took over, allocating two trucks per form. The
tail-gates dropped down and there was a rush to scramble on board.
Tim managed to find a space on the floor between Peter and Frank.
The trucks weren't covered, so it was going to be a draughty ride, and,
if it rained, they would get wet. But what was a little discomfort in the
service of one's country? Fortunately, so far, it was a fine October day.

"Just the day for an outing to the countryside," Mr Cave
remarked to the driver, smiling bravely at the prospect of trying to
keep an eye on 3D at large in the endless acres of Kirkby.

"Will you fire one of those Very pistols, to give the signal to
move off, Sir?" Frank asked the Major, grinning, "like they do in the
army?" The Major wasn't amused, but, at that moment, as if to answer
the question, the engines sprang to life, another cheer went up, and
one by one the trucks pulled away, with 3A in the lead. Eyes peered
down, enviously, from the school windows, as they headed north.

People stared at the convoy with its almost invisible, chattering
cargo, and by the time they had reached the outskirts of the city, the
chatter had changed to singing. There were the usual favourites, with
variations, such as 'One man and his dog went to pick potatoes', and
'Old MacDonald had a farm...and on that farm he had some spuds'.
Then 3A started up with 'There'll always be an England, and England
will be free', and the others joined in '...if England means as much to
you as England means to me!' They felt inspired, and couldn't wait
to get their hands on the precious spuds.

People stopped to smile and wave as the trucks swept past.

Some held up two fingers, Mr Churchill's V-for-Victory sign. Some joined in the singing, until the sound died away, as the column rolled on. By now their voices had almost gone, and the last few miles were spent reflecting on the soreness of their bottoms.

Soon the column divided into twos, each heading in a different direction. The two carrying 3D headed along a cart track, in and out of ruts in the dark loamy earth, and finally jerked to a halt, side by side, on the cobbles of a farmyard. The tail-gates were lowered and the workers jumped down, gratefully.

A red-faced man in Wellingtons, overalls and Trilby hat, emerged from the farmhouse and strode towards them. They were expected, and Mr Cave stepped forward, smiling.

"Good morning. You must be Farmer Birtles. My name is Cave, and this" - he waved towards the boys - "is form 3D, your workforce for the day." The boys stood more or less to attention.

The farmer adjusted his spectacles to peer at them.

"Work force, d'you call 'em? College puddins if you ask me, and little ones at that. Never picked a potato in their lives! Well, I didn't ask for 'em, and I don't think they'll be much use. But the Government says I've got to 'ave 'em and the Government'll be payin', so I suppose they'll be better than nothin'!"

The workforce didn't like what they were hearing. Like Tim, many of them had only recently spent two years in the countryside. They might not have picked potatoes before, but they knew their way around a farm and weren't afraid to get their hands dirty. Mr Cave had read their minds. The farmer was out of order!

"Well, Mr Birtles," he said, "these College puddings, as you call them, might be a bit on the small side, but they'll be more useful than you seem to think!"

The farmer frowned, but said nothing. The work-force grinned. Good old Sir! That stumped him!

The farmer pointed to a younger man who had just arrived on the scene.

"That's my manager, Ernie. 'E'll show 'em what to do." He

glared at them again.

"Just make sure you do what he says!" he growled, then spun round and marched back to the house, muttering.

"College puddins!"

"Follow me, lads," said Ernie, cheerfully, and led them down a track along the side of a field of potatoes just waiting to be unearthed.

"So he thinks we're 'better than nothing', does he? " said Tim, as they trudged along...." and little! Well on the wireless it says that kids in Germany not much bigger than us are being sent to fight the Russians!"

They tramped on in silence, and a hundred yards further on, Ernie stopped.

"Right. Gather round, lads, and don't take too much notice of Mr Birtles. His bark's worse than his bite! Now...I hear that you're Form 3D so, if you don't mind, I'll call you my Threepenny Squad!" They grinned. He waved a hand towards the rows of potatoes.

"In case you didn't know, these are spuds. I know you can't see 'em, but they're the best in the county! Well now, there's thirty-six of you, so that'll be twelve to a row, which makes four groups of three. Each group has its own patch and there are markers at the side of the field to show you where each patch starts and finishes. Keep your eyes on them, so there's no arguments! The plough digs up three rows at a time. The potatoes will be lying on the ground. Just pick 'em up, dump 'em in your basket, and when that's full, take it to the main bin over there," he pointed. "...then come back for more. And be quick, 'cos the tractor'll be coming round again, to start on the next three rows, and Joe, 'e's the driver, won't hang about!"

Mr Cave, the mathematician, divided them into three groups of twelve, and allocated each group to a row. Peter, Frank and Tim asked if they could be together, and were allocated the second patch in the third row. They picked up their baskets and took up their positions.

A few minutes later, a tractor and plough turned into the field. The plough-blades were lined up with the first three rows, the tractor surged forward, turning over the plants, throwing the potatoes clear, and the Threepenny Squad went into action. What surprised them

was the number of potatoes on each plant, and, after only a few
minutes, Peter glanced anxiously after the tractor, which was more
than half-way to the end of the row.

They had already filled and emptied their baskets twice and
they had only covered half of their patch.

"We'd better get a move on," he said, "or we'll be left behind."

They put on a spurt and were loading the last few potatoes into
the bin just as the tractor arrived to start the next three rows.

"That was close!" said Frank.

"Keep going, boys!" said Mr Cave, in his new, self-appointed
role as team coach. "You'll find that it'll get easier as you get the
knack. It's a bit like grooving in your batting strokes. You know...
practice makes perfect!"

"I hope so," muttered John Lightfoot, who was in the next row.
Cricketing metaphors meant nothing to him. Known as 'Tubby' or
just 'Tub', he was the least athletic member of the form, and already
out of breath.

The coach was right. By the time they had completed their third
row, their technique had improved. It saved time, and allowed them a
few precious, extra seconds' rest before starting on the next row. But
now the tractor seemed to be coming round more quickly. Was Joe
putting his foot down harder, or were they starting to flag already?

Whatever the reason, by the time eighteen rows had been plundered, they were ready for a rest, and Ernie had read their minds.

"Alright," he shouted, "We'll take a ten minutes break."

"Only ten!" muttered Harry Noble.

"My back's killin' me!"

"Me too!" said Peter.

Tubby had thrown himself down on a heap of potato tops.

"I can't go on!" he gasped.

"You've got to, Tub" said Tim, "or we won't keep up."

"Remember we're saving our country from starvation, Tub," added Frank, grinning.

"Time!" shouted Ernie.

"Already?" muttered Frank.

"This is hard labour!" said Harry.

"Take a tip, boys," Ernie said, "and don't start off too fast. Pace yourself. That's the farmer's way!" They nodded. They would try anything, and when Ernie shouted 'Time' for lunch-break, another twenty-one rows had been plundered.

Lunch-break was spent stretched out on a bed of potato tops and there wasn't much talking. Tubby was snoring.

After half an hour, Ernie called 'time', and they had just reassembled at the start of the fortieth row when the farmer appeared.

"That's thirty-nine rows completed, Mr Birtles," said Ernie.

"Is that all? D'you call that war-effort? My nine year-old grandson's class could do better than that! Put your backs into it!" he barked. "I want to see another forty-five finished by five o'clock!"

"Jah vol, mein Fuhrer!" said a voice from the back.

"Who said that?"

"Me, sir," said Frank.

"And what's your name?"

"Wilson, sir."

"Well, Master Wilson, I'll be havin' a word with your teacher about you and your cheek. It'll be the cane for you, my lad, when you get back to school. That'll take the grin off your face!" He turned around and stomped back in the direction of the farm.

"So the old buffer wants forty-five more rows, does he?" said Peter. "Well, I vote we do forty-eight. That'll show him!"

"That's an awful lot, Pete," said Harry.

"Hear, Hear!" said Tub, who was feeling suicidal.

"And he doesn't deserve it," said George, "poking fun at us!"

"But we're not doing it for him, are we?" said Peter.

"You're right, Pete," said Frank. "I say we vote on it. Hands up those who agree." Everyone raised a hand, including Tub who said he would do his best. So, when Joe started the tractor up, they were ready, and the picking began. By four o'clock they had completed another thirty four rows.

"There's still fifteen to go," said Frank. He had changed places with George who had been helping Tub.

"We're never going to do it, "muttered Harry, anxiously. "I vote we settle for forty-five. Then, at least, old Macdonald can't laugh at us."

"No!" said Peter. "We can do it!" Peter the British bulldog!

At that moment Mr Cave was spotted walking towards them.

"You look as if you're feeling the pace, boys. I'll take your place, Lightfoot. You can stand by the bin and help the others to empty their baskets."

"Oh, thanks very much, Sir!" said Tub.

Good old Sir, playing the game, helping them out in their hour of need.

The teacher tucked his trousers into the tops of his socks, and took Tub's place just as the tractor started its run up the next three rows. There was no talking now, and by twenty to five, the forty-fifth row had been picked clean. They had twenty minutes to complete the last three rows. Their backs and fingers ached, but now they could see the finishing line.

At three minutes to five, the rest of the squad gathered at the end of the rows, and as the last group emptied their baskets into the bin, everyone shouted...

"FORTY EIGHT!"

"Mission accomplished!" said Mr Cave. "Well done, boys!" and thirty-six weary College Puddins tramped back to the farm, where Ernie reported to the farmer that the Threepenny Squad had picked three rows more than he had demanded. They might be little and few, but they had proved him wrong, and grateful mums up and down the land would soon be able to get their hands on those very potatoes. As Mr Churchill would probably have put it... 'So many owe so much to so few!'

"I wouldn't have believed it!" muttered the farmer, as the trucks swung out of the farmyard and headed back to the city and Shaw Street. Their backs ached and it would take hours to get the soil from under their nails; but they had done their bit, and now they found their voices again. 'There'll always be an England!' had never sounded more certain, and they each had two bob in their pockets.

Back at Shaw Street, Frank was chatting with George, when Mr Cave walked up.

"So, Wilson, I hear that you were trying out your German on Mr Birtles!"

"Yes, sir, and he didn't like it!"

"Well, as they say... 'If the cap fits!'"

Frank was reprieved. There would be no caning, the half-term holiday was due at the end of the week, and Tim had decided that he never wanted to touch another raw potato.

CHAPTER TWENTY-TWO

TIM AND FRIENDS HEAR ABOUT SCHOOL HEROES

"Let us now praise famous men and our fathers that begat us."

The half term holiday had come and gone and, in the Great Hall, a thousand pairs of eyes focussed on the Head Boy who had resolutely made the ascent to the stage, close to where the Headmaster and Vice-Principal sat in state, flanked by the Chairman of Governors and a hodgepodge of dignitaries.

With feet apart for balance and firm grip on the lectern, as recommended in hand-books on How to read the Bible in public, he now launched into the Book of Ecclesiasticus, words which were read every year on Founder's Day. It was the one bit of the ceremonial that most of them would remember, long after they had left the school. Then came the main business of the day, being reminded of past pupils, especially those who had made a name for themselves and the old school. They would be held up as an inspiration to the present generation. That was the task of the Guest Speaker.

The Reverend Charles Morgan was a Chaplain in the Royal Navy whose ship had recently returned from action in the North Atlantic, and had tied up in Gladstone Dock. He began by describing the Battle of the Atlantic, being stalked by U-Boats, and the awful loss of ships and lives. For ten minutes nobody moved. Then he reached his conclusion.

"The text said, 'Let us now praise famous men!' But what is fame? Some say it's to star in films, on the stage or the sports field, being hunted for one's autograph, having one's name picked out in bright lights or inscribed on honours boards. Sometimes we call it 'celebrity'. But there is a different kind of 'celebrity', an even better one. Today, in fact at this very moment, as I am speaking to you, the young men and women of our Empire and Allies are risking their lives in the air, on the land and at sea, opposing a powerful, evil foe, to put an end to tyranny and oppression, and secure peace and freedom, across the world. Among them will be many old boys of this great school, who have sat where you are sitting now." He paused, to allow the last statement to sink in. The Headmaster, Vice Principal, the Governors and dignitaries were nodding, gravely. The Chaplain continued...

"When this conflict is over and the victory is theirs, as we trust it will be, they won't be hunted for their autograph or see their name in lights. Nor, I believe, would they want to." Again he paused, and the silence was deafening. He went on. "Jesus Christ taught us that true greatness is best measured by the unselfish service a person gives to his world and generation, even at the cost of his life, if necessary, and he modelled it himself, perfectly. So who are today's celebrities who deserve our praise? I will leave you to decide." He paused, smiled and turned to the Head. "And now, Headmaster, I would like to request that the school be given a half-holiday!" It was the speaker's privilege, and as he sat down, there was an ear-splitting burst of applause. Was it to acknowledge a moving speech or a daring request? The answer was - probably both, and as the applause died down, the Head and Vice Principal looked at each other as if there might be some doubt that such a request could be granted, although, to human memory, the same request had never been turned down. But one shouldn't appear too keen to dish out half-hols! The school held its breath until the Head stood to give the official nod of approval, and there was more applause. The Reverend Charles had made a thousand young friends-for-life, not to mention quite a few older ones among the masters, and that was the cue for the school song. Vivat haec sodalitas, decus Esmedunae. 'Long live this fellowship, second to none on earth, a mighty cradle of heroes'. Like school songs up and down the country, it was a mixture of exaggeration and optimism, thinly veiled in Latin, a thunderous wall of sound circling all six sides of the Hall. Not many of those present understood the words they were singing so confidently; but those who didn't were happy to take their meaning 'on spec' and make up in gusto what they lacked in understanding.

Next came the National Anthem, a prayer for the King, courageous as well as 'noble and gracious', manfully refusing to run for safety during the dark days of the Blitz, and still sticking to his post even with buzz-bombs landing in his back garden. 'Send him victorious, happy and glorious, long to reign over us!' etc., and on this patriotic note, the Founders Day service ended. The Head now steered the dignitaries back to his study and down to earth with refreshments of sandwiches, modest slices of Victoria sponge-cake and cups of tea. The boys headed for the dining room and a choice of sausage and mash or cheese pie.

A few minutes later, wrestling with a particularly uncooperative sausage skin, Tim was thinking about famous Old Boys, the school's past celebrities. People kept reminding him that his father had been one of them, and seemed to expect Tim to follow his example. But that, one-to-one chat with his form master was an uncomfortable reminder that, so far, he wasn't having much success.

Only the previous week he had had a run-in with Ma' Hill. They had been playing about with magnets and iron filings, creating clever, spidery patterns, which he thought was fun, but could be done far more easily with a protractor and pencil, and without all the mess. He had pointed this out to the teacher, who thought he must be joking, which was not the thing to do with Ma' Hill. Fortunately she had given him the benefit of the doubt, explaining that he had missed the point of the experiment, something to do with 'magnetic fields'. It had all gone over his head, and, soon afterwards, while she was writing on the blackboard, he was whispering behind his textbook to Alex McMinn, about the latest Everton match with Aston Villa. The teacher spun round and pointed at him.

"Boy! Talking! Stand!" The words came in a rapid, machine-gun-like burst, as she stepped down from the dais and headed straight for him, rubbing the knuckles of her right hand up and down the inside of her left arm, as one might sharpen a razor on a leather strop. The form football captain was in for it! Magnetism was put on 'Hold' and there was a deathly silence, like that which indicates the descent phase of a V1 rocket. Tim stood up, bracing himself to ride the right-hook which he was sure was on its way. Instead, the teacher came to a halt a few feet away, and stared at him.

"So you think, master Oliver, do you, that, because your father was a leading light at the Collegiate School, you have the right to spend your time chit-chatting to your friends, while my back is turned!"

"No, Miss. Sorry, Miss." A soft answer might turn away wrath.
"Write out the first law of magnetism fifty times!"

"Yes, Miss." He had no idea what that particular law was, or even that there was one; but Alex was keen on Physics. He would explain.

At break-time Tim was telling Yozzer what had happened.

"She seems to have eyes in the back of her head! "

Yozzer grinned. "She has, in a way! I thought everybody knew that! When she's writing on the blackboard she angles her head so that she can see what's going on behind her, reflected in her specs! Anyway, you got off lightly! When you've done your lines, come around and we can listen in to the six o'clock war bulletin."

Tim brightened up. The half-holiday would be an opportunity to try his hand at the crystal set and be somewhere near Myfanwy.

The half-holiday was the next Monday afternoon, and when he arrived, Yozzer already had the earphones on. He looked up.

"The Americans have given the Jap fleet a good hiding! Two hundred and eighty ships fought it out for three days somewhere in the Philippine Islands. The newsreader said it was the biggest sea-battle in history. The Americans lost two warships, but the Japs lost twenty-eight, including their last four aircraft carriers. That means they can't send their fighters to defend their bases. They're in real trouble! But they weren't going to give in. The Japs never do, Dad says. They don't believe in surrendering. They sent in the Kamikazes - they're suicide pilots. They fill their plane with high explosives, have a strong drink, say 'Bye -bye', salute, take off and, when they've dropped all their bombs, dive right into an enemy ship. Imagine that, Tim!"

"Wow!"

Tim was trying to.

"It's strange how brave some people can be, even though they're on the wrong side!"

"They don't think they are! They're dying for the Emperor. To them, he's a god, so they think they must be on the right side!"

"Well, he might be a god, but now he's lost his last Carrier, Dad says, it's probably 'curtains' for him.

"I bet he's sorry about Pearl Harbour, now!"

****

The trouble with a half-holiday, Tim reflected, gloomily, as he turned into the yard the next morning, is that it isn't a proper holiday; just a brief pause, a breather, as in a boxing match, a chance to take refuge in one's corner, only to be summoned by the bell a few moments later, to take more punishment. Myfanwy hadn't put in an appearance; so, despite all the euphoria, the half-hol had come and gone, almost unnoticed.

The gong rang, the doors at the south end swung open and a great wave swept through and up the staircase towards the first floor where the Headmaster had taken up his usual position, his gown hooked up behind him, and mortar-board under one arm, scrutinising each one, or so they imagined, row by row. It was like walking past a policeman in the street. Who knew what long-forgotten offence might be brought to his amazing memory by a guilty glance? Head down, eyes focussed on the next step, it was as near to the Head as most of them would find themselves, or would want to. That was certainly true of Oliver, 3D, who already had several reasons for wanting to reach the first floor unrecognised.

Apart from his early morning vigil, the Head would put in an appearance at Assembly, to be seen to be leading from the front, say a prayer and make an announcement or two. Otherwise he would spend most of his time at his vast desk in his vast study issuing orders for the day. He rarely, if ever, reached for his cane, preferring to leave the administration of justice to the Vice-Principal, his right-hand man in more ways than one.

Mr Crofts, the Vice Principal, better known as the VP or, less respectfully, 'The Viper', was the school troubleshooter. A visit to his study on the first floor was known to be the last stop on the line for the under-performing, uncooperative or downright rebellious pupil, and since Oliver, T, 3D, fell into all three categories, more or less, it was obvious to everyone in 3D that the form football captain and The Viper were probably on a collision course.

****

Back at Sixty-Five as 1944 drew towards its end, the blackout had officially ended. At last, the gloomy curtains could go, and Grandma had come out of retirement to direct operations. Gertie had spent two precarious days up a step-ladder, taking down thirteen sets, whistling, through her teeth, odd snatches from the latest popular song, *'When the lights come on again all over the world'*.

Dumping them in a pile at the end of the garden, she struck a match, and Grandma, arms folded, looked on as the ugly mound caught fire. It was all rather symbolic in a way, she thought - the powers of darkness being brought down and going up in smoke; a kind of funeral pyre for the Third Reich. She was happy to be alive to witness it. Grandpa would have opened a bottle or two.

The garden gate opened and Tim appeared. She spotted him and waved.

"Come and join the celebrations, Timothy! The black-out's ended, unless you happen to live in Berlin, of course, or Dresden or Hanover. Such beautiful cities. Now they're on the receiving end!" She sighed. "Ah well, as the saying goes - 'Sow the wind, reap the whirlwind'" She paused, peering thoughtfully into the flames. "They do say the bombing will help to shorten the war, but I hope our boys in blue aren't overdoing things."

Tim was reminded of his discussion with Mrs Taylor about fire-storms. He nodded, dumped his satchel on the path, and went over to the fire.

"Now tell me, how's your first term going?"

He gulped. He was afraid she might ask; but should he own up? Admit that, so far, it had been a disaster? If Shirley's bit of sleuthing was correct, and he owed his place at the Collegiate to Grandma's generosity, she would probably be upset. At that moment, as a cloud of dark smoke billowed around the bonfire, almost hiding him from sight, he decided to put down a smke screen of his own. He would keep his reply short and off the point.

"Alright, thanks, Grandma. I've got some quite interesting teachers."

That was the masters damned with faint praise, en masse. He reserved Mr Cave for special mention.

"My form master's quite nice and he's keen on cricket. I'm form football captain, and I've been picked for the Chicks football team."

Grandma smiled slightly. She was good at reading between the lines. Obviously, lessons weren't a priority where her Grandson was concerned.

"That sounds exciting, dear boy!"

CHAPTER TWENTY-THREE

TIM FINDS 'THE NETS'

"Little brothers need bags of fresh air," declared Gertie, one Saturday morning, "and Sandfield Park is an ideal place to push a pram." She walked through it every day on her way to and from Sixty-Five, and was sure it would be quiet and safe enough for someone with little or no previous experience, such as Tim, to take a little brother for a walk. It was a favourite beat for nannies with prams, she said, and the sidewalk, if not exactly level, was wide enough to accommodate the family pram, with room to overtake, if necessary.

Tim had been allowed to try his hand once or twice before, up and down a short, quiet stretch of Quarry Road, which ran behind Sixty-Five. But Sandfield Park would be a completely new challenge, and, although he loved his little brother, he wasn't too keen, for at least three reasons. Firstly, as everyone knows, pushing prams is what girls do. Suppose he was spotted by a 3D boy. It would be around Room 21 and probably along the corridor, in no time. Secondly there was the prospect of jostling for right-of-way with the local nannies, some of whom were in the heavyweight category, to say the least. In the world of the nanny, where might is right, he and Roger could easily find themselves in the gutter, together with the pram. Thirdly, there was the gleaming, streamlined pram, with ultra-modern suspension, extra-wide wheelbase and large wheels. It would be impossible to push such a pram in the open, undetected.

On the other hand, bearing in mind the final report from the Prep and other factors, such as getting out of bed at the very last minute and leaving his bedroom, according to Shirley, looking 'like a bombed site', his general behaviour rating was bumping along the bottom again. An hour's jaunt in the sun, pushing little brother around the park, was bound to raise it a notch or two. So he agreed to venture out that afternoon, in charge of Roger and pram.

Waiting until the coast was reasonably clear, he steered the pram over Queens Drive and into Sandfield Park. As he had expected, people's heads turned automatically to admire the infant or the pram or both, perhaps thinking 'what a kind big-brother the little chap has got! After all, not every boy would be seen doing that!' The low, late-autumn sun streamed pleasantly through the park trees, no Collegiate boys had turned up, the nannies were either enjoying a well-earned siesta or on strike, and little brother was chortling. He smiled. This he could cope with.

By the time they had to turn back for home, however, the novelty had already worn off, and he was bored. Even Roger was bored, judging by the way he was bashing the inside of the pram with his plastic trumpet. The little fellow needed some entertainment, and Tim decided to liven things up.

First they zig-zagged at a brisk, walking-pace, which seemed to please the passenger; then at a trot, which pleased him more. But zig-zagging with such a hefty pram was proving tricky, so he reverted to steering in a more orthodox, straight line. Then it occurred to him that, with its special suspension, large wheels and streamlining, the family pram was more like a Roman chariot than a run-of-the-mill perambulator. This was more promising! He accelerated, and found that, on gentle bends, it developed a chariot-like roll and, on the occasional slight dip, a tendency to pitch, as if at sea in a storm. That seemed to delight Roger, although Tim noticed that, as he clung onto the sides, his little knuckles had turned white. He thought he would check the passenger harness, and was glad to find that it had been fixed securely. Big sister, knowing Tim's liking for adventure, had foreseen a possible mishap and had checked the harness before they set out. Little brother couldn't possibly be ejected.

The sidewalk ahead was clear and, with the Park gates almost in sight, he decided that here was an opportunity for one last manoeuvre, a sort of Grand Finale. The chariot was bowling along quickly on a slight, downward slope; he gave it an extra-vigorous push and let go of the handlebar. Now it was pilotless, with the pilot striding alongside, grinning and waving his hands about, as if to say 'Look Roger, no hands! You're on your own!' and Roger was positively whooping.

This pram-pushing is a pushover, thought Tim. But, as one version of the saying might go, 'smugness goeth before a fall'. As they approached a bend, the front wheels dropped into a dip which Tim hadn't noticed before, the suspension couldn't compensate for the sudden, downward momentum, and, as he grabbed at the handlebar to slow it down, the family chariot nose-dived onto its front-end, leaving all four wheels spinning and Roger suspended, vertically, in mid-air, and positively howling. Tim gulped. What to do next? Roger was probably alright, judging by the volume of sound coming from his little lungs. But what about the pram? What would Mum say if the paintwork was scratched? He grabbed the handlebar and pulled the pram upright. A quick glance at the paintwork revealed only a slight scuffing which, with a bit of luck, wouldn't be noticed. But the howling hadn't stopped. He had better check the passenger.

"Don't cry, Roger," he whispered. "You're not frightened, are you? Brave boy! You're quite safe, but not a word to Mum, PLEASE!" and whether or not Roger had got the gist of his brother's desperate plea, he stopped howling; and was that a little nod? Tim hoped so. In any case, suppose Mum did spot the scuffing and subjected Roger to one of her in-depth interrogations, probably with an offer of extra sweets in exchange for a confession, how could an under-two-year-old say something like 'Suspended at speed in mid-air?' Big brother's secret would be safe with Roger.

By now people were arriving to offer assistance. They had heard the howling, and feared the worst. Among them, Tim spotted Gertie, the one person in the world he would have wanted to see, under the circumstances. She was on her way home. She had recognised the howling and was already feeling Roger's little rib-cage to check for damage, while explaining to the anxious onlookers that she was an employee of the family. The ribs felt in good order, she announced, but, to be on the safe side, she would ensure that the little chap would be properly checked over. She thanked them for their concern.

The crowd now dispersed, leaving Tim trying to explain what had happened. Gertie would understand. She had the knack of understanding.

"The pram hit a bit of a dip, Gertie, when I wasn't looking." It was the truth, if not the whole truth, and Gertie half-smiled. Knowing Tim as well as she did, she had guessed what had probably happened; but she was pleased that he had been treating Roger to some fresh air, as she had suggested. If the scuffed paintwork was spotted, she would be ready with a less-incriminating explanation than the whole truth. Now they made their way back to Sixty-Five, Gertie in charge of the pram, and Tim listening to a lecture on the dangers of pushing prams containing little brothers, at speed.

****

Meanwhile, back at school, Tim had found The Nets. A quick glance, on arrival, confirmed that Room 35, situated on the second floor, might have been designed with a Detention Centre in mind - windows heavily-latticed to discourage the temptation to gaze down on the free world below; bare, picture-less walls, to prevent wandering thoughts, and elevated teacher's desk, for easier surveillance, as from a gun-tower. And silence. If he took the trouble to check, he would probably find tell-tale scratching under desk-lids done by previous, despairing occupants, to keep a tally of the slow, passing hours. Seated well towards the back, Tim thought of the luckless Count of Monte Cristo, unjustly incarcerated, wasting away in one of the Chateau d'If's infamous dungeons. He could sympathise!

He looked around at his fellow offenders. For which crimes had they ended up here, on this particular Thursday afternoon? A hater of P.T, caught trying to burn the Gym down, although that would carry a Saturday morning sentence? More likely, someone caught smoking behind the toilets, propelling a sausage-skin along the dining-room table from the prong of a fork, or reading a comic during prayers. The list might be endless. He did a quick count of detainees. There were sixteen in all, the select few out of a school of a thousand, for all the wrong reasons.

Judging by facial expressions, Room 35 wasn't the jolliest of places to spend an hour after school, when everyone else was happily wending their way home. This was Tim's first visit, although he had had several close-shaves, usually to do with non-production of homework, lateness, or straightforward inattention. He had already taken a strong dislike to Room 35, especially as, in his opinion, he hardly deserved to be there in the first place.

It had happened during a music lesson in the Hall. Sitting uncomfortably on the choir benches below the organ, they had just sung something from Dr Wallace's repertoire of 'Folk Songs for the Younger Male Voice', about frolicking about in a woodland glade and, apart from Ted Langley, who had so far avoided the ignominy of a breaking voice, there wasn't much sound coming forth. Sensing that these particular younger voices weren't entering into the spirit of the music, the Doctor decided to inject something vivace as well as patriotic, into the proceedings.

"We will now sing Rule Britannia, by the great Thomas Augustine Arne."

Not again! There were frowns all round which the Doctor immediately noticed. Annoyed, but undeterred, he pressed on.

"With our courageous Royal Navy keeping the Germans away from our beloved shores," he snapped, "this is a song we should all sing with enthusiasm and pride!" and in one eye-catching movement, he slid along the organist's bench, pulled out most of the stops, hands and elbows working furiously, in unison, and launched into the stirring opening bars. The singing began and they had reached the chorus... 'Rule Britannia, Britannia rules the waves...' when the organ groaned to a halt. The maestro spun around, glaring.

"Someone was singing the wrong words!" he barked.. "Who was it?" The words echoed around the Hall. No one moved. Then two hands were raised. It was Frank and Tim, and sliding from his seat, the Doctor descended to the platform in order to make eye-contact.

"And what were you singing?"

"Erm...marmalade and jam, Sir," Tim muttered, sotto voce.

"What do you mean, marmalade and jam?"

"That's what we sing on the bus on the way to football matches...'Rule Britannia, marmalade and jam. It's just for fun, really, Sir."

"Just for fun!" The Doctor's face was turning a bright pink. "And are there other unpatriotic words which you sing just for fun?"

"Well, there are a few, Sir...but we wouldn't sing them in lessons,Sir! "

"I should think not, sir! And whose idea was it, to jest unpatriotically in my lesson?"

"Mine, Sir, "said Tim. "We didn't mean to be unpatriotic....and we did sing quietly, Sir."

"Well, I heard you quite clearly." Tim now noticed that the Doctor had unusually large ears, which would account for his uncanny ability to identify a wrongly sung lyric. The Doctor went on...

"I have noticed you before, boy, not paying attention, smirking and so on." Tim had to admit that he did tend to smirk a lot, especially in music lessons.

"What is your name?"

"Oliver, sir."

"Ah yes, Oliver, 3D. You seem to be making a name for yourself, and not a very commendable one! Well, I won't have you fooling around in my lessons. You will report to room Thirty Five after school next Thursday, and write five hundred words on 'Why I am proud to be British.' You might start with a reference to our wonderful composers, such as Thomas Arne."

The duty-master now made his entrance, frowning. Mr Banyard, known affectionately among the older pupils as 'Bertie', was obviously unhappy at the prospect of spending an hour in The Nets with the criminal element of the school. Known for a tendency to throw a blackboard duster about, when order needed restoring, he wasn't one to tangle with. Those who knew this now came to attention, as he checked that everyone on the blacklist was present, and no comics had been smuggled in.

Some masters were known to take this opportunity to give a brief pep-talk on the folly of not toeing the line, slacking, smirking and so on, and ending up in detention. Mr Banyard must have decided that, in this case, that would be a waste of breath. He took out a fob watch, and checked the time.

"Right! No talking! You've all got work to do. Carry on!"

To cut his losses, Mr Banyard took out a copy of The Times and seemed to be tackling the long crossword. Tim picked up his pen to tackle his patriotic essay.

Chatting with Frank and Yozzer after lunch, he had collected an impressive list of British things to be proud of - a green and pleasant land of hope and glory, Mother of the free, etc.; winner of various wars, such as the Boer one, although there seemed to be some doubt as to who actually won it; the Crimean one, the Great, 1914-18 one, admittedly with a lot of help from others; and not forgetting the one about to be won, all being well; a nation of great inventions such as football, rugby, cricket and the Coronation Scot; lots of famous people such as Sir Francis Drake, Dixie Dean, Winston Churchill, Errol Flynn, and Lord Shaftesbury. He was spoilt for choice, but left the glorious Mr Arne off the list. The Doctor would be gnashing his teeth. On a topical note, he mentioned Field Marshal Montgomery, 'Monty', as he was known, who had cleaned up in North Africa and, according to Yozzer, was doing the same in Italy at the time of writing, together with the Americans and a few Italians who had changed sides, which was no surprise. To end 'on a high note', if a pun might be allowed during detention, (although probably lost on the Doctor), there were the heroic Battle of Britain pilots, en masse, the few to whom so many owed so much.

He could have knocked off a thousand words with no difficulty, but, on the hour, to the second, Bertie called 'time', and Room 35 emptied quickly, leaving The Nets to the gathering dusk.

CHAPTER TWENTY-FOUR

TIM AND THE VIPER COLLIDE

TIRPITZ SUNK!

Tim couldn't miss the headline on his way to the butchers to collect the family's sausage ration, one Saturday morning. According to the Echo, the TIRPITZ, Germany's new flag-ship, was the last remaining symbol of German sea-power. It could out-gun any single Allied ship, but German Admiral Donitz wouldn't risk it being caught and sunk by a pack of smaller vessels, so it had been holed up in a Norwegian Fjord, where it was spotted and sunk by the Lancasters of Bomber Command's 617 Squadron.

Now there could be no doubt who ruled the waves, even though the U-Boat fleet was making a last stand in the Atlantic. In the air, the Luftwaffe was powerless to stop swarms of allied bombers, a thousand at a time, raiding key targets all across Germany, and on the land, the territory which Germany had grabbed in 1940 and 1941 was being grabbed back by the allies. The Fuhrer was fast running out of room to manoeuvre.

Sadly, the same could be said about Oliver 3D, as Mr Cave wrote in his end of term report.

He seems to pick and choose which subjects he is prepared to take an interest in, of which there seem to be very few. This will not do! I have spoken to the Vice Principal. R.Cave.

Form master, 3D
December 1944

Oliver T, 3D and the Vice Principal were about to collide.

At break one morning, Tim joined a queue outside the Viper's study. He noticed that none of the others looked particularly confident, and when it was his turn, his hand shook as he knocked, then entered.

Mr Crofts turned around and peered at him over his spectacles. It was a few moments before he spoke.

"Well now, Oliver, we meet for the first time." He smiled faintly.

"I wasn't a master here when your father was a pupil, but his name has been passed down to us today as one of which you should be proud. His illustrious reputation at the school is something we presume you would want to emulate. But after just one term here you already have a reputation which is anything but illustrious. Most of your masters complain that you don't show much interest and your form-master's comment is extremely serious. Well, here at the Collegiate, we demand the very best from our pupils, so you must make up your mind quickly why you wish to be here. That is all. You may go."

Tim nodded, said nothing, and went. The one-sided interview had lasted four minutes and, as he closed the door, he was still trembling.

****

"This sounds like the writing on the wall, Tim!" Gertie wasn't her usual, glowing self. She had read his report. He frowned.

"What d'you mean, Gertie, '...the writing on the wall'?"

"Well, it's a way of saying 'You have been warned!' It comes straight from the Book of Daniel in the Bible."

Tim grinned faintly. Gertie the Methodist! She probably knew the Bible from cover to cover!

She continued.

"It's the story of young King Belshazzar who ruled over Babylon. It was the world's biggest Empire at the time, about 550 BC. Today we call it Persia. His father, King Nebuchadnezzar, had made the mistake of thinking that, because he was all-powerful, he could do as he liked.

He became what's called 'a law unto himself.' But his past finally caught up with him and, for a time, he even went out of his mind. It's all there in chapter four! At last, with some advice from Daniel, a brave Jewish prophet, he changed his ways, and when Belshazzar took over, the Empire was strong and prosperous. But the son hadn't learnt from his father's mistakes. He also became a law to himself. He ruled badly and all his father's achievements were being squandered.

"One night he gave a great party for a thousand of his most important officers. He ordered the holy vessels which had been plundered from the Jewish Temple at Jerusalem to be brought in and used to eat and drink from, as they 'praised the gods of gold and silver, bronze, iron and wood'. Then, 'the fingers of a man's hand appeared, writing on the plaster of the wall, '*Mene, mene tekel, upharsiin*'. The King's face turned pale and his knees knocked!' It's all down in chapter 5! His wise men couldn't interpret the writing, so Daniel was summoned.

"O King, the writing says 'You have been weighed on the scales and found wanting!"

"What did that mean, Gertie?"

"Well, imagine these are a set of weighing scales." She held her arms out sideways, palms facing upwards. "On one side are God's laws, the just standards which he has set for nations and their rulers. On the other side, here's King Belshazzar!" She raised the other hand high in the air. "Judging by God's standards of right and wrong, he was a failure, a light-weight!"

"I see. Is that what you meant about my form-master's report?"

"Yes, Tim," she said, sadly. "Judging by his this report, my friend Tim Oliver is a bit of a law to himself. He thinks he can do as he likes and get away with it; but his form master says he can't and won't! The writing's on the wall, Tim!" He nodded, biting his lip, as Gertie continued.

"Now I'll tell you how the story ends. The Bible puts it very neatly, in chapter five verse thirty. 'That same night, King Belshazzar was slain!' While they were feasting off the holy dishes, and laughing at Daniel's God, the armies of the invading Medes and Persians diverted the river which ran through the city, crept up the river bed and put an end to him and his Kingdom! For Belshazzar, the writing on the wall had come too late! But there's another reason I told you that story. Belshazzar seemed to think his Dad couldn't teach him anything. Young men tend to think like that at times. Don't make the same mistake, Tim. D'you remember what I said the last time we talked about your troubles? Talk to your Dad! It's not too late!"

"Thanks, Gertie. I'll think about it!"

"Good. But don't take too long !"

****

"I hope you're all wearing fresh, clean socks today," said Mr Cave, grimly, one morning. "A government inspector is in school to find out who qualifies for extra shoe coupons. Put your books away and file to the Gym in an orderly manner."

Straightaway there was a flurry of activity. If it meant missing algebra, they would put their books away and file anywhere in an orderly manner. Only James Allen seemed to be in no hurry. He had done his newspaper round before school and, as usual, he had run all the way. His socks would be far from fresh.

They reached the gym changing room just as 3C were leaving. Norman Harrison spotted them and ran over.

"There's nothing to it! Just make sure you press down as hard as you can. That'll make your toes spread further. Oh, and don't forget... use your left foot. It's supposed to be bigger than the right one."

A few minutes later, they were squatting on benches, minus their left shoe, waiting for the Inspector to appear, and Tim glanced along the row of socks. As well as the official light grey, there was an eye-catching splash of colour, where conscientious mums had darned heels and toes with any bit of wool they could find. In some cases there was more darning than sock and, in others, even the darning had been darned.

Peter Eccleston had tucked his foot out of sight, under the bench.

"Why are you doing that Peter?" asked Frank.

"There's a big hole in the heel". He pulled his foot from under the bench and pointed to the hole. "My mum'll kill me if anyone sees it!"

"Why don't you just swap it with the other one?"

"It wouldn't make any difference. That one's just as bad!"

The Inspector, a tall, pale gentleman with shiny black hair, parted in the middle, now entered.

"Good morning, boys," he began. "The Government has decided to give extra shoe coupons to pupils with feet over a certain size and that's why I'm here this morning."

They nodded. His fame had gone before him. He continued...

"Now I need to measure your feet." They knew. Norman had tipped them off.

With a flourish, as a conjuror might produce a rabbit from a hat, the Inspector took out a flat piece of wood from his briefcase and waved it about, smiling.

"And this is what we use. When it's your turn, just step forward and place the sole of your foot on it with your heel against the piece of wood at the end. And this"...a long, bony finger pointed to a white line, "is the magic line which the tips of your toes must reach to qualify for the extra coupons."

Tim glanced at the leather sole of his shoe. It was almost worn through. At any time a hole would appear and he would have to use pieces of cardboard to keep the rain out. He had only himself to blame, his Mum said. "It's all that football in the school yard!" He badly needed some of the precious coupons.

James Allen was the first to be measured, and the Inspector leaned down, adjusting his spectacles for a closer inspection. The rest looked at each other.

What a horrible job!

"That's just over the line!" announced the Inspector smiling broadly, handing James his extra coupons. They wondered if they should applaud.

Tim did a quick count. He would be fifth in line, and watched nervously as, one after another, the first four went forward, and returned in triumph, coupons in hand. They must all have big feet, he guessed. He glanced down at his own. By comparison it seemed rather small. Would he be the only failure?

"Oliver next!" He gulped, put his foot on the block and leaned forward to press down. He daren't look down, and the Inspector seemed to be taking ages to make up his mind. At last he looked up and smiled.

"You're in luck, Oliver! Your toe has only just touched the line, but I'll give you the benefit of the doubt."

As he sat down he waved his coupons at the others. It was like winning a laurel, if only a small one. Now he could relax and watch, as the rest attempted to reach the line. Only Brian Jones and Ted Simmons failed. Ted was almost in tears. Couldn't he be given the benefit of the doubt, too? The Inspector sympathised, but in Ted's case, there was too much doubt. There would be another examination in six months, he said, and, from long experience of foot-testing, he felt sure that, by then, Ted's feet would have grown enough to get his toes over the line.

****

The Christmas holidays meant more visits to Yozzer's, and Mum noticed that, on such occasions, as he left the house, he had combed his hair. She smiled. Yozzer's sister must be very pretty!

On the crystal set they heard that the Russian army was smashing its way through Poland, heading for Berlin, and the rest of the allies were closing in.

The writing was on the wall for the Nazi tyrant!

****

On Christmas morning there were at least some of the usual minor mysteries hidden away in stockings. The tangerine, an old favourite, was missing, which was no surprise. Nobody had seen one for five years. The sixpenny tanner, once retrieved from the toe, would come in useful, and there was a selection of sweets. The government had increased the ration for Christmas. "And not before time", said Auntie May. Shirley would make hers last well into the New Year. Tim's might last a few days at most. Among his presents there was another feast of Amazing Wilson exploits in the Wizard Annual for 1945.

****

The Spring Term brought the high moment of the football season, when the Junior Shield, a knock-out competition between the city's Grammar Schools was held. By mid-January, the first two rounds had been played. The Collegiate had reached the semi-final and their opponents would be Quarry Bank. The match would be played at Holly Lodge, and the reward for winning would be a place in the final at Anfield, Liverpool FC's famous stadium. It would be the most important game in Tim's life, so far. He could think of nothing else.

After school on the Wednesday before the match, there was a

kick-about on the Recreation ground. It was almost dark when he got home, tired out, and there was homework to be done. A punctuation exercise took just a few minutes, and a brief glance at Geography revision. That left Latin verbs to be memorised, but he was too tired. He would check them on the way to school; but, as it happened, the tram was full, and he had to strap-hang, which made revision almost impossible. To make matters worse, Latin was the first lesson and, worse still, he was the first to be singled out for a homework check.

"Oliver, take us through the imperfect tense of the verb desidero," said Mr Evans.

For what seemed like ages, he stood looking at the ceiling, but saying nothing.

"It would seem that you can't." said Mr Evans. "You didn't do your homework. So I have decided - another pun - that you must do it on Saturday morning in detention." He wrote a note on a pad.

"But it's the Junior Shield semi-final on Saturday morning, Sir, and I should be playing!"

"You should have thought of that!"

"Please let me off, Sir!"

Mr Evans shook his head.

"You don't deserve to be let off. Your homework is usually most unsatisfactory."

"But, Sir." Now he was desperate. Should he grovel? Perhaps throw himself at Mr Evans's feet? After all, he did say that he had been a boy himself once.

"PLEASE, Sir!"

"No. I'm sorry, but there's nothing more to be said."

Tim slumped down in his desk. The world was about to end. At break-time, he ran to the staff room, and asked to speak to Mr Welsby, who was in charge of the team.

"I'm in detention on Saturday, Mr Welsby, because I didn't do my Latin homework. Will you ask Mr Evans to let me off, please."

Mr Welsby frowned. "I'll speak with him. But I can't hold out much hope. See me at the end of school."

The afternoon dragged slowly by. Mr Welsby was waiting outside the staff-room when Tim ran up, searching for a sign that the news was good, but it wasn't.

"Mr Evans says you don't deserve to be let off. You fool around in lessons, and this isn't the first time you haven't done your homework. It's a pity, but you'll have to take your medicine, and I will play a reserve in your place."

Now he was on the point of tears, but there was one other person he could turn to. The sporty Mr Cave would put up a good defence.

The next morning, the day before the match, he was waiting at the form-master's desk when he arrived to call the register. Tim had prepared his case, explaining that he had been doing 'extra training before the important match, and didn't have time' to do his homework. Would he please beg Mr Evans for clemency?

Mr Cave looked down sadly on the troubled football captain.

"Ah, Oliver, when will you learn that there are some things in life even more important than football? You want me to act as an umpire on your behalf, perhaps because you have a famous Collegiate name." He frowned. "I have advised you to play a straight bat and so on, but you haven't! I'm sorry, but I think Mr Evans is right, so I cannot ask him to change his mind, and I think I know what your father would say."

Tim knew exactly what his Dad would say. He was letting everybody - the team, the school and the family down. He hadn't thought about it like that. He had been so busy feeling angry with Mr Evans and sorry for himself. But Mr Evans was right. He didn't deserve to be let off.

At five to ten the next morning, he took his place in Room 35. It felt more prison-like than on his first visit.

Mr Gillespie, the duty master, was checking the names and looked across at him.

"Shouldn't you be playing in the semi-final, Oliver?" He frowned. Everyone seemed to know. It added to the misery. He could picture the scene at Holly Lodge - the crowds, the chanting, the excitement. If the Collegiate won, they would be in the final, and he would be able to play. Please WIN, Collegiate!

The time crept by. They were the longest two hours of his life, and when Mr Gillespie called time, he ran for a number 12.

He got off at Sandheys and cut across to the playing fields. Groups of Collegiate boys were standing about chatting sadly. The Collegiate had lost 2-1. So that was that! There would be no final, no Anfield Stadium, no Junior Shield, and he might have made a difference! He hoped he wouldn't bump into the team. How could he look them in the eye? He had never been so miserable. He turned round and trudged home. It was time to take Gertie's advice.

CHAPTER TWENTY-FIVE

TIM BREAKS THROUGH

The Drawing Room at Sixty-Five was the most spacious, quietest in the house, usually reserved for special occasions. At the far end, a bay window overlooked the front garden. The blackout curtains had gone, replaced by more uplifting, floral ones. A large wicker sofa with matching armchairs and an 'occasional' table took centre ground.

At the opposite end of the room from the windows, prominently sited on a mahogany sideboard, stood two silver-framed photographs. One of a youthful Auntie May in tennis outfit, racquet in hand; and another, much larger one, of two athletic young men in football 'togs', muscular-kneed, arms folded across the chest, faces set and unsmiling, as was the custom for sporting photographs - Bill and Tom, family heroes of the '20's, Grandma's boys, the apple of her eye, who could do no wrong. This was a kind of shrine, where Tim would sometimes stop by, to pay homage, and it was here, one evening in late-January, that he met the junior of the two heroes to discuss his report which was lying open on the table. He had asked for this meeting, to test out Gertie's theory about fathers and sons.

For the allies all across Europe, success was in the air, but there was little here to suggest success for Oliver T, 3D, who, it seemed, was doing little that was right. All the usual indictments - 'could do better', 'doesn't pay attention', 'shows little interest' leapt from the page to point an accusing finger, and Dad was frowning.

"Your Mum and I are very disappointed, Tim" he said quietly. That was an understatement.

In fact, when the report was first read, there was quite a scene. Mum had already decided that, in such situations, tears didn't achieve very much, and was talking of imposing more serious sanctions, such as a total ban on evening football and strictly limited time at Yozzer's. Dad had decided on a calmer, more constructive approach.

"I think I can help you with some of your subjects, Tim. Shirley's doing well at school, so I'll have some spare time on Thursday evenings. We'll start with Latin. It was my favourite subject at school."

Tim frowned. He had seen this coming.

"But Latin's my worst subject, Dad! I just don't get it, and I'm not the only one! Even Yozzer says he doesn't always get it, and he's really clever."

"Well, sometimes it's not cleverness that's needed when you're learning something like Latin. Once you've got the basics, the secret is knowing where to look, and I can teach you. It's a bit like fishing. We'll tackle it together," he smiled, "one to one, every Thursday, seven o'clock prompt!" Tim nodded, biting his lip. If the sporty Tom Oliver enjoyed Latin, there must be something in it!

"OK Dad, I'll give it a try."

"Good! So don't arrange any football or visits to your wireless friend and his pretty sister on Thursday evenings!"

So Dad had noticed!

The following Thursday evening, a notice appeared on the handle of the Drawing Room door.

DO NOT DISTURB!
LATIN IN PROGRESS

But the progress was extremely slow and very little. Dad, the most patient of tutors, was struggling to get through, and every now and then, upstairs in her bed-sit, Grandma picked out his voice.

"You're NOT CONCENTRATING!" or "THINK, Tim!"

There was frustration on Tim's side, too. Cries of despair or resignation, or both, could be heard.

"It's NO USE, Dad!" He had already decided that Gertie's theory wasn't working. "I'll NEVER get it!"

Even the tutor was beginning to despair. Then, one Thursday evening, after Tim had gone to bed, he was leafing through the textbook, hoping for some inspiration, and a picture caught his eye. He jumped to his feet.

"If this doesn't work, nothing will!"

On the following Thursday evening, sitting across the table from Tim, he pointed to the picture. It was of a Roman amphitheatre, high terraces packed with spectators.

Tim leaned forward, and Dad took note.

"The Romans were very keen on sport, Tim. Most large towns had a gymnasium, and there were hundreds of arenas like this one scattered all over the Roman provinces. You can see the remains of many of them to this day. Games were usually in honour of the Emperor. It was a clever way of keeping the people in outlying provinces loyal to the Emperor and less likely to make trouble."

"On the day of the games, trumpets would announce the arrival of the Emperor or another celebrity. Then the gladiators, you've heard of them - tough, muscular types - would make their entrance, with an interesting variety of weapons - nets, tridents, lances, short-swords and shields, and a particularly nasty one which looked like a canon ball covered in spikes on the end of a chain." He pointed. "Here they are, lining up to salute the guest of honour. They raise their right arm and shout, in Latin, of course,

'We who are about to die, salute you!'"

Tim grinned.

"Just like the Kamikaze, saluting the commanding officer and taking off for a certain death!"

Dad nodded and went on. "Then the signal to start the entertainment would be given. The gladiators would split up, to fight with one another and hope to be standing at the end!"

Tim nodded. It wasn't his idea of entertainment, but one-to-one combat would be more interesting than a full-scale pitched-battle, where nobody seemed to know which side was winning; and it would be a lot more interesting than 'Everyday Life in a Roman Villa' or 'Cassius Goes to School'.

The clock on the mantelpiece said ten to eight, and he hadn't even glanced at it. Dad smiled. At last, in crystal-set terminology, they were on the same wavelength.

"Let's look at what the Gladiators shouted to the Emperor. It'll give us some clues about the way the Romans used words and put their sentences together." He pointed to the caption below the picture. "Look at that word salutamus. You can guess what it means."

"Salute." Tim grinned.

"That's right, Tim. In this case it means 'We salute'. The Romans were very practical. They didn't like to waste words, so one word in Latin, like 'salutamus', can mean two or even three words in English - 'we salute' or 'we are saluting'".

Tim nodded. "I see." He remembered Mr Evans saying something like it, but it hadn't registered.

Dad went on. "To find its English meaning we look at the first part - 'salute' - that's easy in this case; then we look at the ending, 'amus' which tells us who's doing the saluting - 'we', as we've seen. So saluto means 'I salute' and salutamus means we, that's the gladiators salute. They just changed the ending. The word nos goes with it. It means 'we' and it's hardly needed. It's for emphasis. Now we can look ahead - 'morituri' means 'about to die'. I'll explain that soon. 'Te' means 'you', the person being saluted. In Latin, the verb, usually comes at the end of the sentence, like here. Remember that, then the rest will fall into place. So nos morituri te salutamus - that's four words in Latin meaning eight words in English! 'We who are about to die, salute you!' There was no need for words for 'who' and 'are'. People just took them for granted."

"I get it!

At last the penny was dropping! Now he knew where to look! He was already beginning to think like Cassius, and couldn't wait for the next session. Thursday evenings were the highlight of the week. It was useless the local footballers knocking, trying to persuade him to come out for a kick-about. Even the opportunity for an hour or two searching the air-waves with Yozzer and a word or two with Myfanwy couldn't tempt him away.

Meanwhile, Peter, Frank and the others noticed that something extraordinary was happening in Latin lessons. Until then, the football captain had struggled in the very lowest reaches of the form, but as the Easter holidays approached they looked on, in amazement, as he passed them by on his way towards the top.

In his end-of-term report, Mr Evans wrote 'His new-found enthusiasm is astonishing!' He could even hold Tim up to the others as a shining example, someone who had put 'Nil desperandum' to the test, and had prevailed!

"If Oliver can do it, why not you?"

Now he was up and running! If he could lay the dreaded ghost of Latin, what was to stop him doing the same with all the other subjects, even Physics, for example? Unfortunately there was no one like his Dad to mentor him. Ma' Hill was out of the question, so that particular ghost would remain unlaid, and it was the same with Algebra. Even Mr Cave couldn't do the trick.

Otherwise, he had decided that education wasn't a complete waste of time, after all. He couldn't cram enough books into his satchel to meet the demands of homework, and in his Easter Term report, one compliment followed another. Mr Riddle wrote 'Has suddenly developed a remarkable appetite for grammar.' Mr Hall was impressed when Tim offered to bring a selection of Grandpa's stamps to a 'swaps' session, which his Dad immediately vetoed. After all, he might easily swap a priceless British Colonial for a brightly coloured, worthless Eastern European. Mr Griffiths wrote 'Is acquiring an uncanny flair for irregular verbs!' and Mr Kneen commented - 'Is showing a pleasing interest in Roman architecture, especially amphitheatres.'

On a negative note, Miss Hill, who had long since recognised that Tim's was a lost cause, but was obliged to make a comment, wrote 'Evidently hasn't the foggiest idea of what Physics is about. Often seems to be concentrating, but one wonders what he is concentrating on." This was quite a complimentary report by Miss Hill's standards.

Mr Cave's general summing up was a complete reversal of the previous one.

'This is more like the Olivers of yesteryear! At last he has started to play a straight bat! Now he must keep his eye on the ball!'

Back at home, he gave a modest interpretation of Mr Cave's mixed metaphors. Mum cried tears of restrained joy. Dad patted his protegé on the back, and, at last, Grandma could be told the truth. Shirley offered him a hug, which hadn't happened for ages, and Gertie, Bible-teacher supreme, beamed down on her young friend one of her special, 'just between you and me' smiles.

Time on the Crystal Set had to be strictly limited due to homework commitments, but Yozzer kept him up to date on the war. The Allied armies had crossed the River Rhine and, like the Russians, were closing in on Berlin.

****

In the last game of the season, the Chicks were playing SFX. There was no trophy to play for, just boasting rights in Shaw Street. So it was still a 'needle' match and, with Mr Harris's permission, would be played on the hallowed First Eleven pitch. Tim couldn't believe his luck.

Crowds lined both sides of the pitch. Tim's Mum and Dad were there and, to Tim's surprise, Yozzer had brought Myfanwy. The butterflies were on the move.

At half-time the score was 1-1. When the second half began, the Collegiate were pinned back for several minutes, and the SFX centre-forward coolly side-footed the ball into the Collegiate net.

That was 2-1 to SFX. Maroon caps went into orbit.

"SFX! SFX! SFX!"

The Collegiate hit back, and Gordon Howard, the captain, scored with a powerful shot from outside the penalty area. The score was 2-2, as the Collegiate supporters found their voices. Tim picked out his Mum's. Please stay well back, Mum!

Now it was the Collegiate's turn to press forward, and the 'home' crowd was chanting...

'Boomaranga, boomaranga, boom, boom, boom,' as Doug McQueen, the inside left, made a run into the SFX half and played a long ball out to Tim on the wing. Tim took the ball down the touchline, to draw the defenders, then cut inside, almost to the goal line. He saw that Ken Keates had made a run into the penalty area, and 'chipped' the ball across. Ken, who never missed such opportunities, headed it firmly into the corner of the net. It was 3-2. The crowd erupted, black and blue caps flew into the air and the chanting was deafening.

'Ooh, aah, ooh, aah-aah, Coll, Coll, COLLEGIATE!'

SFX pressed again, but ran out of time as the referee blew the whistle to signal the end. Tim spotted his Mum, proud and happy, hovering near the corner flag. He daren't go across, knowing that she might want to make a public expression of her pride and happiness. Dad just smiled and nodded his approval. Tim waved, then headed for the pavilion. He had to get changed quickly. He and Yozzer were going to the pictures.

Yozzer and Myfanwy were standing at the entrance to the pavilion as he ran up. Yozzer grinned.

"Te salutamus, Timothius!" He was already talking like a Roman!

"Well played, Tim" said Myfanwy, sweetly.

Timothius blushed and hurried past, to change.

****

At the CARLTON, the interval was coming to an end and the lady selling soft drinks had retreated to the foyer as Tim and Yozzer settled down in the fourth row from the front, in the middle. This was Tim's reward for the glowing report.

The lights were dimmed and the projectionist went into action. The familiar cockerel appeared on the screen announcing the PATHÉ NEWS, showing Russian tanks bursting through German defences. Tim remembered the newsreel pictures at the GRAND, three years before, when the German tanks were racing towards Moscow. Now they were back-pedalling. The caption said RED ARMY FORTY MILES FROM BERLIN.

"Pity the Gerries, now!" Tim whispered. Then, as the tanks disappeared, one word came on the screen and, all over the cinema there was a loud gasp, as pictures of what looked like living skeletons came on the screen, peering hollow-eyed through barbed wire fences. Most were wearing striped, pyjama-type trousers and jackets, some just rags. Many sprawled on the ground as if too tired or ill or hopeless to stand. The word was BELSEN.

All around them, people turned to look at each other in disbelief and shock. The lady in front of the boys was covering her eyes.

On the screen, groups of British soldiers looked on, grim-faced and bewildered. They were the first of the allied forces unlucky enough to discover Belsen; but now, according to the commentator, all over Nazi-occupied Europe, allied troops were stumbling on places like this, with names like Buchenwald, Auschwitz, Treblinka and Dachau, names which would go down in history as a witness to twentieth century man's cruelty to man.

But who were the living skeletons? Convicts? Criminals? The commentary was answering the question on everyone's mind. The boys picked up words like 'political dissidents', 'communists', 'gypsies', 'disabled', 'mentally ill', but, over and over again, 'Jews' - the 'undesirables', for whom Adolf Hitler had no room in his 'perfect' Third Reich. That was their crime, and Belsen was their punishment, to be starved, beaten, shot or gassed to death.

There were no guards in sight. They had fled for their lives. The only people in uniform were Red Cross workers who seemed as dazed as the soldiers. A nurse was being interviewed.

"In our work, we see terrible things," she said, "but never anything like this."

The Carlton had never been so silent. The only sound was that of the projector as it poured out the horrifying story, and the exit door opening and shutting, as people got up and left.

Yozzer glanced at Tim. Reflected in the light of the projector, his face was white.

"You look terrible, Tim!"

Tim just nodded. He felt terrible!

The interview and newsreel came to an end, and the big picture started, but it was difficult to concentrate, and when the programme ended, everyone made for the exits in silence and out into the fresh air. Yozzer looked at Tim.

"You don't look much better in the daylight, Tim!"

"You don't look so good yourself!!"

They caught a tram, and sat, deep in thought.

"How can people treat other people like that?" Tim said what they were both thinking. Yozzer nodded.

"My Dad says that Hitler made the Nasties swear an oath of total obedience to him. So they can do what they like, and can say they're just keeping their promise...obeying orders...that kind of thing."

"So Belsen is really his idea."

"Yeah, him and his chief cronies. I wouldn't want to be in their shoes when the Allies catch them, and that won't be long. On the wireless it said that Berlin's completely surrounded!"

********** .

"They can't catch Adolf now!" Back at home after school, a few days later, Yozzer was listening to the news when Tim arrived. He had taken his head-phones off.

"He's dead! His gang, too, or most of them. They committed suicide just before they could be nabbed! The Russians didn't take long reaching the Reichstag, that's the German parliament. There was hardly anyone to stop them, just some kids and old men. The German Generals have surrendered unconditionally. It's all over, bar the shouting, Dad says. Tuesday's VE Day- that's Victory in Europe Day. Everyone's got the day off!"

CHAPTER TWENTY-SIX

VE DAY

At a minute to ten on Tuesday, May the 8th, the bell ringers at St James's Church took a deep breath and a firm grip on their ropes. In West Derby, the shouting was about to start. They would be ringing a 'peal', which would take about three hours, to celebrate Victory in Europe, two thousand one hundred and seventy five days after war was declared. Ringing at number three, wearing a smart red and white striped blouse and blue, pleated skirt, was Myfanwy, the object of Tim's undying, if hopeless, admiration.

Now all eyes were on Mr Bleasedale, Captain of bells at number one, who glanced at his watch, smiled around the circle, nodded, and pulled down on his rope. The PEAL began, and, more or less simultaneously, church bells up and down the country rang out in a deafening, united explosion of sound. With a brief break on 'El Alamein' Sunday, they had been silent since the start of the war. Now they intended to make up some of the lost time and practice.

At Sixty-Five, Tim was determined to be in the thick of the celebrating. After all, in a way, he had been involved from the very beginning. Now he was keen to celebrate the end of the ending, as Mr Churchill might have put it.

The two friends had agreed to set out early and catch a tram to the Pier Head. That was where some of the main celebrating would be, Tim's Dad said, but, as Tim approached the tram stop at the Jolly Miller, he frowned. There was a long queue. He might have known. The trams started from West Derby village with its thousands. Suppose they had all decided to start celebrating early?

Yozzer was waiting, and they joined the queue. All eyes were focussed past St James's where Myfanwy would be toiling away, towards the village, and there was an optimistic murmur as a Number 12, signed CASTLE STREET, approached and squealed to a halt. The queue inched forward, hopefully.

"Three on top, two inside," said the Conductor, standing resolutely on the platform, holding one end of a chain, and counting the lucky five as they climbed on board. Someone else put a hopeful foot on the platform, but the conductor quickly put the chain across. He had said five, not six!

"That's all. Sorry," and the foot was withdrawn.

"Can't you let one or two more on?" a lady called out. "After all, it is VE Day! We wouldn't mind squeezing in, would we?" She looked around, to address the queue over her shoulder. They nodded. On a day like this, they would consider hanging onto the side, if necessary, like they do in India and places like that.

"Sorry luv," the Conductor said, "it's more than my job's worth." He tugged the bell-rope to let the driver know that he should get going, before trouble broke out. The tram moved off and the queue retreated, to re-group on the pavement.

Several minutes passed before another Number 12 came into sight and swept past, packed, with the chain across. Nobody was getting off, so nobody would getting on! There were groans.

"It's hopeless," said Yozzer. "We could be waiting all day!"

"Let's walk," said Tim. "It'll be easy to get a tram back."

They set off past the CARLTON where a poster declared RULE BRITANNIA!

The clock on St John's Church said ten to eleven. The bells were in full swing and the pavements were busy. Most people had settled for the long walk. Trams rattled past, all full, some over-full, where a soft-hearted conductor had bowed to public pressure.

In street after street leading off both sides of the main road, bunting fluttered over busy activity below, where tables were being set up for a street party.

"Will your street be having a party, Yozzer?" Tim asked.

"Yes, but we're going to the one in my Granddad's street in

Bootle. Will you be having one?"

"I don't think so. Mum says the people in Kremlin Drive aren't keen on that kind of thing. Grandma wants to have a quiet lunch in the garden, with a glass of champagne, and listen to the Prime Minister on the wireless."

The crowds on the pavement were thickening all the time, and the boys had to dodge on and off, to forge ahead. There were Union Jacks and St George's flags everywhere, a sprinkling of Welsh Dragons and, here and there, a Scottish Lion and the Stars and Stripes. The singing had already started. They could hear snatches of 'There'll always be an England', and 'Land of hope and glory.'

After a few minutes they reached the Hippodrome, where the face of Winston Churchill, the toast of the nation and most other nations, looked down from the hoarding, complete with V for Victory sign and famous cigar. The caption underneath said 'WE WILL NEVER SURRENDER! People pointed, waved and cheered.

For the walkers, it would be almost all downhill now, and the pace quickened as they dropped down towards the Collegiate. It was strange to imagine the corridors and classrooms empty and silent on such a noisy day. By now, walking was stop-start in places, and Tim's dribbling skills were proving useful as he zig-zagged his way through the crowd, with Yozzer not far behind, trying to keep up.

They crossed St George's Hall plateau, smothered in flags where children had taken possession of the lions, and people were already reserving places on the steps, to witness the Victory parade in the afternoon. Sailors, soldiers and airmen of the Empire and Commonwealth would be marching past the Lord Mayor and City Councillors, and Scouts, Guides, Church Lads Brigade, Salvation Army, almost anyone with a uniform, would be muscling in on the celebrations. Would the Colonel be marching, Tim wondered?

Soon the boys were heading uphill, for the last time, into the business centre of the city. Offices were shut for the day, and instead of the buzz of business-talk, the sound of singing echoed along canyon streets. As they reached Castle Street and the Victoria monument, the overpowering smell of the sea reminded them that they had almost reached the river and docks, where the Luftwaffe had done its worst and failed. To add to the cheering, singing and chatter, there was a continuous barrage of sound from the river, all but drowning the bells at St Nick's, the Pier Head Church, where the ringers were gathering themselves for the final push.

The boys trotted under the Overhead railway onto the Pier Head, and started to squeeze their way through dense crowds. They could slip through gaps where a grown-up would think twice, and after quite a bit of ''scuse me' ing, emerged at the railings running along the quayside

Tim had often seen the river in war-time conditions, but everything was different now. The only troop-ship on view had tied up, and the heroes were disembarking, kit-bags over shoulders, waving to families and friends waiting on the landing stage, only to be submerged in a deluge of hugs, kisses and tears. Then there was the steep climb to the quayside and more hugs and kisses from people, most of whom they had never met before and would probably never see again. It was the Liverpudlian way of saying a heartfelt 'Ta'!'

Further out on the river there wasn't a Destroyer in sight. The planners under the City streets had done their job well. The U-Boat menace had been seen off, so escorts weren't needed any more. Sir Francis would have been proud. But another war, against hunger, was still being waged all over Europe, and streams of merchantmen made their way in and out of docks or to and from the Ship Canal, reducing speed to DEAD SLOW as they passed the Pier Head, and sounding their horns to join in the celebrations.

Everywhere on the river there was action. Tugs dodged in and out, specially dressed for the occasion with every flag they could find in their lockers. The faithful old ferries were there, packed to the rails and low in the water. They had earned their place in the lime-light. Now, smothered in flags, they were doing a profitable line in sightseeing trips. Any spare space on the river had been taken over by smaller craft of one kind or another. It looked as if anyone with anything that would float was determined to take to the water for the chance of an unscripted part in the celebrations, and all the pilot-boats were out on traffic duty, throwing their weight about.

On the quayside, surrounded by a group giving a loud rendering of 'Land of Hope and Glory", Tim was watching the pilots, imagining, taking over the wheel of a Cunard liner, guiding it past the tricky sandbanks at the mouth of the river and into port, without the risk of being lost at sea. He would think about it.

He glanced up at the Liver clock, which said ten to one.

"Mum said be home by half past one. We'd better be going."

They squeezed their way back to Castle Street, with a brief glance at Queen Victoria. If she was still alive, she would be in her element, what with all the flag-waving and ballyhoo; but what would Prince Albert be thinking?

There was a number 12 waiting. They bagged seats at the front, and were soon on their way back to West Derby. Tim got off at the Jolly Miller, while Yozzer stayed on, as the tram rumbled on its way. The bell ringers at St James's had survived the rigours of the peal and had retreated to the vicarage lawn for tea and cake, provided by the vicar and Mrs Crewdson.

Back at Sixty-Five, Tim was on his way to his bed-room when Shirley called out.

"Billy Thompson's Mum telephoned to ask if you'd like to go to the Welbeck Avenue party this afternoon. We said we were sure you would."

"You bet!" He grinned.

"It starts at four. You'll need to be on a bus by half past three."

Grandma's Victory Lunch would be held on the back lawn. Shirley had been busy making bunting out of old sheets and stringing it up over the table laid out in the middle of the lawn. Tim was happy to see Gertie in attendance, with her glorious smile to fit the occasion. As Sixty-Five didn't possess a decent-sized Union Jack, she had brought one, dating back to the Great War celebrations, faded and frayed, but 'still dignified,' she hoped. She had attached it to the end of the washing-line pole, and propped it up against the end wall for the benefit of passers-by.

Auntie May and Uncle Arthur and Grandma and Grandpa Dodd had just arrived. Grandpa Dodd was commenting that, having served in the Great War, he was getting used to victory celebrations over the Gerries! Auntie May was complaining, bitterly, that there was still no sign of an end to 'the scandalous sweet rationing', but, ever thoughtful where her 'favourite evacuees' were concerned, she handed over two 'celebratory' bags of assorted boiled-sweets.

Lunch was served promptly at 1.30pm, and Grandma Oliver had excelled, as usual, making a little go a long way. The main course, chicken salad, was delicious, although Tim was more interested in the pudding and, to his undisguised joy, Gertie brought out a tray of home-made éclairs. However did she do it, he wondered, and had she kept one or two in reserve?

Grandma now produced Grandpa's celebratory bottle of Champagne, and it fell to Uncle Arthur to propose the loyal toast. He was already on his third glass of wine, but determined to rise to the occasion. He now rose to his feet, with glass raised.

"THE KING!"

"THE KING!" Everyone stood to chime in, sipping solemnly.

"God bless him!" added Grandma, "...and not forgetting the Queen!"

"THE QUEEN!" All responded.

"THE PRIME MINISTER!"

"THE PRIME MINISTER!"

"Good old Winnie!" Grandma exclaimed, sprinkling champagne on the grass, as Uncle Arthur soldiered on...

"THE SAILORS, SOLDIERS AND AIRMEN OF THE EMPIRE!"

"THE SAILORS, SOLDIERS AND AIRMEN!" was the abbreviated response.

"THE ALLIES" Uncle Arthur was now in full stride. Tim sipped his fizzy drink, frowning. How long was Uncle's list? He had a party to go to!

"THE ALLIES!"

"THE HOME GUARD !" Uncle didn't want to leave anyone out. Shirley was determined to make sure that he wouldn't. She moved into position close to him.

"Don't forget the fire-watchers, Uncle Arthur," she whispered.

"THE FIRE-WATCHERS, of course," Uncle raised his glass. Shirley squeezed Dad's hand, as glasses were raised in his direction.

"THE FIRE-WATCHERS!"

"And finally." Uncle became solemn. "Two brave young members of the family who had to leave home and run for cover from Goering's cruel Luftwaffe, far away from their Mum and Dad, away from grandparents...and aunts and uncles!" At this point Auntie May was sobbing into her handkerchief, as Uncle flourished his glass. "OUR EVACUEES!"

"SHIRLEY AND TIM!" Everyone responded, glasses raised, and Shirley smiled back, shyly. All her worries were behind her. Tim was worrying about the time. It was almost three o'clock, and Grandma led the way to the drawing room, to hear the Prime Minister's speech to the nation. There was the usual crackle and whine, followed by the voice which had done so much to keep Britain's hopes and determination alive during the six, long years of the war. Up and down the country there was a deafening hush, as Mr Churchill spoke.

"The German war is at an end. Advance Britannia!...Long live the cause of freedom!...Long live the King!" And that was the signal for the celebrating to begin, as people spilled out into the streets, to dance and sing and party until late into the night.

At Sixty-Five the celebrators returned to the garden for a more restrained celebration of tea and cake.

Tim drew alongside Mum.

"Can I go now, please?"

"Yes, Tim. I'll explain to Grandma. Say 'hello' to Mrs Thompson, Mr and Mrs Impitt and Mrs Ferguson and anyone else who remembers us. And if there's jelly on the menu, don't make a pig of yourself!"

He left by the back gate, heading for the bus stop, and after a few minutes wait, the number 60 arrived. He jumped on, found a seat and reflected. It was so long since they had said 'Good bye' to Welbeck Avenue. Would it all feel strange?

He got off at Ullet Road, and was soon running past the kiosk, where the headline said WE WON! Was Mr Erskine lost for words, for once? He wasn't there to ask. It was his holiday, too! Tim ran on, and turned into Welbeck Avenue. Down the centre, under a canopy of bunting, tables had been set out, end to end, covered with heaps of sandwiches, sausage-rolls, cakes and what looked mouth-wateringly like a sea of jelly-creams. The residents, including the new folk at number 6, Mr and Mrs Collins and their two children, were already taking their seats. He had arrived just in time!

Billy had been on the look-out and ran over.

"Hi, Tim! I thought you weren't coming! Come on, I've kept a seat for you."

They reached their places just as Mr Impitt called for silence for Grace, to give 'grateful thanks for the victory of right over wrong, that Harry Simpson had come home safely from the high seas, and 'for what we are about to receive, Amen!' - the signal for an all-out assault on the sandwiches. Harry, in full Royal Navy uniform, was Guest of Honour, sitting in state at the top-table next to his Mum, proud and radiant in a home-made red, white and blue hat and matching dress. Completing the favoured top-table was Mrs Ferguson, Grandma of the Avenue and unwitting heroine of the 'dud bomb' episode. She had brought Henry out in his cage to share the honour. He had picked up a new phrase - 'Danke schon', in perfect German, to the surprise of Mrs Impitt, as she offered him a fish-paste sandwich. Tim spotted old Welbeck friends and waved.

The time, like everything on the tables, was going quickly, as wartime reminiscing and gossip criss-crossed the tables. Ken had won a place at the Holt High School, said Billy, and Sid was at Quarry Bank. Billy was at the Institute, which, he said, was 'better than the Collegiate.' Tim wasn't going to argue on VE Day. There was bad news about the Den. Ken's Mum had finally convinced Mr Cox that there wasn't much likelihood of a further outbreak of hostilities, and wanted her rhubarb patch back. The boys would be looking for another HQ. Tim talked about his clever new friend and his five-penny Crystal set, and the mysterious good friend of the family, who had paid for his place at the Collegiate Prep, and was probably Grandma.

By five o'clock, the food was gone, the party was over, and most of the residents had drifted indoors. The tables were being dismantled, and the Avenue was deserted, except for a few mums, clearing up, and the two friends, reunited after two years, chatting about old times - Mr Donaldson, football and the SCOT. There was one treat still in store. The SCOT would be passing by on its return run from Euston to Lime Street.

"Come on!" said Billy. "It'll be going by in a few minutes!"

Together they ran to the end wall. Before the war they had needed three footholds to reach the top. Now, one was enough.

"Pity the others aren't here," said Billy. Tim nodded.

Not a word passed between them as they waited for the Pride of the London, Midland and Scottish Railways to go by on its return run.

Then it appeared pounding through Mossley Hill Station and past their ring-side seats. Tim glanced at his friend, and grinned. The same old SCOT! and the driver waved! Nothing really important had changed - not Welbeck Avenue, not Mrs Ferguson and Henry, not THE SCOT. The song was right. There'll always be an England!

After a few minutes they dropped down, and strolled back to number 7. Tim said 'Bye, bye' to Mrs Thompson, in exchange for a rib-crushing hug, and the two friends walked to the bus stop. The bus arrived, Tim jumped on and stood on the platform for a few moments as the bus pulled away, then he turned and waved.

"Be seeing you, Billy!"

"Be seeing you, Tim!"

They both hoped so, as Tim climbed upstairs and out of sight.

CHAPTER TWENTY-SEVEN

A CHIP OFF THE OLD BLOCK

Back at Holly Lodge, the start of the cricket season seemed to symbolise the return of peace and tranquillity to the troubled world.

Tim had been picked to play for the Chicks. Mr Morgan, the master in charge, had noted that he was 'good with bat and ball'. His favourite fielding position was at 'point', close to the batsman, where the best of the action would be. It would have been his Dad's position, he felt sure.

An 'away' match had been arranged against Kingsmead, a Preparatory school on the Wirral with a reputation as a good cricketing school. Kingsmead were batting first, and one batsman in particular was hitting the ball all over the field. It was during the third over that he accidentally drove the ball straight at Tim who saw it coming, just in time. He grabbed at it, but could only deflect it onto his forehead. The next moment he was flat on his back, holding his head. Mr Morgan ran over to check that he was breathing normally, then picked him up and carried him back to the pavilion. One of the Kingsmead mums brought him a drink of orange squash, and he had soon recovered enough to notice a table laid-out with what looked like mounds of sandwiches and cakes.

A doctor among the spectators came to examine him.

"A mild concussion. He'll be alright after some rest, but he should sit-out the rest of the game."

Tim, however, had no intention of sitting anything out. He was sure that, in his place, his Dad would have played on; but Mr Morgan agreed with the doctor, and a reserve took Tim's place. That left him free to enjoy the sympathy of the Kingsmead mums and the chance to be the first to help himself to the tea. He had landed on his feet!

Unfortunately, the Chicks hadn't fared so well. Kingsmead won the match by fifteen runs.

In Room 21 the next morning, a circular bruise, orange with a hint of blue, surrounding one eye, told the story of Tim's encounter with the cricket ball. Mr Cave was impressed.

"Bravo, Oliver! An honourable scar of battle!" Tim nodded modestly. Oliver 3D, Martyr! As if he had deliberately put his head in the way.

****

At Sixty-Five there was still no news from Hong Kong, but Dad had heard that Dave Bone, his great friend and rival for the Victor Ludorum cup, had been taken prisoner by the Japanese.

****

Sports day now loomed up, a final hurrah for the school year, and Mr Harris's chance to demonstrate how, with a bit of Irish genius, a playing field can be turned into an athletics stadium. The quarter-mile track, with six lanes, would be mown to a bowling green finish. There would be a lot of Union Jacks and bunting everywhere.

The day arrived and the kind of feelings Tim was becoming used to, on such occasions - a mixture of excitement and nerves. Excitement because he loved all the action; nerves because he would be taking part in it, and the family had come to see him in action - Mum in one of her neat crocheted hats, and as nervous as himself; Dad cool and calm in old school tie and well-worn trilby hat, revisiting the scene of former glories; Shirley looking very pretty in her dark green school uniform, keeping a sisterly eye on Roger who wanted to take part himself. Grandma had come to see her Grandson in action, and perhaps to compare him with her son; and Gertie, an honorary family member for the day, to cheer on her young friend. To complicate matters further, Yozzer had said he would be coming, and would bring Myfanwy. The butterflies were already on the move.

There was a carnival atmosphere, with parents, grandparents and other assorted relatives and friends crowding the finishing straight, ten or more deep.

Looking around, as he was warming up, Tim picked out familiar faces - Mrs Taylor and Miss Sterland, representing the Prep, flamboyant in home-made hats; the Headmaster and Mrs Gibbs entertaining a gaggle of governors in the tea tent; the Vice-Principal on duty as head timekeeper. Mr Cave had drawn the short straw. He was officiating at the Throwing the cricket ball, having to retrieve the ball from wherever it had finally come to rest, and return it to the next thrower.

Tim caught sight of 'The Wasp', a popular prefect, conspicuous in a vest with gold, black and yellow hoops attended by an admiring group of juniors. He was favourite to become this year's Victor Ludorum.

Tim was entered for the One Hundred Yards. The track was laid out in lanes divided by strings running along the tops of sticks. He had seen the same thing in photographs of the 1908 London Olympics. It was the nearest that Sam could come to giving Sports Day an Olympic flavour, and added to the excitement.

As the competitors lined up Tim glanced at Alf Turner in the next lane. He was half-Chinese and half-British and muscular. It must be all that rice, Tim thought. His family came from Hong Kong, where the Japanese were still in charge, so the crowd would probably be cheering for Alf, which didn't seem fair, in a way. He looked down the track and noticed Yozzer and Myfanwy standing not far from the finish. Myfanwy seemed quite excited. Would she be cheering for him...or Alf?

The starter raised the gun. "ON YOUR MARKS!" "SET!" ... BANG! The competitors launched themselves down the course. At half way, Tim was just in the lead, but Alf was catching him and, at the finish, it looked as if he might have won. What would the VP and the other judges decide? Was it Alf or Tim, Hong Kong or England?

The announcer picked up his loud speaker.

"Third form One hundred yards. First equal, Turner 3C and Oliver 3D." It was a dead heat.

The crowd applauded enthusiastically and the boys shook hands.

"That's a fair result!" said Mum. "Uncle Joe Quie would be quite pleased."

But Tim wasn't. After all, this was where Dad had been Victor Ludorum all those years before, and he was watching. But first equal would have to do. There would be more Sports Days.

He was walking away from the finish, and the Vice Principal stopped him.

"So, Oliver, we meet again! I hear from your Form Master that you have begun to make a name for yourself." He emphasised the last word. "And for the right reasons!" He smiled.

Tim nodded, the VP went on...

"And it seems that we have another Oliver athlete at the school."

"Yes, Sir." Again Tim nodded, then as he turned to go, he almost bumped into Mrs Taylor and Miss Sterland.

"That was splendid running, Timothy!" Mrs Taylor smiled. "Let us hope it will be the first of many laurels!" She frowned slightly. "Oh, and I do hope you are enjoying poetry a little more these days!"

"Thank you, Miss. But we don't do much poetry in 3D." He was trying to sound disappointed, but didn't want to get Mr Riddle in trouble for dereliction of duty.

"And how is the war-correspondent getting on in the Big School?" Miss Sterland joined in, brightly, "...and your friend... Yozzer, I seem to remember." She smiled. "Well, we finally polished the Gerries off, didn't we? Tell me, is the crystal-set still working?"

"Yes, Miss. We think it won't be long before the Japs give in...or fall on their swords!"

"I agree, Timothy. Any time now!"

He nodded. If you say so, Miss!

Now he joined the crowd for the last event on the programme, the Senior Four-Forty (short for four hundred and forty) yards, and all eyes were on The Wasp as he stepped onto the track and led from start to finish, which gave him the points to become Victor Ludorum.

The prize-giving was held in front of the pavilion.

Having detached himself from the tea-tent, the Headmaster said a few words, then Mrs Gibbs, resplendent in a blue, wide-brimmed hat, presented the prizes. It was a long list, but at last Tim and Alf walked forward together, to extra-loud applause.

The last prize to be awarded was the silver Victor Ludorum Trophy and, as the Wasp went forward, Tim glanced at his Dad. This was the cup he had won all those years ago! He was smiling, but with a slight frown. Was he thinking about Dave Bone?

That brought Sports Day to a close. The competing was done, the shouting was over, and Tim ran over to show his certificate to the family. They basked for a few minutes in the reflected glory, then moved homewards, leaving Yozzer and Myfanwy to pay their tributes. Tim gulped. This might be tricky!

"A great run, Tim!" said Yozzer. "I thought you beat Alf by a whisker!"

"I agree, Tim," added Myfanwy, sweetly. "And you have a very nice running style!"

"Oh, er...thanks, Myfanwy." He had been practising pronouncing her name, and hadn't thought about his running style. After all, aren't all styles pretty much the same...moving the legs and arms in time, no looking back, keeping your eye on the finishing tape, and so on?

"See you in school on Monday," said Yozzer.

"See you, Tim!" said Myfanwy, with a dazzling smile.

He gulped. Did she really mean it?

"See you Yozzer!" he replied. "See you, erm, Myfanwy!"

Slightly dazed, he headed back to the pavilion which was deserted except for the groundsman. Sam had been showered with compliments all afternoon, no one had annoyed him, and he was about to lock up, when he spotted Tim in the doorway. He waved a hand at the honours boards.

"That was good running, Tim Oliver! You're a chip off the old block, as we say in Ireland, to be sure!"

Tim grinned. That was a great compliment! "Thank you, Sam... Mr Harris I mean!"

That was one small step out from his Dad's shadow.

He turned and ran to join the little procession making its way towards Kremlin Drive - Mum, Dad and Grandma in the lead, Shirley with Roger in his push-chair, waving the Certificate to passers-by and, a little distance behind, Gertie talking quietly to the hero of the hour.

"You've come a long way since you were an evacuee, Tim, and I've been thinking about the fierce teacher in the country school, who gave you such a hard time. You mustn't go through life holding a grudge against her, however much you think she deserves it. You're not a war casualty any more. That's all behind you now, Tim. Leave it there!"

He smiled and nodded, and Gertie's smile shone in the late afternoon sunshine as she took his hand, and mentor and pupil hurried to catch up with the family, and stroll back to Sixty-Five for tea with éclairs.

POST SCRIPT

A month later, on August 5th, the first atomic bomb was dropped on the Japanese city of Hiroshima. The Japanese Emperor Hirohito surrendered on the 14th. World War 2 was over.

A letter from Hong Kong brought the news that the Japanese occupiers had left. Uncle Joe had lost a lot of weight, but his family were well and free. Shortly afterwards the sad news came through that Dave Bone had died in the pison camp. Dad was devastated, and worse news was to come over the weeks and months. Exactly one hundred Collegiate Old Boys had lost their lives in the war, to add to the one hundred and eighty-eight who died in the First World War. Their names, including that of Dave Bone, are inscribed on a memorial in the entrance hall to what was the school, in Shaw Street.

Tim (or perhaps we should call him Tom from now on) continued to make good progress through the school. Although not an academic 'high-flier', he gained the Higher School Certificate in English Literature and Latin. He played fly-half and goal-kicker for the Rugby First Fifteen, was Captain of athletics and Victor Ludorum in 1950 and 1951, exactly thirty years after his father, and a Senior Prefect.

By this time he had made up his mind about a career. He wouldn't be a soldier, sailor, farmer or even footballer. Instead he became a teacher specialising in Physical Education and Religious Education.

In the meantime, his rabbit-running was paying off! He was British (AAA) champion at 400 metres hurdles in 1957* and at 800 metres in 1960. He represented Great Britain in the Melbourne (1956) and Rome (1960) Olympics, and captained the British team at

---

* Setting a UK record of 51.0 seconds.

the 1958 European Championships in Stockholm.

Grandma Oliver died in September, 1955, so, at last, Dad was able to reveal that she was the 'mysterious friend of the family', as Shirley and Tim had guessed. Sadly Tim, wasn't able to say 'Thank you!' but would never forget her kindness.'

There was one final change of direction. In 1971 he was ordained as a Church of England minister, and the following year he was chaplain to the British athletics team at the ill-fated Munich Olympics.

His love for football never left him. He played for the Collegiate Old Boys in the top Liverpool (I Zingari) Amateur league for several seasons, finally getting that chance to play on the (vast!) Anfield pitch in the semi-final of the Lancashire Amateur Cup, losing to Maghull 2-1 after extra time.

"I've never been so tired!"

ACKNOWLEDGEMENT

I owe so much to so many people. Sylvia Hogbin, unfailing source of advice and encouragement. Dr Gardner Thompson, friend and mentor on the war aspects of Evacuees Return, (even while writing two books of his own). Ed Fenton of Writers' Workshop, who, once again, has gone far beyond the terms of his remit, reminding me of the basics of good writing. Shirley's daughter, Helen, gave much helpful advice on style and vocabulary. And how would I have kept going if it wasn't for my young advisers...Granddaughters Amber, Abby and Grace; neighbours Hannah and Peter, and, when the book was in its formative stages, Ella Littlewoood and Faith Davis, then pupils at Dovedale Road Juniors.

My special thanks to my brother, Roger, a fellow Collegiate Old Boy, for assiduous proof-reading; and to Peter Galvin and Lionel Ross, also Old Boys, for invaluable advice on the second half of the book. Above all, to Peter Rogers, my one-time pupil at Dulwich College, now illustrator extraordinary and friend, for putting Evacuee's Return together.

I am so grateful to them all.

Tom Farrell was born and brought up in Liverpool. Educated at the Liverpool Collegiate School and Loughborough College, and has a Divinity Degree from London University.

Before being ordained he taught in several schools, and, after ordination, served as a curate at Woolton Parish Church, Liverpool, Chaplain at Dulwich College, Vicar of Wonersh in Surrey and Rector of St Margaret Lothbury, in the Square Mile.

He is married to Liz, with three children and nine grandchildren. First-cousin to twice Booker Prize-winner, J.G.Farrell, in retirement he continues to play an active part in church life, runs regularly 'for fitness', and is writing his 'running' memoirs, 'The Making of an amateur Olympian'.

Lightning Source UK Ltd.
Milton Keynes UK
UKHW01f2357050718
325309UK00002B/144/P